Secrets of a Kept Chick, Part 2

Renaissance Collection

Secrets of a Kept Chick, Part 2

Renaissance Collection

Ambria Davis

www.urbanbooks.net

Urban Books, LLC
300 Farmingdale Road, NY-Route 109
Farmingdale, NY 11735

Secrets of a Kept Chick, Part 2: Renaissance Collection
Copyright © 2017 Ambria Davis

ISBN 13: 978-1-62286-608-3
ISBN 10: 1-62286-608-8

First Trade Paperback Printing September 2017
Printed in the United States of America

10 9 8 7 6 5 4 3 2 1

*This is a work of fiction. Any references or similarities
to actual events, real people, living or dead, or to real
locales are intended to give the novel a sense of reality.
Any similarity in other names, characters, places, and
incidents is entirely coincidental.*

Distributed by Kensington Publishing Corp.
Submit orders to:
Customer Service
400 Hahn Road
Westminster, MD 21157-4627
Phone: 1-800-733-3000
Fax: 1-800-659-2436

Secrets of a Kept Chick, Part 2

Renaissance Collection

Ambria Davis

Chapter 1

Jayden

It had been three weeks, and we hadn't come close to finding Kaylin. We'd been by all of his hangout spots and his clubs. We even got at some his workers, and we hadn't come up with anything. Not to mention that Mark's girl Troy got shot by one of his sidepieces. Hell, we even tortured her ass before putting her to sleep, but she didn't know shit.

It was gonna be hard to say good-bye to Mimi. I mean, I'd just met her and, yeah, I knew people may have felt some type of way because I met her and fell for her. Shit happens. A lot of people have one-night stands, some be together for three or four months and the next thing you know, they getting married and shit. Things like that happen. It's life. I met Mimi, and I knew that she was the one for me. You can tell a person by the vibe that they send and her vibe was phenomenal and outstanding. I wanted her to be my one, and now that shit couldn't happen. I guessed I'd have to chalk it up to life and that wasn't okay with me. I was pissed off about the way it went down.

The thing about Mimi that got me was that you could tell from the beginning that homegirl was a boss. Even when she wore something as simple as a T-shirt, shorts, and sneakers, she wore it well. The chick was just that bad. She became my A-one on day one, and I was going to end that bitch-ass nigga's life for cutting hers short.

We'd been at the hospital all day with Troy. They were supposed to release her from the hospital today, and I was glad. Hospitals made me feel some type of way ever since I lost my mother and younger brother last year. I didn't like going there because every time I went there, somebody died. The only time I'd been there for a pleasant experience was when my four-year-old son Cameron was born.

I was in need of a good blunt, so I went to the car to fire up the blunt that we had in the car. Taking my phone out of my pocket, I decided to call my li'l dog Chucky back in Virginia. I had left him in charge while I was gone and he was doing great so far, but I needed an update on how shit was going now. Last week we took a loss, and that shit ain't sit well with me. I knew for a fact that it was some nigga in the crew, because I was never one to have the same routine for too long. I stayed switching my shit up for that purpose. That's how I knew it was a setup within the crew. Let me find out who it was, and it would be game over. I didn't play 'bout that shit. Not only did they take money out of my mouth, but they went against the grain. I made sure all my niggas ate good, so I knew there was no reason for them trying to be greedy. One thing was for sure: I would put an end to that nigga as soon as I found out who he was.

"Yo, what's up, boss?" Chucky said, answering the phone.

"Ain't shit, man. How's everything going over there?" I asked, waiting to know if we had any more issues like last week.

"Everything is good right now. Shit is back to normal. Well, almost. I had to put ya boy Deuce in his place today."

"Oh, yeah? What happened with that?"

"Man, that nigga was talking that slick shit. Talking 'bout we taking orders from a nigga who ain't here. Nigga wanted to try to take over, talking 'bout we could take over your throne since we're basically doing it right now. I had to check that nigga about his loyalty to the crew, 'cause that was some slick ho shit he was popping out his mouth."

"Oh, yeah? Where he at now?" I asked, already knowing the answer.

"Man, you already know where that nigga at. I put that nigga in the basement with the dogs, where the rest of them disloyal-ass niggas go out."

"What you plan on doing with him?"

"Nothing. I'm leaving that nigga there until you get back."

"I'ma have Mark do that nigga in. You know he ain't like him from the beginning," I said, knowing Mark would enjoy fucking up Deuce's ol' bitch ass. "Is there anything else that I need to know?"

"Oh, yeah. Yo' baby mama came here with Cam. I started to kick her in her ass."

"What the fuck that bitch wanted?" I was annoyed. My baby mama Shelly was a real bitch. She wasn't nothing but drama. That's why I stopped fucking with that ho. She always wanted to make a scene when the shit wasn't called for. She was ghetto as fuck, and if it weren't for Cameron, I would've been had that ho missing.

"Man, she came over here looking for you and, when I told her that you wasn't here, she made a scene. Talking 'bout she was going to call the police and have all of us arrested," he said, sounding heated. I knew he was. Hell, if I were him, I'd be heated too if somebody had threatened to put me in jail.

"That bitch came 'round there stunting like that?" I asked, not believing Shelly's stupid ass would fuck around like that, but then again, I didn't know what that crazy bitch was capable of.

"Man, you already know who that ho is. I shouldn't have to tell you that."

"All right, man, I'ma handle her ass. Just make sure to keep them niggas in line and keep that paper flowing. I should be back real soon," I said, while I spotted Mark walking in my direction.

"All right, man, I'ma hold it down until you get back, but don't be long too soon. You know them niggas get big-headed when they don't see your face around here."

"Oh, trust, I already know how them niggas are. I'll be down there sooner than you think."

"All right, man, see you soon."

"Bet," I said, hanging up the phone. I took a toke from the blunt that I was puffing and just inhaled the weed, letting the smoke full my lungs up.

"Sup, man?" Mark said. He knew the only time that I acted like this was when some shit was going down or was about to go down. I didn't say anything as I took another puff from the blunt before I passed it to him.

"Man, Chucky said he had to deal with ya boy Deuce today. Said that nigga on that bitch shit, talking 'bout taking over and shit," I said, blowing the hair out of my mouth.

"Nah, man," Mark said, shaking his head as if he couldn't believe it. "That nigga on that shit like that?"

"Apparently, that nigga is. But I got something for that nigga," I added, taking the blunt out of his hand. I then gave him that, "Yeah, nigga, that's yo' work you 'bout to put in," look.

"Hell yeah, nigga," he stated, rubbing his hands together, with this crazy look in his eyes. That nigga lived for crazy shit like that, like killing was a game or something that he enjoyed doing.

"You know I'ma let you get at that nigga since you ain't never liked his ass from the get-go. I just can't believe that I trusted that nigga and considered his ass to be my li'l homie."

"Man, I told you from the get-go that nigga wasn't to be trusted, but that don't mean that you have to fault yourself for trusting his snake ass. Nowadays snakes come in all forms and sizes. It's really hard to spot one, especially if you done been cool with one for so long. I mean, you really have no way of knowing. You just have to believe people when they show you who they really are the first time." Mark passed the blunt back to me. "But I'ma enjoy handling his bitch ass though."

"I know you will. That's why I'ma let you do it."

"That's what's up."

"I gotta do something with Shelly. That bitch over there threatening to call the police on our folk and shit. She gonna to make me hurt her ass." I really didn't know why I started fucking with her ass in the first place. If it weren't for the fact that she had my son, some good pussy, and a fire-ass head game, I would've been cut her ass off.

"She over there tripping like that again?" he asked, shaking his head.

"Man, you already know how Shelly is when she don't get what she wants."

"I told to you to stop fucking with that girl from the beginning. I told you not to mess with her ass, because she wasn't nothing but trouble. You ain't wanna listen to me, and now you get to see that for yourself." He repeated what he always said whenever I would say something about Shelly. He never did like her and, like he said, he had always warned me about her, but I was thinking with the wrong head and got myself trapped by a bitch with a fucked-up mind frame.

"I know, and I should've listened to you then, but I didn't. Only good thing that girl ever did was when she gave birth to my damn child. Then, after that, she became even crazier and shit." I sat silently for a moment, remembering what she did a couple of days after our son was born. "I can't deal with all of this shit no more, man. I already have a lot on my plate."

"What you wanna do about it then?"

"I don't know. I'ma think about it," I said, just as my phone started ringing. Looking at the caller ID, I saw that it was Shelly's triflin' ass calling me now. "Speak of the devil. What?" I answered with an attitude.

"Don't 'what' me, nigga. Where the hell you at?" she screamed into my ear.

"Bitch, don't be questioning me. What the fuck do you want?"

"Nigga, I don't know what bitch got you feeling some type of way, but you better stop playing with me. When you coming home?"

"Bitch, is you stupid, simple, or just damn slow?" This loony ho either couldn't or wouldn't take a hint.

"I'm none of 'em, nigga. What I know is we ain't over until I say we over, and if we were over, why did you come fuck me before you went on that little run?"

"Bitch, I fucked you because I was horny and you was there at the moment. That shit ain't mean nothing else but a quick nut to me. I don't want you, ma. It's time to move on."

"You must didn't hear what I said, huh, boy?" she shouted, sounding like a crazy lady. "We ain't over until I say that we're over, nigga!"

"Shelly, I don't know what part of 'I don't want you no more' that you didn't get, but hear me when I say this: stay away from Chucky and the rest of the crew. You threaten to put them niggas in jail one more time, you won't like what happens. Next, stop calling me. If the shit don't have anything to do with Cameron, then don't call me. We're done, over, finished. I don't want you or ya pussy, so leave me the fuck alone. Yo' ass ain't nothing but trouble and drama. I ain't got time for that type of shit anymore," I yelled, hanging up the phone in her face.

I looked at Mark, who was just standing there laughing. "What's so funny, nigga?"

"Hey, man, don't chew my head off," he said, throwing his hands up. "You know she's going to be causing a lot of problems, since you done made it clear that you don't want her no more, right?"

"Yeah. I know. I'ma handle her though," I said, as my phone started ringing again. I didn't have to look at my phone to know that it was Shelly calling back. I didn't bother answering the phone. Her ass really didn't get the point, but the minute I stepped foot back in VA, I was going to handle her.

"See what I'm saying? You gotta do something about her, man."

"I will." I cussed as my phone started ringing again. "Fuck this shit." I powered my phone off because, if I didn't, I knew Shelly would be ringing it all damn day.

"Don't say nothing, man," I warned, knowing Mark was about to say something. He always did.

"Hey, I wasn't about to say nothing." He smirked.

"Uh-huh, I bet. Come on, man, let's go check on shorty."

"All right, man, come on."

As we made our way toward the hospital, I thought about what I was going to do with Shelly's ass. Hell, if she weren't my son's mother, I wouldn't have hesitated to kill her ass. I had Cam to think about though. I didn't want him to grow up without a mother. If she would only just keep her ass still, then there wouldn't have had to be no shit. I knew one thing though: if she continued to act the way that she was acting, I wouldn't have no choice but to rock her ass to sleep.

Ambria Davis

Pushing that to the back of my mind, I started to prepare mentally for three things. First, I had to say my final good-byes to Mimi tomorrow. Next, I had to find her no-good-ass baby daddy, get Mimi's kids to Troy safely, and put that nigga down for a dirt nap. Finally, I was going to take the state of Virginia by storm. When I returned, all them niggas were going to feel me.

Chapter 2

Kaylin

It'd been weeks since we left Atlanta and I really missed Mimi a lot. Lately, I'd been kicking myself in the ass for reacting without thinking. I knew that what I did to Mimi was wrong, but I couldn't help it. I cheated on her, and she knew about it, but when she did it to me, I couldn't forgive her that one time. I snapped. Even if she had planned to leave me, I should've let her live. That was the love of my life and the mother of my kids. I had planned on marrying her, but I fucked that shit up the day I started fucking with that cutthroat-ass bitch Stacy. I didn't know where my head was at to make me cheat on my girl with a bitch like Stacy. We'd been through everything together, both good and bad, yet somehow we'd always managed to stay together as one. Even after she found out about me and I went to jail, she was there for me, pregnant and all.

I should've known better than to bring the shit that I did in Louisiana to Georgia. From the day that Mimi found out about Stacy and me, up until the day that we got back together, I had to basically kiss my girl's ass. I did any- and everything that I could to win her back, and I promised that I wasn't going to do it again, but I broke that promise. Now, because of me, my girl was dead, and I was on the run from the boys in blue. My life was fucked up right about now.

I stood there staring out the window at my kids playing in the yard. I had bought a house out here in Mississippi for the time being. Even though Mississippi ain't really that far from Georgia, I wanted to settle down in a state where they wouldn't think about looking for me. Once the heat died down a bit, I'd be making my way back, when I knew what was good and what wasn't. I still had my property there, so I'd be heading there in a minute. I wasn't worrying about them coming to kick in the door, because none of my properties were in my name, so I was good. I just needed to come up with a plan to get rid of Stacy's hood ass.

"Kaylin, Kaylin, Kaylin," I heard a shrill voice repeatedly calling me. I wished like hell that I could mute her ass.

"Yeah, what's up?" I replied, never bothering to take my eyes away from the window.

"Why you always do that?" she whined, sounding like a big-ass baby.

"Do what?" I asked, snapping at her.

"Ignore me. You've been doing that shit for forever now, Kaylin," she continued to whine.

"Bruh, don't start with that shit today. Right now ain't the time for ya whining and bitching!" I quickly turned around. "You're really starting to get on my last fucking nerve, girl!"

"Well, when is the right time, huh, Kaylin?" She ran up in my face.

"Never, so keep that shit to yourself!" I pushed her aggravating ass backward.

"Kaylin, that ain't fair. I've been through too much shit trying to be with you so we could be a family."

"Bitch, I never once said that I wanted a family with you. I wanted that shit with Mimi, not you. You been nothing but bad news from the beginning. I was too young and dumb to realize that I already had what I needed at home. If it weren't for you showing up at my house, Mimi would pro'ly still been alive. But no, you just had to get big-headed and not listen to me like I told your dumb ass," I yelled as I walked away from her. I needed to get far away from her, because I couldn't stand the sight of her right now.

"You can't put all that shit on me, Kay. I never forced you to do anything that you ain't wanna do. I never forced your dick inside of me, never forced you not to wear a condom, and I never forced you to nut in me. I never forced you to take me on trips nor did I force your money out of your pockets. You did all of that shit on your own, nigga. You're just as much to blame as I am. She was yo' bitch, not mine. I wasn't supposed to give a fuck about her, you was!" she replied, following me.

"Yeah, yeah, yeah, I did all that, and you was cool wit' it. Now I gotta pay for the mistake I made from fucking with a bitch like you. Hell if you ain't had no loyalty to the two bitches who had your back through whatever, why would I think you'd have my back?" I said, walking into the kitchen. "You been hating on Mimi since before I came into the picture. Just admit it: you wanted to be her. You've always wanted to be her."

She didn't say anything. She just stood there looking at me. I knew what I said might have pushed a few buttons, but I was tired of playing the nice guy. I wanted the bitch to just leave me the fuck alone.

Shaking my head, I grabbed my keys to go for a drive. I desperately needed to clear my mind and get away from here before I ended up killing this bitch.

"Kaylin, where are you going?" She started running behind me, but I kept on walking.

I walked over to my kids and gave them all a kiss on their cheeks. "I'll be back later y'all," I said to them. They

all looked like they wanted to cry, especially Kayson and
Kaylon, but they kept it in. I headed over to my car and got
in while Stacy was still walking over to me.

"Kaylin, where are you going?" she asked, beating on
the window.

Still ignoring her, I started the car and drove off. I had
one destination in mind, and it wasn't Louisiana. I was
going to see Mimi for the very last time. I was headed to
Atlanta, and even though I knew it was a stupid decision,
my heart was telling me otherwise.

Chapter 3

Troy

I just sat there, staring into space as the doctor started explaining what I could and couldn't do or eat for the next two weeks. My body was there physically, but my mind was not. My mind was still on the fact that Kaylin's bitch Star had caught me slipping. I couldn't believe she shot me. It was a good thing that Kayla wasn't shot when that shit happened to me, because I would've been devastated. I wouldn't have been able to live with myself, knowing that she was hurt just because she was with me. So, to keep her out of harm's way, I sent her back to Louisiana with Jayden's mother. She didn't want to go, but I promised her that I would see her soon. I wondered where that ho Star was at though. The news said that they couldn't find her. I wondered if she was somewhere dead, because I knew for a fact that I shot her ass two times. So, why didn't the police find her body? That evil bitch probably survived and got away. Shit, now that was something else that I had to add to my list of things to worry about.

Tomorrow was the day that we'd be laying Mimi to rest. It was kind of a bittersweet moment for me. I'd accepted the fact that she was gone and not coming back, but what I couldn't accept was not being able to bury her body. I still couldn't believe that no one knew where her body was. How they could lose a whole body like that was crazy. I still hadn't been able to speak with Detective Webber, but I would after the funeral tomorrow. I wasn't letting this shit go. I'd sue the state of Georgia if I had to. Somebody would give me an explanation, instead of giving me the runaround all day.

That reminded me, I hadn't been able to tell Mark and Jayden about what had been going on this past week. So many things had been happening that I never got a chance to, but I would today. I didn't want them to be clueless when they got to the funeral tomorrow and found out that it would be a closed casket. I knew everyone would be expecting an open casket service. People would want to see Amina's beautiful face tomorrow for one last time, but that wouldn't be happening. They'd be seeing an empty-ass casket.

I was so happy that I was going home today. I couldn't wait to get home to my bed. I didn't think I could spend another day in the hospital. I barely got any rest, because of the people coming back and forth. Staying in the hospital and that disinfectant smell started to get to me. I hated being cooped up in one spot for too long.

"Ma'am, do you hear me?" Dr. McKenley asked, snapping me from my thoughts.

"Yes, sir, I hear you," I lied right through my teeth. I ain't heard a word he said since he'd been in here, and I wasn't trying to. I was too busy worrying about everything that had happened.

"You have to follow up with your doctor in about a week."

"Okay, I'll make an appointment when I leave from here."

"Make sure to take it easy. You don't want to do too much at one time. It could cause you to come back and see me."

"Trust me, I'm not a fan of hospitals, so I won't be coming back here to see you no time soon," I said to him. He smiled, showing a perfect set of white teeth. I suddenly realized that Dr. McKenley was a good-looking brother. He was about six feet tall, and 200 pounds of solid muscle. That banging body, caramel complexion, and dazzling smile were the truth.

"Okay. I'll send the nurse in shortly with your discharge papers and your prescriptions." He removed his gloves from his hands and threw them into the trash.

"Okay, thank you," I said sincerely. He'd taken good care of me since I'd been in here.

"Welcome. Take care of yourself."

"I will."

I sat there thinking about my life. I remembered when I was younger and life wasn't so rough. Minus all of the things I went through with my family and past lovers, I'd have loved to be a child just one more time. Unfortunately, things like that can't happen, so I made the best of my life as it was now.

My phone started ringing as I sat there waiting for the nurse to come with my discharge papers and medicine so I could get out of there. Since I didn't want to be bothered, I let the call roll to voicemail. I'd call whoever it was back later. I needed a little peace right now.

Grabbing the remote, I searched for something to watch when my phone started to ring again. Grabbing my phone, I fished it out of my purse. Looking at caller ID, I thought my eyes were playing tricks on me. "I know this nigga ain't calling me now," I groaned, rolling my eyes. "Hello." I answered the phone with as much attitude as I could muster.

"Hey, ma, it's me," he replied softly.

"I know who this is. What do you want, Weedy?"

"Damn. Oh, so now I can't call to check up on you?" he asked, sounding hurt.

"Nah, because I called you three weeks ago, and you just now decided to return my call. How come you ain't called me back then when I called ya ass?"

"What you mean? Ma, you didn't call me three weeks ago."

"Wanna bet? Oh, but then one of ya little females answered when I called, so I'm guessing she never told you that I called you."

"What are you talking about, ma?"

"Like I said, I called you three weeks ago, but one of your females answered giving me a hard time. Talking 'bout she was ya woman and whatnot."

"Man, come on, are you serious?"

"Does it sound like I'm playing, Weedy? Now, what do you want?"

"You, ma. I want you. You thought about what we talked about?"

"Weedy, not right now. I've been through so much shit the past couple of weeks, I ain't had a chance to collect my thoughts."

"What's up? What's going on?"

"Nothing." I felt some type of way. His ass wasn't nowhere to be found when I needed his ass, but now he wanted to be concerned. He needed to leave me the hell alone right now.

"Come on, ma, don't be like that."

I tried sitting up so that I could give his ass a piece of my mind, but the pain in my shoulder prevented me from doing so. "Ugh," I screamed as the shooting pain raced across my chest.

"What's wrong, ma?"

"Weedy, leave me alone and go play with ya females, because I don't have time for your games."

"Troy, go 'head with all that there. You know I don't have no damn females. So stop trippin'."

"Shit, you could've fooled me, with that chick answering your phone and all." I hoped he didn't think that he was running game on me, because he wasn't. Weedy was a man ho, and he wasn't going to change for nobody. He was one of those types of dudes who needed a whole team of females. Ever since I'd known him, he never had just one woman. There was always a sidepiece lurking somewhere.

"Chill out and tell me what's going on with you, ma," he said, trying desperately to get me to talk to him. I had to admit that I did miss him a little. He was a crappy-ass boyfriend, but a great friend.

Sighing, I removed the phone from my ear. I needed a shoulder to lean on for the moment, because if I kept all this shit inside of me, I may have ended up exploding.

"Troy, you still there?"

"Yeah, I'm still here, Weedy."

"Are you going to tell me what's wrong, ma?"

I thought about it and figured I had nothing to lose. Without giving it any more thought, I decided to give him a shorter version. "Three weeks ago, my best friend was shot and killed. Then someone broke in the shop and damaged the place. And, to top that off, I have some unknown stalker stalking me, and I got shot a week ago."

"My God, Troy, why didn't you call me?"

"I did, Weedy, but you wasn't there. You're never there when I really need you to be. It's always the same thing with you."

"Ma, don't do this, please," he begged, because he knew what I was about to say.

"How you gonna try to be there for me now, but when I needed you the most, you wasn't there? What about all them times I had to fight your hoes? Where were you then, huh? With another ho. And what about that time I got in a car accident because of one of your stalking ass bitches? Where were you when I miscarried our babies, Weedy? Whenever I needed you the most you wasn't there," I yelled with tears flowing down my face.

He didn't answer. Hell, he couldn't. I'd been holding this shit in for a while now. I needed to get that out. I actually felt a bit better now that I'd gotten that off my chest. It'd been years since I experienced a breakdown talking to him.

"I can't go through that no more, Weedy. You've cut me too deep already. I can't look past that." I sobbed, wiping the tears that had fallen from my face. "I just can't."

"Ma, come on. That's the past; this is the present. I'm not the same dude I was before. I've changed. Let me prove that to you, Troy. Let me be there for you in your time of need." He said it like he really meant it, but then I had to remind myself that this was Weedy we were talking about.

"Weedy—" I started to say something, but I was interrupted by Jayden and Mark walking through the door. "Let me call you right back," I said and hung up without waiting for him to answer. I quickly tried to wipe my eyes before they could see me, but I was a little too slow.

"What's wrong, ma?" Mark asked, walking over to the bed. "Why are you crying?"

"I'm just emotional with the funeral being tomorrow, that's all," I said, trying to play it off.

"Are you sure?"

"Yes, I'm positive," I snapped as a nurse entered the room, pushing a wheelchair with my discharge papers in the seat.

"Hello, Miss Miller, I'm here with your discharge papers."

"Okay."

"Umm, is everything okay?" she asked, looking from me to Mark, then to Jayden. I guessed the look on Mark's face, along with the fact that my eyes were red and puffy, gave her the impression that something was wrong.

"Everything is fine. I'm just ready to get out of here," I said, cracking a half smile.

"Okay. I need you to sign here." She pointed to the bottom of the page. Something about the sexy look she gave Mark made me heated.

"I need a pen," I said with attitude.

"Sure." She handed me a pen. I jacked the pen out of her hand and hurriedly signed my name at the bottom. I wanted to get this bitch out of my nigga's face and get home ASAP.

Ten minutes and three signatures later, they finally wheeled me out of the hospital. The minute I got outside, I desperately sucked in some much-needed fresh air. Staying in the hospital was something that I never wished to do again. Mark and I stayed by the entrance, while Jayden went to get the car from the parking lot. I decided to use this time to apologize for snapping on him earlier.

"Mark, I'm sorry for snapping on you in the room earlier. It's just that I've been through a lot," I said softly, rubbing the hand that he had sitting on my shoulder.

"It's cool, ma, I'm not even trippin'. Just remember that I've been by ya side this whole time. If something is wrong, you can tell me."

"I really appreciate you for that. Not a lot of dudes would stick by a woman's side when they need them," I mused, referring to Weedy. I couldn't believe I almost fell for his shit yet again.

"Ma, I'm sure you've realized that I'm not like most men. I'm a different breed," he said, just as Jayden pulled up with the car.

"Yes, I've noticed that," I replied, smiling. "Thank you."

"No need to thank me, baby. You're my girl, so I'm going to do what I'm supposed to." He opened the back seat door for me and helped me to get in. He then jumped in on the other side, and we were on our way.

"Y'all niggas got me playing taxi and shit. Where to?" Jayden asked, laughing from the front seat, making us laugh also.

"To my house," I replied, laughing.

"Yes, ma'am," he replied, trying to fake an accent, and I couldn't help but chuckle some more.

He pulled out of the hospital parking lot, straight into the morning's traffic. I knew it was going to take some time for us to make it to my house, so I used that time to think. I had lots of things to do. I needed to stop by Mimi's house to get a few things, and I needed to call Candy down at the salon. Yes, we were still doing business. Mimi always said that, no matter what, the shop should be open. Tomorrow it would be closed for the funeral. I also needed to find out where Kaylin and Stacy were. Once Mimi's funeral was over, I'd give that my full attention. I was going to find them no matter what it cost me.

Pulling my phone from out of my purse, I sent Weedy a text.

Me: I need a favor. I set the phone on my lap as I waited for a reply.

Weedy: What's up?

Me: I need you to look for Kaylin for me. I've been having a little trouble locating him. I know he's not here and I'd bet my last dollar that he's headed that way.

Weedy: I'll look into that for you. Are you okay?

Me: Thank you. I'm okay, Weedy. I just need some time to think about this. I'll give you an answer after all of this is over.

Weedy: Okay, ma, I understand. I'll give you some time to think about it.

Me: Thanks.

I tossed my phone down in my lap and decided to use the rest of the drive home to prepare myself mentally for the talk we'd have once we made it home. I had no idea where to begin, but I knew they wouldn't be too happy after I told them everything that'd been going on. I just hoped they didn't flip out, because I couldn't deal with all that right now. I was just going to have to take it slow, and give them a little piece at a time.

Chapter 4

Mimi

I sat there in the dark for the seventh day in a row. I couldn't eat, sleep; I barely could breathe. My mind was clouded, and my heart was broken in two. It took me a week to finally accept the fact that Kaylin was the one who shot me. I couldn't believe it. Hell, I didn't want to. I thought that when I called his phone and it was disconnected, it was because of other reasons, not because he was in hiding. Now I had to face the fact that Kaylin shot me, left me for dead, and now he was on the run with my kids.

I still didn't understand why he would shoot me though. I remembered bits and pieces, like Kaylin and me fighting, but I didn't know why. That part was still unclear to me. Whatever happened prior to me being shot must have been serious if Kaylin felt he had to shoot me. Hell, I needed some answers, and the only one I could think to call was Troy. I had a major problem though: I couldn't seem to recall her number. I racked my brain, but I couldn't remember a damn thing, and that shit was frustrating as hell.

I needed to get out of here as soon as possible. I couldn't do shit locked up in this hospital like a prisoner. I needed to get home. I needed to see my kids. I needed answers, answers that this fake-ass detective couldn't give me. It was time to come up with a plan. I was leaving this hospital today.

I sat there waiting on Nurse Margie to come. For the past few weeks, we'd gotten close. She'd been my day nurse since I'd been in here. She'd been helpful. Any- and everything that I needed, she made sure that I got it. She'd been doing a little research on what happened the day that I was shot and, so far, she hadn't come up with anything. It's like they never even put the shit in the papers, or on the news. You'd think the shit had never even happened. I wondered what the hell was going on out there. I got shot four times, and it didn't even make the news.

Pushing the call button for the nurse, I decided that this time was the best time. Since Detective Webber was gone on a little break, I needed to make a break for it. If there was a perfect time to try to leave, now would be it. Throwing the cover back, I sat up on the side of the bed, waiting on Margie. It was taking her so long that I started to think she wasn't coming.

I attempted to get out of bed, but I sat back down when I realized that my strength wasn't at 100 percent. Holding on to the side of the bed, I inched my way up. I was about to take a step when I heard someone walking through the door.

"What are you doing?" Margie asked, running toward me. "Why are you out of bed?"

"Making a break for it. I'm getting out of here while I have the opportunity. I need some answers, and Detective Webber isn't trying to help me, so I'll have to help myself," I said, standing to my feet.

"But you're in no condition to leave."

"Don't matter what condition I'm in, I'm getting up out of here," I grunted.

"Now you know you can't go anywhere like that," she said, trying to stop me.

I looked in her eyes with a straight face and said, "I can and I will. Now you can either help me, or you can let me go."

I stared at her intently. I could see the wheels in her head turning, wondering if she should help me. Hell, she was probably scared of losing her job.

"If you're worried about losing your job, I can help you. I have money, I can give you some," I said, trying to ease her burden.

"I don't want your money, Amina, and although I know that you're in no condition to leave, I'm going to help you. I like you. As a matter of fact, I care deeply for you. You're like the daughter I never had. All I ask is that you be careful and take care of yourself," she said with her voice cracking.

"Aw, that's sweet. I promise that I'll take care of myself, Margie. I just can't stay in here not knowing what's going on. I don't know how I got here. I don't know where Troy is, where Kaylin is, or where my kids are. I wanna be able to see, hear, and hug my kids, but I can't do that. I need to find them and I can't if I'm locked up in here."

"I understand all that, baby, I really do. Now I'm going to help you get out of here, but you have to be patient," she replied, looking at the door like someone was standing there.

"Okay. Thank you so much for helping me. I really appreciate it," I said, hugging her.

"Child, you don't have to thank me, just get out there and find those babies. When you find them, make sure you bring them by to see me." She hugged me back.

"Okay."

"All right, now, let me go get you a wheelchair. Lord knows you can't walk up out of here in your own," she said, preparing to leave, but she stopped just as she was about to open the door. "Will there be someone here to pick you up?"

"Hell, no. I didn't even think about that. I can't remember anybody's number to try to call them," I replied, looking stupid. I thought about a lot of shit, but finding a ride away from here wasn't one of them.

"It's okay. I'm going to get you away from here. Stay here."

I sat down in the chair while I waited for Margie to return. I ain't gonna lie, I was a nervous wreck right now. So many questions were flooding through my mind. What if Detective Webber came back and caught me? What if Margie was caught and lost her job? I would have been devastated if any of that were to happen. I made up my mind that I wasn't going to do it.

"What are you doing?" Margie asked, seeing that I was trying to walk over to the bed.

"I'm not doing it, Margie. I can't. So much shit can go wrong, and I don't want you to lose your job behind me."

"It's okay, really. I'll just act like I'm taking you for a walk, then act like I forgot something. When I get back, you'll already be gone in my car." She smiled, handing me the keys.

"Won't you have to report your car stolen and shit? Margie, I ain't trying to go to jail." I handed her keys back.

"I won't. I'll give you my number, and you can tell me where you are. I'll catch a cab to come pick it up, and I can check on you at the same time."

"Margie, I don't think we should do this."

"Amina, it's going to be all right. Now while you're standing over there wasting time, we could be getting you out of here before Detective Webber gets back."

"Okay," I finally agreed, walking toward the wheelchair. "But if you get caught and lose your job, you have to promise to let me help you."

"Okay, little lady, just come on before we both get caught," she replied, shooing me into the chair. I sat down and waited for her to move. Opening the door, she peeked out of it first before grabbing the chair and pushing me out.

"Be real quiet, but if anyone asks where we're going, tell them that we're going for a walk," she whispered to me. We passed two patients who being wheeled out also. Smiling, we waved at them and kept on about our business. I could hear my heart beating super loud. The shit felt like it was going to come out of my chest. It wasn't that I was scared of getting caught. I was scared of not getting up out of here and finding my kids. Shit, by the time they let me out of here officially, Kaylin might be long gone with my damn children.

We made it all the way to the elevator without getting caught. It actually went smoother than I expected. Now if the rest of our little journey went like that, we'd be on easy street, I thought as the elevators opened. Moving quickly, we bumped right into Dr. McKenley.

"Morning ladies, how is it going?" he asked, stopping to talk to us.

"G . . . good morning, Dr. McKenley. Everything is going good," I stuttered.

"Good morning, Dr. McKenley. Everything is great. We're just going for a walk," Margie spoke from behind me. I was glad that she interrupted the conversation, because my nervousness would've given us away.

"Where's Detective Webber?" he asked, looking through the elevator doors.

"Oh, uh, he stepped out for a little bit," Margie replied. "He said he'll be back shortly."

"Oh, okay. Remember to take it easy."

"We will."

"Okay, then, have a great walk." He walked off toward the nurse's station.

"I thought he was going to catch on to us," I whispered the minute the elevator had closed.

"Or get us caught," Margie said chuckling, as the elevator started to move. It felt like the elevator was taking forever to get to the first floor. If I didn't know better, I'd have sworn it wanted us to get caught.

"Come on, elevator," I complained. My nerves were all over the place. I wanted to get away from here as fast as possible. I needed to get to my children.

"Finally," I yelled when the elevator stopped on the first floor. We carefully made our way out of the hospital toward the front entrance. We were almost home free when we spotted Detective Webber outside, smoking a cigarette.

"Oh, shit, what are we going to do, Margie?" I started to panic.

"Child, calm down. We're just going to have to go around back," she said, pushing me in the opposite direction.

"Margie, we can't do this. We're going to get caught. Just bring me back upstairs."

"We can and we will. Now hush up and save your energy for when you get out of here," she fussed, picking up speed. We made it to the back of the hospital in no time.

"My car is parked on the left side of the parking lot. It's a black Chevy Malibu with tinted windows." She gently helped me out of the wheelchair. It took a minute for me to get my bearings, but I was fine after that.

"Thank you so much, Margie. You don't know how much this really means to me," I said, turning around to hug her. "I'm so happy that I've met you."

"Aw, baby, you're welcome. Now go out there and find those babies. Don't you forget to call me when you get settled in." She gave me a little push.

"Okay, I will. Thanks again," I replied, heading out of the entrance. My legs felt like Jell-O at first, but after the first few steps, I was back to normal.

I slowly made my way to the left side of the parking lot in search of Margie's car. When I couldn't find it, I used the remote on the keychain to make the headlights flash. Once I located the car, I got in and started it up. I took my time as I backed out. I didn't want to cause an accident because I hadn't driven a car in a minute. On my way out of the hospital parking lot, I spotted Detective Webber by the entrance. I passed by him slowly, praying I didn't alert him or hospital security. Once I drove past him, I turned out of the parking lot and headed for the expressway.

Pulling onto the highway, I finally breathed a sigh of relief. I'd been holding my breath from the minute I spotted Detective Webber by the hospital's front entrance. Now that I was a good distance from the hospital, I could breathe right.

I had no plans on where I'd be staying. I knew I couldn't go home, because that was the first place that they'd look for me. I could go to Troy's, but I didn't want her to know that I was alive and well right now. I needed a place to rest, gather my thoughts, and to form plan. I spotted a service station and decided to make a quick stop.

Pulling into the parking lot, I parked on the side away from the gas pumps. Looking in the glove compartment, I found a loose five dollar bill. I figured I could pay Margie back, so I took it and went in.

Walking to the back by the coolers, I reached in and picked up an AriZona tea. After getting my drink, I went to the front and got a pack of Skittles and a sample pack of Tylenol. Then I paid for my things, and I was out the door. The minute I stepped outside, I spotted a white Camaro. I thought it was Kaylin. I slowly crept over to where I had parked the car. I got in and waited to see if he got out. When the Camaro's car door opened, I frowned. It was Kaylin's car for sure, but he wasn't the one driving. It was his stupid-ass friend Arthur. I never liked his loud, obnoxious ass, because he always thought he was all that.

"What is he doing with Kaylin's car though?" I wondered aloud as I started up the car and drove off. Once I made it back on the freeway, I knew exactly where I was headed. It was the one place I'd be safe, and no one would find me.

Chapter 5

Troy

It felt like it was taking forever and a day to make it back to my place. The whole ride there, I was getting a bit agitated. I didn't know how I was going to get through this. I had a feeling that something was going to go wrong. I didn't know how or why. I just had that feeling.

The minute we pulled up on my block, I felt an empty feeling in the pit of my stomach. When we passed by the spot where I was shot, I felt like I was about to hallucinate. I knew it'd been a week now, but I still couldn't believe that Kaylin's sidepiece shot me. I mean, I knew I gave that ho one hell of an ass whooping, but she should've taken her problems out on Kaylin, not me.

"Where's my car?" When we pulled up in my driveway, I immediately noticed that it wasn't there.

"It was a little messed up, so I put it in the shop," Mark said, looking at me. "I hope you don't mind."

"Oh, okay. That's cool. I don't mind at all."

We all just sat in the car as if we didn't want to go inside. I didn't know about them, but I knew I wasn't ready. I hated coming back to my condo. It made me think too much about everything.

"You ready to go in, ma?" Mark asked me softly, breaking me from my thoughts.

Clearing the lump that had formed in my throat, I gulped and said, "Yes."

He then got out of the car and walked over to the other side to open my door. He reached out one of his hands and helped me out of the car. While he grabbed my things, I quickly glanced around. It suddenly felt good to be home. It just dawned on me that I could've died a week ago.

"All right, come on." Mark grabbed my arm to assist me. I wanted to object and remind him that I wasn't a child, but I didn't. He was just trying to help me out, and I was thankful for that.

The bright sun beat against my face as I slowly made my way toward my front door. I felt like it was going to take me forever to make it to there, because my legs were unsteady and I was afraid I'd fall.

"Where are your keys, ma?" he asked, once we made it to the door.

"They're in my purse." I pointed to the purse he had in his hand.

"Hold on to my shoulder." He handed me the purse, and I fished out my keys and gave them to him. He opened the door and allowed me to go in first. "Where do you want me to put these?" he asked, holding up my bags.

"You can put them on the kitchen table," I replied, pointing to the kitchen as I took a seat on the sofa. I had gotten tired just that fast.

"You good, ma? You need anything?" He patted my leg as he took a seat on the sofa next to me.

"Nah, I'm all right."

"You sure?" he asked again.

"Yeah, I'm sure, boo," I responded by scooting a little close to him. Looking into his eyes, I leaned forward and gave him a passionate kiss, the kind that takes your breath away.

"What was that for?" He looked surprised.

"Just because. What, I can't give my nigga a kiss now?"

"Nah, ma, it's cool. You just took me by surprise, that's all."

"Uh-huh." I folded my arms across my chest.

"Come on, ma, don't be like that." He looked hurt, but I ignored him.

He tried to move over to me, but I raised my hand, stopping him in the process. "Get Jayden in here so we can discuss everything," I said to him. I wasn't really mad at him. I thought I was still feeling some type of way about what had happened between Weedy and me earlier.

"Cool," he said, pulling out his phone. He dialed Jayden's number and told him to come up.

I got up from the sofa and went into the kitchen to get me something to drink. When I came back, he was still sitting over there pouting. I walked over to him and sat down on the coffee table in front of him.

"I'm sorry, Mark. Everything is just too much for me right now." I apologized yet again today. "I want to thank you for being there for me. I really don't know what I would've done without you being by my side. Not just through this, but also when Mimi got killed. You've been everything I need and more."

Getting up, I sat on his lap and started kissing him. I was trying to make up for getting mad at him when he was only trying to help me. I needed him to know how much I appreciated him.

Looking directly in my eyes, he stopped kissing me and said, "Ma, I told you time and time again that you don't have to keep thanking me for doing what I'm supposed to do. I don't know how dudes used to treat you before, but I'm different. I'm with you, so I'm going to be there for you, no matter what."

Hearing him say those words made my heart skip a beat. Other than Mimi, no one had spoken to me like that, especially not the niggas I'd been with. Hell, my parents weren't even there for me, so to hear him say that made me teary-eyed. Leaning my forehead against his, I let the tears fall freely.

"Why are you crying, ma?" He leaned my head back, but I couldn't say anything, and I didn't want to. How would it sound if I told him about everything that I'd been through with Weedy? He might have thought I was all kind of dumb bitches and shit.

"I'm fine, Mark," I said as Jayden knocked on the door. "Come on in, Jayden."

"Sup with y'all?" he asked as soon as he saw me crying on Mark's lap.

"I'm just emotional, that's all," I replied, rising up from Mark's lap. I sat next to him on the sofa as Jayden sat down on the loveseat across from us.

"Y'all want anything, something to eat or drink maybe?" I nervously bit my lip.

"Nah, I'm good," Jayden replied.

"Me too," Mark responded after him.

"Okay." I exhaled. "Well, I need to discuss a few things with you guys. I already told y'all about the stalker, the salon being trashed, and the notes. Y'all also already know that we can't find Kaylin or the kids."

"Yeah, we know all that," Jayden replied.

"Well, Mimi's funeral services are scheduled for tomorrow." I took a deep breath and exhaled, then continued. "But what y'all don't know is that Mimi will be having a closed casket."

"Why? I thought she was shot in her back. Why she gotta have a closed casket?" Jayden asked, looking confused.

My heart started to pound while my stomach was doing back flips. "The reason she gotta have a closed casket is because they can't find her body."

"Say what?" Jayden exclaimed, leaning forward.

"The people at the funeral home cannot find her body!"

"What you mean?" Jayden jumped up in anger.

"I'm saying that they can't find her. As in it wasn't there when the coroner went to pick it up," I said.

"Where is she? How can someone lose a whole body out here? That's impossible! Somebody had to see something, or knows what the hell happened," he said, pacing back and forth. From the way he was pounding his hand in his fist, I thought he was about to spazz out.

"I don't know. I went through all that with them. Nobody knows anything, so they say."

"This shit sounds fishy as fuck, ma. You talked to the detective about this shit?"

"No, I haven't had a chance to talk to him yet."

"Why though? This shit is serious. You can't just lose a fuckin' body and not expect the family to ask what's goin' on!"

"Every time I call him, he doesn't answer, and when I went down to the station, they gave me the runaround."

"Oh, yeah. We 'bout to see 'bout this shit now," he growled.

"No, Jayden, it's no use. We're just going to have to wait until after the funeral to find out what happened to her body. I already have too much stress on me as it is, and I'm sure you guys have a lot going on yourselves." I was trying to talk a little sense into him, because I needed him to wait. Now was not the time to be starting trouble, especially when Mimi's kids were out there somewhere.

"I'll wait, but just know I'm not waiting too long," he said, slamming the door.

I turned to Mark for comfort. He took me into his arms, and I snuggled up closer to him.

"He's just mad. Give him some time to cool down," he said, rubbing my arms.

"I already knew that he was going to be mad, but I had no idea that he was going to act like that. I just need him to wait a little while for me, that's all." I laid my head on his shoulder.

"Jayden is a hard dude. He doesn't let nothing get by him. If there's a problem, he always wants to fix it right away."

"Hell, I can see that!"

"It's going to be all right, ma. He won't be mad forever."

I was about to reply when I heard a ringing coming from my purse. I was confused, because my phone was actually sitting on the table. For a few seconds, I was scared to touch my purse. Suddenly, I remembered that I still had the phone Mimi had given to me.

"What the fuck?" I grabbed my purse and fished out the phone.

"What's going on?" Mark asked, but I didn't answer him. Looking at the phone's caller ID, I saw it read, "Private Caller."

"I don't know. This is the phone that Mimi gave me before she was killed. She's the only person who's supposed to know this number." I sat still, staring at the phone in my hand.

"Maybe someone got the wrong number or something. Just answer it and see," he said, hunching his shoulders.

"Hello," I answered. "Hello, who the fuck is this?" I said when they didn't say anything.

Pressing the phone closer to my ears, I could hear shallow breathing on the other side. "Helloooo," I said, stretching the word, but the person still didn't say anything. "I know you're there, so you might as well just say something!"

The person on the other end still didn't respond. Instead, they just disconnected the call. Throwing the phone on the sofa in frustration, I huffed and took a seat.

"What's wrong, ma?"

"I'm just tired, Mark. Someone has been calling me for the past few weeks and won't say shit. It's starting to piss me off."

"Well, get your number changed then."

"I will. I'm going to do it later. Right now, I just need to get some rest for tomorrow," I said, getting up. I walked in the bathroom and started running my bathwater.

"Well, do you need me to get you anything? Something from the store? Something to eat? Anything?" Mark asked, walking in the bathroom behind me.

"Nah, I'm straight. But you could go and get me a bottle of water and them pills out of my purse."

"Okay," he said, walking out of the bathroom. I kicked off my shoes, took my pants and panties off, and waited for him to get back so that he could help me take my shirt off. I knew my shoulder was too sore to try it alone.

"Here you go," he said, handing me the pill bottle and water.

"Set it right there for me." I pointed to the bathroom counter. "Can you help me take my shirt and bra off please?"

"Sure." He placed the things on the counter, and then carefully helped me out of the rest of my clothes.

I removed two pills out of the bottle, opened the water, and took my pain medicine. When I was done, I got into the tub to relax my sore body.

"Hand me a washcloth and my body wash right there on the stand, please."

Getting the washcloth and body wash like I asked, he came back over by the bathtub, but he didn't hand them to me. Instead, he got down on his knees and wet the washcloth in the water.

"What are you doing?" I asked, suddenly becoming shy.

"What do you think I'm about to do?" he asked, chuckling. "I'm about to bathe you. Is something wrong with that?"

"Uh, no, no. Nothing is wrong with that," I stuttered.

"Okay, then." He shrugged as he took the washcloth and drenched my body gently with water. He made sure to soak every inch of my body, and when he got to my shoulder where the bullet hole was, I flinched a bit. I didn't want him to see my scars.

"It's okay, baby. I love every part of you." He kissed me lovingly on my shoulder, and when I heard that, I thought, *I can't believe he just told me that he loved me. Hell, this is his first time saying it.*

"I love you too," I replied sincerely, looking into his eyes. I couldn't believe I almost let Weedy get next to me again. I should have whooped my own ass for even thinking about messing with Weedy after all of the shit that he had put me through. Why would I want to go back to a man I had to share when I had my own man right here?

He squeezed some body wash into the washcloth and began to bathe me. I wanted to object, but I didn't. It not only felt good, but it was actually nice to have someone cater to me.

"Stand up," he said, getting up off the floor.

I stood up with my hands covering my breasts.

"You can put your hands down, ma. I already seen all of that," he said, smiling.

I let my hands fall, and I started to breathe slowly as he started washing the top half of my body. My heart was beating like a bass drum. That's how afraid I was. When he got to my midsection, he stopped.

"You can breathe normally, ma. I'm not going to bite you," he said as he rubbed the washcloth against my stomach.

"Okay," I said, taking a deep breath. He proceeded to wash the rest of my body and, when he was finished, he turned on the shower and rinsed me off.

"Where are the bath towels?" he asked, turning off the water.

"They're in the linen closet in the hallway."

"Okay." He left the bathroom.

I stepped out of the tub to examine my body in the full-length mirror. Lately, I'd added on a couple of pounds. It went lovely with my body, and no one else could tell the difference, but I could, and I didn't like it. Moving a little closer, I turned to see the holes left in my shoulder and side. They weren't too big, but they looked huge to me. They were already starting to form into keloids. My eyes got misty as I looked over my once-perfect body. I figured no one was going to want me once they saw me completely naked.

"You're still perfect, ma. Them little war wounds ain't nothing. You're just a gangsta chick to me, and I've always had a thing for your kind," Mark murmured, walking up behind me. Wrapping the towel around my body, he began to dry me off. When he was done, he handed me the robe that was hanging on the back of the door, and I put it on.

I turned toward him and gave him a long kiss. I wanted him in the worst way. I needed him, and if things were different, I wouldn't mind having him right this moment. "Call Jayden and tell him that you're staying over tonight," I said, looking intently at him.

"Okay." He pulled his phone out.

"Y'all still staying at the motel?" I asked.

"Yeah."

"Well, look, y'all go and get y'all things. I'll let y'all stay in one of Mimi's properties not too far from here."

"Ma, you really don't have to do that."

"I can and I will. Why would I let y'all stay in some sleazy motel, when Mimi has a lot of properties around Georgia?" I went straight into my room to get some clothes to put on.

"Where you think you goin'?" Mark asked as I took out a pair of pants and a shirt.

"I'm going with you guys to pick up y'all things," I said letting the robe fall from my body.

"Man, you don't need to be going nowhere, ma."

"Yes, I do," I said, slipping on my sweatpants. I didn't even bother to put on a pair of panties, and I knew there was no way in hell I'd be able to put on a bra.

"Ma, you don't need to be going back out this time of night. You just got out of the hospital, bruh."

"Mark, don't fight me on this. I'm going with you guys to get your things so that y'all don't have to sleep in that hotel no more." I slipped on my tennis shoes and then went into my closet to get me a jacket, because it was getting kind of chilly outside.

"Come on," I said, stopping in front of him. He said nothing. All he did was look at me, shake his head, and walk out of the room. I'd make it right later on, but right now we were leaving, and I didn't have time to argue.

I went to look for my keys so that I could take my own car, but then I realized that my car was in the shop. "Shit." Suddenly, I remembered that one of Mimi's cars was still parked in the garage at the house.

"I'll just use her car until my car comes from the shop," I said to myself as I cut the light off and went to meet Mark in the living room.

Chapter 6

Mimi

I was waiting on Margie to come and get her car. I was tired and hungry. I needed to go out to the store and get myself a few things. It was a good thing that I had clothes over here and that I was able to take a bath, or else I would have stunk and been hungry. Normally, I kept this house fully stocked, but since I was supposed to be dead, there was nothing in here to eat.

I'd only been here for a couple of hours, and I'd already damn near walked a hole in the carpet. Every time I spotted a car's headlights, I thought that it was Margie. She was supposed to be here fifteen minutes ago. I hated being in one spot for too long, which was part of the reason why I broke out of that hospital. I was tired of being there, and I was especially tired of not getting any answers. That was one of the things that Troy and I had in common: we were always on the move. We never stayed in one spot for too long.

I was about to walk into the bedroom when I heard a car pull up in the driveway. Taking baby steps, I calmly walked to the window to peek out of it. I moved slowly, not wanting anyone to see me. I slowly peeked out the window to see Margie getting out of a cab. I walked over to the door and opened it, but I didn't go outside because I didn't want any of these nosy-ass neighbors seeing me.

"Girl, I didn't think anyone was at home the way the house was all dark and stuff," she said, walking up to the door.

"Oh, I decided to keep the lights off. I don't need no one getting suspicious and calling Troy," I said, moving to the side and allowing her to enter.

"So you haven't called her yet?" she asked, walking into the living room.

"No, I haven't," I said, closing the door and following her.

"Why?" She removed her jacket and threw it on the back of the sofa. She then took a seat and waited for me to answer.

"Because, Margie, I can't. I mean, I've called her a few times, but I never said anything. I always blocked my number and just listened to her voice until she hung up." I sighed, plopping down on the sofa next to her.

"Child, you will never get any answers unless you call her. You need to call her. Never mind what Detective Webber said. Call your friend. She holds the keys to all of your unanswered questions," she replied.

"What will I say to her? She probably won't even believe it's me when I call. She thinks I'm dead, along with the rest of the world."

"You won't know until you try."

"Okay, I'll call when I come back from the store."

"Okay."

"How did everything go with Detective Webber?" I asked, changing the subject.

"It went okay. He kept pressuring me about you, but I told him I didn't know where you went. Told him that I had gone to check on something, left you there for a few minutes and when I came back, you were gone."

"I know he had to be mad. He was trying his hardest to keep me in that hospital."

"Girl, I'm telling you. That's why I was late getting here. I drove around leisurely for a little while, just to make sure he wasn't following me. I didn't want to lead him to you when I know you have a lot of things to do," she said, laughing.

"Thank you so much, Margie." I walked over to her and gave her a big hug. "For everything."

"You're very so welcome," she said, hugging me back. "Now let me get out of here. I have a few things to do at home, and you have a lot of things you need to be doing yourself."

"Hold on, I'll be right back," I said, running to the master bedroom. I remembered having a safe in the closet where I kept some of Kaylin's money. Since the safe was behind a lot of clothes, it took me a minute to get to it. It took me a few tries to remember the code, but I got it. Troy was the only one besides me who knew the combination. Kaylin didn't even know it, and that was his money in there.

Opening up the safe, I grabbed a couple of bundles out of there, threw them in a small duffle bag, and shut the door. I safely secured the safe back behind the clothes and shut the closet. I was almost to the living room when I heard what sounded like fussing.

"I'm going to ask you one more fucking time. Who the fuck are you, what do you want, and how the fuck did you get in here?" I heard a female voice that sounded strangely like Troy.

"Who I am and why I'm here doesn't concern you," I heard Margie fire back.

"Bitch, you talking some slick shit considering the position that you are in."

I heard Margie laughing, and I wondered what was funny. "The fuck you laughing at?" Troy yelled. Although I couldn't see Troy, I bet her face was all screwed up.

"I'm laughing at you. You must be Troy. I've heard a lot about you," I heard Margie say.

I inched closer to the living room, where I spotted Troy. She had two fine-ass niggas with her. Who the fuck were they?

"How the fuck do you know my name and what could you have possibly heard about me? I don't know you, but you claiming that you've heard a lot about me. What, you a stalker or something? Don't tell me, you're one of Kaylin's hoes too?"

"Like I said, I've heard a lot about you. Let's just say that we have a little something in common," Margie said, crossing her legs.

I watched as Troy went over by the TV. I knew that she was going for the gun we kept in a secret spot.

"See, I tried to be nice to you, but you don't like nice. I'm already not in the mood. I just got out of the hospital, and my best friend's funeral is tomorrow," she said, removing the gun. She pulled the clip out and then cocked it. "Now I'm going ask you one last motherfucking time and this time I want an answer. Who the fuck are you and what are you doing here?"

"You really think that is going to scare me, little girl?" Margie asked, not looking scared at all. I watched as Troy decided to point the gun in her direction, and I waited to see if the two guys were going to interfere, but they didn't. They just stood there looking.

"Wrong answer," Troy said as her finger inched toward the trigger.

"Troy, wait. She's here with me," I yelled, which brought Troy's two male visitors to full alert.

"Yo, who is you?" she asked, looking in my direction.

I stood there silent. How was I going to tell her that it was me? I knew Troy. She was hardheaded. She wasn't going to believe me.

"It's me, Mimi," I replied, still standing where I was.

"Get the fuck out of here. Amina is dead and gone. I seen her with my own eyes, lying on the floor in a pool of blood. So I know you ain't her."

"No, it's really me, Troy."

"Nah, fuck that. Kaylin must have really done a number on these hoes. Got them out here pretending to be Mimi and shit. Where the fuck they do that at? I already done got shot by one of his hoes, and had to beat another one of 'em up. Now you over here with this shit?" She shook her head. "I tell you what: since you want to be Amina so bad, then I'm going to send you right where she is. Right after I shoot this old lady. Now come on out here and let us see your imposing, stalking, identity-thief-acting ass."

"But it really is me, Troy," I said, trying to plead with her ass again.

"Yeah, I bet. You can save all that fuckery for some-body else. Hurry up and get ya ass over here," she said, motioning with the gun.

I took my time as I walked toward her. Troy really looked and sounded like a crazy woman. I didn't need her ass shooting me. I had cheated death once before in the last couple of weeks. I didn't need it knocking at my door again, because I was pretty sure that I wouldn't be escaping it again. I was almost in the living room when I spotted the dude with the dreads. My mouth damn near dropped to the floor. I guessed he was really surprised that it was really me too, because he was looking at me like he had seen a damn ghost. Well, I guessed to him I was a ghost, since I was supposed to be dead and all.

When I came into view, her hands immediately went up, covering her mouth. Troy gasped, "Oh, my God, it can't be! You're supposed to be dead. I seen you with my own two eyes!"

"It's me, Troy. It's Mimi. I'm alive," I said, taking two more steps toward her so that I was dead in front of her.

"It can't be. I must be dreaming, because my best friend is dead and gone," she mumbled to herself. The look on her face was one of pure confusion. I reached out to touch her so that she could see that I was actually real and she wasn't dreaming, but she jacked her hand away from me.

"Get away from me!" she screamed, sounding like a deranged woman. She then took a couple of steps back and yelled, "Mark, get this bitch away from me before I shoot her!"

My feelings were actually hurt. Troy and I had been through a lot together. I looked from her to the two dudes she was with. The dark-skinned dude with the dreads still had this shocked look on his face, while the light-skinned dude was still looking at Troy. They looked somewhat familiar. I just couldn't place them. Shaking my head, I looked back at Troy.

"Why are you still standing there looking stupid? Y'all know this shit ain't real. Niggas playing with a bitch's feelings, but they need to know that the shit ain't fucking funny," she cried, with tears falling from her eyes. I went to say something to her, but dude with the dreads had beaten me to it.

"Troy, this is as big of a shock to me as it is to you, but it's not a joke, man. This shit is really real. She's alive," he said to her, with his eyes were focused on me. For some strange reason, I felt like I knew him.

"Jayden, this can't be Mimi. Someone has to be playing a joke on me, because if my best friend were alive, I would've known about it," she said, wiping frantically at her eyes; but the tears kept falling.

"I told you that we had something in common," Margie spoke up. For a minute, I had forgotten that she was still here.

"Shut up. Everyone just shut up. This shit ain't real. This bitch ain't no fucking Mimi," she still repeated in denial. No matter what anyone said, she just wouldn't believe it. There was only one way I could think of to get her to believe me. I decided to bring up something that only we would know about. I knew the shit was going to hurt both of us, because we'd vowed to never speak on it again, but I had no choice.

"Troy, remember when I first met Kaylin? I was about sixteen years old." She looked at me and waited for me to finish. "Remember when I stayed home from school the week of finals, you thought it was because of Kaylin and it wasn't?"

She looked at me, stunned. I knew it would convince her. That was a day that she would never forget.

"What happened that week that made me stay home, Troy?" I asked as tears rolled down my face. The memory popped up fresh in my mind like the shit happened yesterday, and it was just as painful as when it first happened. I needed to relive it though so she could believe me, and that was the only way that I knew how.

"Tell me what he did to me, Troy. Tell me what Magilla Gorilla did to me," I said, calling him by the horrible nickname I had given him. Just the mention of his name and remembering everything that man did to me had even more tears rolling down my face.

"He . . . he . . ." she stuttered.

"He did what to me, Troy?" The tears drenched not only my face but the front of my shirt as well.

"He raped you!" Troy wept as she actually realized I was indeed standing in front of her.

I walked over to her and embraced her. She squeezed me for dear life as if I was going to leave her again. "What? How did this happen?"

"A miracle I guess," I simply replied.

"But how?" she asked, confused. "I seen you with my own two eyes. You were lying there in a pool of blood on the floor. You were dead!"

"I guess it wasn't my time yet. They said it was the mortician who found a faint pulse on me." I shrugged. "In fact, Margie was the one who told me that I had died twice, but they were able to revive me both times," I said, pointing to Margie. "She was my nurse at the hospital. It was her helping me get well this whole time. In fact, if it weren't for her, I wouldn't be standing in front of you now. She was the one who helped me escape from the hospital, away from the detective who's been acting like my personal bodyguard. To top all that off, I apparently have some memory loss. I can remember some things, but others are very fuzzy. Doc said my memory could return, or it may never come back."

"Oh, my God, you've been through a lot. That's probably why his old ass was giving me the runaround."

"Who?" I asked, wanting to know who she was talking about.

"Detective Webber," she replied. "Ralph from the funeral home told me that your body couldn't be found. I tried to get in touch with Webber's ass, but I couldn't get him. It's like he got ghost or some shit. Hell, now I know why no one could find your body. You alive instead of being dead."

"Yes, I'm alive," I repeated. "So, who are your friends?"

She looked over to the two guys who were standing by the door, and she motioned for them to come over. They both looked at each other confused, and then they slowly made their way over to us. They were walking like a couple of zombies. They started to make me nervous.

"Umm, this here is Mark," she said, referring to the light-skinned dude with dreads. Homebody was fine as fuck, too. Troy gave me a warning look that said, "I know you, Mimi, and I see it in your eyes. He's my friend. Hands off."

"I'm sorry, boo," I said to her because she caught me. Reaching out my hand, I said, "Hey, Mark, nice to meet you."

"Sup, ma. Likewise," he said, shaking my hand.

"And this here is Jayden," she said, pointing to the dark-skinned dude. I couldn't put my mind on it, but I swore it felt like I already knew him.

"Hey, Jayden," I said, waving. I reached out my hand for a handshake, but he didn't shake it. He picked me up and gave me a huge bear hug.

"I've missed you so much, ma." He was hugging me so tight that I barely could breathe.

"Umm, you're hurting me." I pushed away from him so he'd let me go.

"I'm sorry," he said, putting me down. "It's just that I thought you were dead and, now that I know you're alive, I'll never let you go again."

"Umm, so we do know each other?" I asked him.

"Yes, we do." He winked, flashing a killer smile.

"I had a feeling that we did, because from the moment that our eyes connected, I couldn't help but feel like I already knew you." I gazed into his eyes once more. Dude had a set of dreamy eyes that would send a woman straight to the bedroom.

I was about to ask him how well we knew each other, but I couldn't help but notice Troy giving him this look.

"So, Mimi, do you remember anything about what happened these past couple of weeks?" she asked nervously.

"Well, umm, I don't remember everything, just bits and pieces. That is why I came here. I need your help."

"What do you need help with?" She looked back and forth between Jayden and Mark. I couldn't help but notice the way she was acting like she was nervous.

"Troy, what is going on?"

"What do you mean? Nothing is going on. Why you ask?"

"Because you're acting funny, Troy. Whatever it is, you can tell me," I said, reassuring her.

"There's nothing to tell," she replied.

"Amina, I'm going to head home now," Margie said, getting up from the sofa.

"Okay, hold on a second," I said, going to retrieve the duffle bag that I had left in the hallway. I picked up the bag and tucked up under my right arm. "Here," I said, walking over to her and handing her the bag.

"What's this?" She looked at the bag like it was a disease.

"It's for helping me out these past weeks."

"If it's money, I can't take it," she said, pushing my hand away.

"You can and you will," I said, passing the bag back.

"No, I'm not," she said, taking a step back.

"Margie, if it weren't for you, I wouldn't have been able to make it here. You've been a great friend and a mother when I needed one. Please take it," I pleaded, reaching out my hand with the bag in it again. She looked at me and then at the bag. "Take it, Margie, please!"

"Okay, but I didn't do it for a reward," she said, taking the bag. "I did it because it was my job and you needed someone to guide and help you through your healing process. You needed a friend."

"I know. That's why I'm giving you a reward anyway," I said, hugging her. "Thanks again, Margie."

"You're oh so welcome. Don't be a stranger now. You can call me if you need me."

"Okay. I'll walk you to the door," I said to her.

As I walked Margie to the door, I noticed Troy, Mark, and Jayden in a circle whispering back and forth. I made a mental note to ask about that shit.

"Thanks again, Margie. Be sure to call me when you make it home, okay?" I called out as she made her way to her car.

"You're welcome and I will. Good luck with everything!"

"Thanks," I yelled from the door. I watched as she got into her car and backed out of the driveway. I gave her one final wave as she beeped her horn, and she was gone.

Closing the door, I locked it and made my way back into the living room. When I got in there, I heard Troy whispering. "We can't tell her right now," she said. "She said that she don't remember anything and this will crush her."

"What can't you tell me?" I asked, scaring them.

"Damn, you scared the shit out of me!" she declared, holding her chest.

"I can see that," I replied. "Now what is it that you can't seem to tell me?"

"Uh, nothing. Would you like something to eat or drink?" She quickly changed the subject.

"Nah, I'm not hungry or thirsty."

"Well, do you need anything?"

"What I need is for you to stop trying to change the subject and tell me what is going on, Troy," I yelled. "Where is Kaylin and where are my kids?"

"Ma, calm down. You don't need to be getting all upset. Troy is just looking out for you," the dark-skinned dude with the dreads said.

"Excuse me, what is your name again?" I asked.

He looked both shocked and confused by my question. "Um, it's Jayden," he said, looking like I had hurt his feelings.

"Well, Jayden. Lemme let you in on a thing or two. I've been in the hospital for weeks with no visitors or anything. I was left to look at four white walls, alone! My mind was all over the place, not knowing what was going on. No one wanted to tell me anything, and when I'd ask them, they'd just blow me off and give me the runaround."

I looked around the room, furious. "I'm tired of people keeping shit from me, which is why I came home, to find out those answers. I thought my best friend would be the perfect one to tell me what was going on, but now I'm seeing that I was wrong," I said, looking at Troy. I shook my head at her and then made my way toward the garage. I was heading out there to jump in my car and find my own damn answers.

"Hold up, Mimi. Wait," she said.

"What?" I asked, turning around.

"I asked you earlier what you remembered, because I wanted to see just how much you already knew."

"I don't remember much. All I know us what they've told me."

"Well, ask me. What do you want to know, Mimi?"

"I want to know everything, but I'll save that for later. Right now, you can give me the CliffsNotes version. I'm just tired of being in the dark, and tired of not knowing."

"Well, the day that you was supposed to be leaving Kaylin, you called me to tell me that you were leaving, but you had to stop by the house first. You promised me that you would call me, but you didn't. So I got worried and headed to your house. That's when I found out that he had shot you four times and that you was supposed to be dead."

"I know all that. What I don't know is why?" I said, walking over to the sofa. I took a seat and began shaking my leg. "Know what? I have all the time in the world. You can tell me the whole story tonight."

"Everything? Are you sure you want me to tell you everything right now?" she asked with uncertainty, confusion, and worry plastered on her face.

"Everything," I firmly repeated myself.

"Okay, but I think we may need a drink or something, because this is a lot of shit that I'm about to tell you. So can we do this at my house?"

"Nah, I really don't feel like moving right now. I'm more comfortable here."

"All right, shall we take this to the bedroom? I want you to be comfortable for this."

"Yeah, that's fine with me. Um, will you guys be staying here tonight?" I asked.

"Uh, nah, we'll just go back to the hotel. We don't want to be in your way," Jayden replied, moving toward the door.

"Nah, that's okay. You guys can stay here. We have more than enough room," I said to them. I swear, every time I looked in dude's eyes, my heart nearly skipped three beats.

"No, ma, we're good."

"No, I insist. You guys already looked like y'all was going to stay here, so it would be rude to let y'all leave."

"Are you sure?"

"Yes, I'm sure," I said. "Wait! Are you all killers or something? Because I need to know if I'm going to have to sleep with one eye open."

"Nah, we ain't no killers. We gentlemen," Mark replied, laughing.

"I'm just playing with y'all," I replied as the room erupted with laughter. "Follow me. I'll show you guys where y'all will be sleeping tonight."

I peeped Jayden out while I waited for them to grab their suitcases. I didn't know if he could tell I was flirting, but I damn sure wouldn't have minded getting with him.

When they were ready, I showed them down the hall to the two bedrooms on the right side of the house. "One of you can take this room over here," I said, pointing to the first door. "And the other one can take this one. The bathroom is across the hall right here, and the kitchen is across from the living room. I may have to run out and buy a few groceries."

"Oh, no, ma. That's okay. We'll go and get some groceries. You've already done way too much for us already by letting us stay here," Jayden said, shaking his head.

"You really don't have to. Y'all are guests in my house."

"No, ma, we insist. We'll get settled in first and then we'll go ahead and run to the grocery store."

"Yeah, we can't have you going out there anyway. Let us do something for you since you're letting us stay here," Mark added.

"Well, okay. We'll be in that room over there if y'all need anything." I pointed to the one door at the end of the hall on the left.

"Okay, thanks again," they both said at the same time.

"Y'all are very much welcome." I grabbed Troy by the hand and made my way toward the master bedroom. Once we were inside the room, I slowly closed the door behind me. When I turned around, Troy had this sneaky smile on her face.

"Girl, what the hell is the matter with you?" I asked, playing dumb.

"You ain't slick, Mimi. I know what you're doing," she said, waving her finger at me.

"What? I'm not doing anything," I said, blowing her off.

"Yes, you are. I seen you flirting with Jayden."

"I was not." I broke out in a shy smile.

"Oh, yes, you were."

"Girl, I know I'm wrong for doing that shit, but I couldn't help it. Dude is just so damn fine."

"Yes, you are wrong for that, but you might as well just give it up. He's kind of already taken."

"Damn, really?" I asked, plopping my ass down on the bed. She just looked at me and burst into laughter. I looked around the room trying to find out what was so funny. "Really, Troy?" I asked, catching a slight attitude. "So you just gonna stand there laughing at me?"

"I'm laughing because if you could've seen the look on your face when I told you that he was already taken, you would've laughed ya damn self."

"Fuck all that shit. Tell me where Kaylin and my kids are," I said, changing the subject.

"Well, we've been looking, and we can't seem to find them," she said, changing the look on her face to a more serious one. "That's why I called Weedy for a little help."

"Hold up, who is this 'we'? I can't believe you called Weedy."

"Me, Mark, and Jayden. I had no choice. We couldn't find him, so I needed the extra help."

"What's up with them and why would they help you find my fiancé and kids?" I asked, confused. It was time that I knew the truth, the whole truth at that.

"You really don't remember what happen to you, huh?" She was annoying the shit out of me. "You think if I knew, I would've risked breaking out of the hospital to ask you?"

"I meant that he was taken by you," she said, confusing the shit out of me.

"Say what now?" I didn't think I heard her right.

"Yeah, you heard me right. Before you was shot, you and Jayden had a thing."

"What you mean? What happened to me and Kaylin? Why did I have 'a thing' with Jayden?" My ears were obviously playing tricks on me. Kaylin and I were going to get married. Why would I cheat on him?

"You were leaving Kaylin, Mimi. You finally got tired of his dog-ass ways and decided to leave him."

"What, Troy? I mean, I know about Kaylin cheating on me with Stacy, but I thought I let that go in the past. I was in love with Kaylin, so how did I end up with Jayden?" I was confused because I just didn't get it. Kaylin and I had been through a lot together, and I didn't see myself leaving him. I was mad because, if Troy was telling the truth, I couldn't remember shit, and I hated being clueless. I knew Troy wouldn't lie to me. I trusted her with my life. "Explain this shit to me."

"Well, it's all a part of the story that I'm 'bout to tell you," she said, sitting down on the bed. I just stood there looking at her like she was crazy.

"You might as well get that look off of your face and hop on in." She patted the spot beside her. "Make yourself comfortable, because we're going to be up all night."

I stood still in the spot where I was. I wasn't too sure if I was ready to hear what she was about to tell me. This shit was beginning to confuse me, and she ain't even told me half of the shit already.

"Come on, girl. You said you wanted to know, right?"

"Um, yeah," I said. I slowly walked over to the bed, mentally preparing myself for whatever it was that she was about to tell me. After saying a silent prayer, I sat down and prepared for what would soon be my biggest heartbreak yet.

Chapter 7

Jayden

Words couldn't describe how I was feeling right now. I mean, I was still speechless about this whole thing. I couldn't believe that Mimi was actually alive. I really thought I was dreaming, but I wasn't. *She's really alive, bruh.* I really didn't know how, but we could count this as a miracle. She pulled a Tupac, like when he got shot five times and still survived. I didn't know what it was. All I knew was that I was happy that she was still here with us.

My mind was so heavy, and I was in dire need of some fresh air, so I decided to take the trip to the grocery store alone. Mark tried to tag along, but I convinced him to stay there and look after the girls. I needed this time alone. So much shit had been happening these last few weeks, but I didn't count on no shit like this. I was happy but afraid at the same time. I was happy because she was, in fact, alive, but I was afraid because she didn't remember anything and I hoped like hell that the shit wasn't permanent. I wanted to just wrap her up in my arms and never let her go, but Troy said since she didn't know anything, we'd have to take it slow. I didn't know how long "slow" was supposed to last, and I didn't know if I could dig this slow shit for a minute.

I pulled up into the grocery store parking lot and quickly got out. I ain't know shit about buying groceries, but I was going to learn how today. I was going to get most of Mimi's favorites and a few things for myself, Mark, and Troy. I knew most of the things she liked. I just hoped that she remembered that she liked them.

After getting out of the car, I grabbed a cart and made my way into the store. It was late at night, and the store was rather empty, which made it easy for me to find the things that I needed even faster. I went up and down every grocery aisle and looked for what I needed. I picked up a variety of things such as cookies, chips, and vanilla ice cream. I grabbed up stuff to make mac and cheese, which was Mimi's favorite. She said she liked it cheesy with fried chicken and green beans on the side, so I made sure to get that, too. I also grabbed fruit, water, soda, and Gatorade.

When I was sure that I had enough groceries to last us for a while, I made my way to the checkout line. On my way there, I could've sworn that I passed that dude Kaylin. I looked twice to make sure that I wasn't tripping, but when I turned around, the dude was nowhere in sight. *I must be trippin'.*

It took me a minute to put all the things that I had on the counter, which made me regret not letting Mark tag along for the ride. At least the clerk wasn't slow with ringing me up. It took us all of ten minutes to bag and put all of the groceries in the basket. My total damn near came to $300, but I wasn't tripping because money wasn't a problem for me. I was good in that department. I thanked the clerk and even tried to tip her, but she refused. Instead, she slipped me her number and told me to call her. I took the piece of paper even though I wasn't going to use it, thanked her again, and I was out the door.

After locating my car, I took on the task of loading the groceries in the trunk. I saw why men rarely bought groceries. That shit was a part-time job. After loading up, I returned the cart to its little area, hopped in the car, and made my way back to the house.

On my way back to the house, my phone started to ring. I already knew it wasn't nobody but Shelly, because I had done told all my boys that I would be MIA for Mimi's funeral service tomorrow. Hell, now that she was back, I wondered if she'd be having a service at all. I decided to let Shelly's call roll straight to voicemail. She wasn't trying to do anything but work on my nerves. I didn't know what part of "I don't want you no more" she didn't understand. She was going to drive me to putting my hands on her. She always drove me to that point, but I'd always restrained myself from actually doing it. These days she was becoming more and more determined to make me go over the edge.

It wasn't even a good five minutes, and here she was, sending me a text.

Nigga, I know you see me calling that phone.

I simply deleted the message and set my phone back down on my lap, waiting for her to ring my line with either a message or a call again.

Cam's over here sick, Jay. You gonna ignore your child, too?

The bitch knew what she was doing. Whenever I didn't answer her calls or texts, she would always say some shit about Cameron. She knew my son was my weakness and, since I wasn't there, I didn't know if he was really sick, so I decided to return her call.

"What's wrong with my son?" I asked the minute she answered the phone.

"Well, hey to you too, baby daddy. I see that you ignored me, but when I mention Cam, you hurriedly picked up huh?"

"Bitch, what's wrong with my fucking son?" I yelled at her dumb ass.

"Why are you ignoring me, but yet you run when I say anything about Cameron?" she whined in that needy-ass voice that always seemed to piss me off.

"Bitch, Cameron is my responsibility, not you."

"Nigga, you must not know that we come as a package deal."

"Bitch, is you slow? I told ya ass before that I didn't want you. What part of that statement don't you understand?" I asked through gritted teeth. I loved Cam dearly, but I made a huge mistake when I decided to fuck with this bitch. I was beginning to think that she had a few screws loose or something.

"And I clearly remember that I said we ain't over until I say we over. You must think I'm playin'. I don't know what bitch down in Atlanta done made you trip and bump yo' head but, nigga, you betta think again. I ain't goin' nowhere. I'm here to stay, so tell that bitch I said beat it."

"Bitch, you trippin' hard if you think I'm worryin' 'bout yo' dumb ass. Like I said before, we done. If the shit don't have nothin' to do with Cam, then don't call me."

"You really think I'm playin', huh, Jayden? You think I'm one of them bitches you can just throw away? If so, then you better think again, because that ain't me. Now you got three days to show your face in Virginia. If you don't be here within seventy-two hours, I'm comin' to Atlanta."

I was about to reply when I heard dead silence. *What the fuck? The bitch done hung up on me. Shelly knows better. She can come with that dumb shit if she want to. That's going to be the day that I whoop her ass from here to yonder. I'ma shut that bitch down. That's on everything that I love.*

Not really giving much more into Shelly's bullshit, I powered my phone off and threw it on the seat next to me. I then turned up Migos's "Fight Night" song and relaxed for the rest of the ride. My baby was back, and I was supposed to be happy. I wasn't about to let Shelly's ass spoil my mood. *Fuck her dumb ass.*

When I pulled up to the house, Mark was standing out-side smoking a cigarette. *Good. Since he's already outside, he can help me bring these damn bags up.*

"It took yo' ass long enough. I thought yo' ass got lost or some shit," he said, walking over to me with the cigarette hanging from his lip.

"Man, I didn't take that long," I replied, stepping out of the car.

"Hell, you think so? I started to send a search party after yo' ass, nigga!"

"Yeah, yeah, yeah." I walked to the back of the car and popped the trunk. "Come help me get these bags out of the trunk, li'l nigga."

"I ain't no li'l nigga, homie," he said, grabbing two handfuls of grocery bags.

"Man, why do people do that shit like they just can't come back and get the rest of the bags or some shit?" I asked myself. I always wondered why people would take an assload of groceries that they could barely carry when they could just make several trips.

"Do what?" he asked, looking confused.

"Grab all them damn groceries like it's so hard to make several trips to the car."

"Man, you know how us black folks do shit. We'll damn near try to carry every last one of our bags or die trying before we make a second trip to the car," he said, laughing.

"Hell, I see that shit."

We ended up having to make only two trips to the car. When we got back in with the last of the groceries, the girls were already in the kitchen putting things up. I look at Mimi, who in turn looked at me and smiled. Maybe she remembered me.

"We really would like to thank you guys for all of these groceries. I didn't think y'all would get that much," Mimi said.

"Ma, there's really no need for you to be thanking us. That's the least we could do since you let us stay in your home," I responded.

"What he said. You let us stay in your home, so there ain't no need to thank us. Besides, Jayden was the one who went and got all of this," Mark said.

"Well, thank you, Jayden. I really appreciate it," she said, walking over to hug me.

"No problem." I hugged her. The minute our bodies connected, I felt a magnetic force.

"Oh, my," she said, which let me know she felt it too.

"Um, so what are we going to do about the funeral service tomorrow?" I asked. "I mean, do we go or don't we?"

"Yes, we're going to the funeral tomorrow. We're not quite ready for everyone to know that Mimi is still alive. So, we're going to act like she's still dead," Troy announced.

"Yeah, like she said, I'm not ready for people to know that I'm still alive. To be honest, I wasn't going to tell her until after I sorted a few things out." Her eyes looked sad as she spoke. "It was just in God's plan for you all to come here tonight."

"Well, okay. I feel you on that," I said to her.

"Me too," Mark said. "But you on ya Tupac shit, ma. Besides him and 50 Cent, you the only one I know who done took a couple of bullets and still lived like a G."

"Well, thank for the compliment, I think," she said, laughing. I stood in a trance, just staring at her. I wanted her right now, just as bad as I wanted her before, but I knew that I'd probably have to wait.

"Well, do you girls want something to eat or anything?" Mark asked.

"Um, not right now. Maybe later," Mimi said, looking at Troy. They were looking at each other like they were trying to give each other a sign or some shit.

"Is there something wrong?" I asked, looking at them.

"Um, no," Mimi replied, still looking at Troy.

"Nothing is wrong, Jayden. Mimi just wants to know if you guys want to go with us to her house," Troy explained.

"But, I thought this was her house," Mark said, waving his hand around.

"Technically yes, this is her house, along with several others, but she wants to go to the house that she previously stayed in with Kaylin," Troy answered. Shit, I didn't know my girl was banking like that.

"Uh, sure," Mark replied, looking confused.

"Well, I'm down too, but what I want to know is why she want to go back over there?" I asked feeling some type of way.

"Because I need to," she spoke softly. "Even though Troy's told me everything, I still can't remember it. I want to be able to remember and maybe going back over there will help me."

"Are you sure this won't be a little too much for you?" I was more than a bit concerned.

"No! It won't be. I need this. This is probably the only way I'm going to remember anything."

"Well, if that's what you want, then I'm down," I said, grabbing the car keys.

"Wait, let me go get my shoes on right fast," she said, leaving the kitchen.

"Ay, are you sure your girl is up for this?" I asked Troy the minute she was out of earshot.

"Honestly I don't know. I mean, I tried to talk her out of it, but she insists on going. This is what she wants to do, so I guess we can't do anything but support her." She shrugged her shoulders in confirmation.

"Okay, I'm ready," Mimi called out as she entered the room.

"Well, let's get going then," I said, walking toward the front door. I didn't go to church often, but I did pray some times. This was one of those times I felt I needed to say a silent prayer. I really hoped that this wouldn't be too much for her.

Chapter 8

Jade

I'd been trying my hardest to find Kaylin, but I kept coming up empty-handed. I'd been to his club and the many apartments he had that he didn't think I knew about. They were cleaned out and abandoned. Hell, I'd even been by his house, the one he and ol' girl used to stay in, but by the looks of the high grass, yellow tape, and overflowing mailbox, no one had been there.

The shit was really starting to bother me, because it'd been weeks since my tracker stopped working. I ain't no closer to finding him, then I was a few weeks ago. I was beginning to think that the nigga had left the fucking country or something. All I knew was wherever he was at, he better not let me catch him doing wrong or else it was going to be some shit.

I sat parked outside of Kaylin's and Mimi's old house for the third time. I came to the conclusion that something in there had to give me a hint of where Kaylin was at or where he'd been. I needed to make sure that no one saw me. So I waited until it was late and the streets were quiet before I made a move. I wasn't trying to get caught and thrown in jail. I needed my freedom to find Kaylin's lying ass.

When I thought the streets were silent enough, I slowly got out of the car and walked across the street toward the house. I had to be careful, because there was still yellow crime scene tape all over the place. When I got to the door, I found out it was still locked.

"Shit," I cursed under my breath as I looked for a spare key. I know there had to be one somewhere around here, because rich people always kept one. I searched all over until I located it right underneath the doormat.

"Typical muthafuckers," I said, removing the key. Carefully removing the crime scene tape, I unlocked the door and went inside, making sure to lock the door behind my back. I didn't want anyone to walk in and catch me.

The minute I entered the door, I wanted to walk right back out of there. The place looked a mess from where I was standing. There were dried bloodstains, teddy bears and dust all over the place. The smell was horrible. I wasn't trying to get caught in all of that, so I took my time as I made my way farther in to peep out the rest of the house.

I made my way toward the kitchen and, from the looks of it, you'd swear I'd walked in two totally different houses. The place looked like a restaurant's kitchen. All of her appliances were up-to-date shit, with marble countertops, with floors that looked like you could eat off them. The living room was just as nice. There was a set of cream sofas, famous paintings, and two big flat-screen TVs. I got a bit jealous, thinking about how Kaylin had her living like this while I was barely making it. Moving along, I decided to just search for what I had come for, because I knew the rest of the house would make me go insane.

When I made it upstairs, it took me a minute to locate the master bedroom. They had like five bedrooms and two bathrooms. Hell, what could they possibly do with all them rooms? I cursed myself for falling for a kept bitch's man bullshit and having the nerve to actually catch feelings for the nigga. Now I was in here playing Nancy Drew and shit.

After about three minutes of searching, I was finally able to locate the master bedroom. When I walked inside, I became jealous all over again of how the bitch was living. Not one room in the house looked ratchet. It was like she hired a personal decorator to decorate her whole house. The shit was impressive. I carefully looked around, trying to find anything that could help me find Kaylin. I checked all over, from the dressers, to under the mattress, to under the bed, but I couldn't find anything. So I decided to check his closet. Yeah, they each had they own damn closet.

I pulled all the shoeboxes from their places and snatched all the clothes off the hangers. Still, I didn't find anything. I then went to look through her closet. When I opened the door, I immediately spotted a safe sitting in the middle of the floor, halfway open. I pulled one of her shirts, grabbed the handle of the safe, and opened it. There wasn't anything in there but empty envelopes and broken jewelry. I carefully felt around the safe, and that's when I found a little compartment under a piece of fabric. I moved the fabric, but I didn't find anything except some damn papers. It was a pleasant surprise when I looked at the papers and noticed that they were deeds to properties in Louisiana, owned by Kaylin.

"I bet my last dollar that his ass is headed to Louisiana, but I got his ass," I said, taking the papers and putting them into my purse. I then hurriedly left the closet and carefully made my way downstairs. I was almost at the front door when I heard what sounded like the garage door opening. I picked up my pace and raced for the front door. I opened the door and quickly closed it behind me when a heard a voice enter the living room.

"Are you sure you're up to this?" a female voice said. I recognized it as being that bitch Troy's voice.

"I think so." I heard a tiny voice that I didn't recognize. I guessed that was a child, because the person's voice was so small.

"Well, come on. Let's get to it," Troy responded. "Why don't you guys give us a minute? Y'all make sure that the place is clear while I show her around. Oh, and catch the mail from outside please."

The minute I heard that, I broke out running to my car across the street. I wasn't trying to get caught this time. Troy would've killed me. I already had too much shit to do. I ain't ready to die yet.

It was a good thing that I left the porch when I did, because the minute I sat down in my car someone came to the door. They peeked out the door first, and then they came strolling out to the mailbox. I instantly recognized the dude Troy was with the past few weeks.

I wonder what the fuck they doing over here, I said to myself. I watched as he grabbed the mail, and I glanced down to see where my phone was. When I looked up, he was watching the car. I wasn't worried about him seeing me, because the windows were heavily tinted. He started walking out into the street, which alarmed me. I grabbed my keys and shoved them in the ignition. If he walked over here, I was going to haul ass but, thank God, his friend came to the door and called him. He looked over at the car one last time and then started walking back toward the house.

The minute he walked inside and closed the door, I breathed a sigh of relief. I thought for damn sure that I was caught. Not wasting another minute, I started my car and got the hell out of there. I had already found what I was looking for. I didn't care what the hell they was doing. My only concern right now was to find Kaylin's ass. It looked like I'd be taking me a trip to Louisiana.

Chapter 9

Kaylin

I was almost to the border of Mississippi and Alabama when I turned around. I realized I couldn't go back to Georgia. There was nothing left for me there. The house, club, and cars were all material things. What I wanted the most was gone, so there was no point in me going.

So instead of me staying in Mississippi like I had planned to, I decided to pack up my kids and head on down to Louisiana. I needed me and my kids to be surrounded by people who truly cared about us, and I could only get that from my mother. So that's where I was headed. I was heading home, straight to the Big Easy.

It didn't take me long to get back to the house. I made it there in no time. I had already called Stacy and told her to help the kids pack their things so we could get on the road. When I pulled up to the house, there was only one light on. It was in the living room, which let me know that Stacy was still up. *I really hope she don't come questioning me, because I damn sure don't have time for her shit. I just want to get the kids and our things and be out. I don't want to argue or fuss, because that shit isn't in me no more.*

I got out of the car and walked up to the house. Before I could make it to the door, she had it open already. I brushed past her and went straight to the kitchen to get me something to drink. I thought that since I didn't speak to her, she would know that I didn't want to be bothered. Her simple ass didn't catch the hint. She marched her aggravating ass in right behind me.

"What's going on with you, Kaylin?" she asked as I opened the refrigerator door.

"Ain't shit going on with me. Why you bugging?" I said, grabbing a bottle of water.

"Well, you could've fooled the shit out of me," she said, being sarcastic.

"Man, look, right now ain't—"

"The time for that. Yeah, well, when is the time, huh? According to you, it's never the time for that," she yelled, getting in my face. "It's always the same damn thing with you. If you don't want me, just tell me. Ever since Mimi done died, you changed."

I didn't reply because I didn't want to hurt her little feelings. I just walked past her and went to get the kids' things so that I could load up the car.

"Oh, so that's it, huh? You don't want me? What, you still stuck on Mimi?" she asked, still following me.

I refused to answer her, because I didn't want to fuss over a dead issue. She knew from the beginning that I didn't want her. I never did want her. I only dealt with her because she was the mother of my son. She knew that we couldn't be nothing more than parents to our son.

I walked into the kids' room and grabbed as many suitcases as I could.

"She's dead. You might as well face the fact. Mimi is never comin' back. You'll just have to get over that shit," she yelled.

"Ma, chill out before you wake up my kids." My tone was low and menacing.

"Fuck that shit. I put up with your shit for too fuckin' long, and you over here stuck on a dead bitch. If you want her so much, then go dig up her body!"

"Daddy?" Kailay called out, wiping her eyes.

"Yes, baby," I replied, walking over to her.

"I want my mommy," she said as she began to cry. I took her into my arms and began to rock her. Before all of this happened, I was her favorite person. Now all she did was cry for her mother.

"Shhhh, we already had this talk, baby. Mommy's in heaven with the angels." The minute I said that, she started to cry harder. I picked her up and carried her to my room. I didn't want her to wake the boys up, or else I'd have to deal with three crying children instead of one.

I placed her in the bed and took off my shoes. I then got in the bed beside her, and I started to rock her back to sleep. It didn't take long for her to fall asleep. Once she was sound asleep, I slid out of the bed and went downstairs.

The minute I hit the bottom of the stairs, here came Stacy in my face again.

"So is it time yet?" she said, waving her hands around. I tried to move past her, but she blocked me. "No, you ain't goin' nowhere. This time you gonna talk to me, damn it."

I'd finally had enough of her and her fucking mouth. I grabbed her and pinned her against the wall. "Bitch, check this out. I be tryin' my hardest not put my hands on you, but you keep on postin' with me. I don't know who you think you are, but your mouth always be the one to get you in trouble. You ask me why I don't want to talk to you, that's the reason why. Your mouth is forever writin' a check that your ass can't cash!"

"You're always runnin' away from me, or tuning me out when I'm tryin' to talk to you. You can't keep doin' that to me, Kay. That shit has to stop if we gonna be together as a family." She had the nerve to continue talkin', even after I told her why I couldn't stand her dumb ass.

"Family? I don't know where you got that shit from, ma, but you need to chill on that. We ain't never gonna be a family, ma. You need to get that through your fuckin' head. I don't want your ass. You just the mother of my child and I don't see us havin' a future together. You not Mimi. She's who I wanted a future with, but that can't happen now. So I'm good on having a family. As long as I got my kids, I'm good," I said, bursting her bubble. I tried to be nice, but I was tired of telling her that I didn't want a family with her ass.

"Well, okay," she said, pushing past me. I really wasn't expecting her to be so calm and cool but, hell, as long as she wasn't bitching, then I was cool with that.

"Good. Now, can you please get the rest of the kids' things so that we can get out of here? I'm tryin' to be in Louisiana before the sun comes up." I left her right where she stood. I really didn't care how she felt. I was tired of playing games with her, and she needed to stay in her place.

I was on my way to the kids' room to grab the rest of the bags that I was supposed to get before Stacy had interrupted me. I was almost down the hall when I heard whispering. Walking a little farther, I noticed that the voices were coming from the bathroom. I placed my ear against the door to see if I could hear anything.

"We'll be in Louisiana tomorrow morning," I heard Stacy say to someone. I heard a pause, and then she said, "I don't know where he'll be staying, but I'll try to find out for you." There was another pause. Stacy whispered, "Just be on the lookout for me. I'll call you when we make it there. See you in a minute."

I started to interrupt her, but I didn't want her to know that I knew what was going on. I wanted her to think that I was still clueless. I backed away from the door quietly, hoping like hell that she didn't catch me. If she wanted to play, then I was going to play right along with her.

I quietly went back into the kids' room, grabbed the bags, and went outside to the trunk. When I came back inside, she was walking down the hallway with two bags. I grabbed her and kissed her. I'd caught her off guard, and she let the bags slip out of her hands. Before she could respond, I let go of her and went to grab the rest of the bags. When I came back, she was standing in the same spot that I had left her in. I passed by her like nothing had happened. When I was done loading all of the bags in the car, I grabbed Kailay, woke up the boys, and we were out the door.

When I got outside, she was standing outside by the car. I made sure the kids were safely in their car seats, and I hopped in the car. I then beeped the horn to get her attention. She hopped in the car and looked at me. I still said nothing as I started the car and hopped on the highway, making my way home to Louisiana.

Chapter 10

Stacy

I didn't know what had gotten into Kaylin, but I was tired of playing with him. I wasn't about to be his little play toy anymore. I was 'bout to look out for me and Kaylin Jr. Fuck running behind a nigga. Sad thing was I done played the back end to Mimi for too damn long and, now that she was dead, I still found myself doing the same thing. I couldn't compete with a dead person, and I wasn't trying to. I was done with that shit. I was about to get it how I lived.

I couldn't lie. I was hurt when he said that he didn't want a family with me. It crushed my heart. Hell, why not have a family with me? I'd been the side bitch for so long, and now that the main bitch wasn't here anymore, he still wanted me to be the side bitch? Hell, it didn't work like that no more. I didn't think so. I had something for his ass this time. I would not be assed out and looking sad as hell this time.

I decided to go ahead and call up Mister. Since he wanted Mimi and couldn't get her, I decided to give him Kaylin. After all, he didn't want me. Why not let this nigga suffer for putting me through all of that bullshit? He didn't give a fuck about my feelings, so why should I have given a fuck about his ass? The only ones I felt sorry for were the kids, because after tomorrow they were going to be both motherless and fatherless.

The plan was for me to find out where he would be laying his head, give it about a week or two, then rob and kill him. Did I feel bad for what I was about to do? Hell no. I thought this was long overdue. I was tired of letting Kaylin think he could just play with me. Enough was enough. I was done being his dummy. I wouldn't continue to play a fool no more.

After I got off the phone with Mister, I went to grab the kids' bags so that we could head out. I was walking along, bringing the bags to the car, when Kaylin grabbed and kissed me. To say I was surprised would be an understatement. This dude had just said he didn't want a family with me, and now he was kissing all on me and shit. How was I supposed to take this?

I wanted to just grab him and kiss him back, but when I started to, he had done pulled away. I stood there feeling stuck. I had done already made a deal with Mister, but now Kaylin was here, doing the most. I didn't know if I should go on with the plan or just call the whole thing off.

I picked up the bags and put them in the car. Pulling out my phone, I stood there like a deer in headlights. I wanted to call this thing off, but I had already made the deal no more than five minutes ago. I couldn't just close this shit.

I entered Mister's number in the dial pad but, when I went to call him, Kaylin came walking out the door with the kids. I didn't want him to hear my call, so I decided to wait. *I'll just tell him that we had a change of plans,* I thought as Kaylin beeped the horn. I placed my phone inside my pocket, got in the car, and mentally prepared myself for whatever tomorrow may bring. I just hoped like hell that nothing would go wrong.

Chapter 11

Mimi

I sat in the back seat of the car, still trying to process everything that Troy had told me. Some of the shit was so unbelievable. I had lived it, and I almost didn't believe it. I was numb to the pain though. I guessed my feelings had temporarily left with my memory. Maybe that was a good thing though, because I was sure the minute my memory returned everything would hit me like a ton of bricks. I couldn't believe that, after all of the things we'd been through, Kaylin would do me like that. He had me wondering what I ever did to him to deserve that. Was he missing something at home that caused him to continue to cheat on me, even after we left our past in Louisiana?

"You don't have to think so hard about it. Your memory is going to come to you," Troy whispered in my ear.

I nodded my head in agreement, but it was easier said than done. It was hard for me not to worry. Her memory was already intact, while I had to go searching for mine. The other thing that threw me off was when she said that I had another daughter, who I remembered nothing about. "My God, what's been going on?" I whispered to myself.

"We're here," I heard Troy say. I was so deep in my thoughts that I hadn't even noticed the car had stopped.

I looked at the house that was once mine, and I wondered what secrets it held. From the outside, it looked like a regular house, except for the uncut grass, yellow crime scene tape, and overflowing mailbox. The house looked like it had once been a beautiful home for a family—my family—and now there wasn't a family staying there.

"Are you gonna get out or do you need a little time?" Troy asked me.

"Oh, I'm coming," I said, snapping out of my daze. Reaching for the handle, I got out of the car and strolled up the walkway. I stood still as I waited for Troy to catch up to me.

"Do you want us to come in with y'all or do y'all want us to wait in the car?' Jayden asked.

"Y'all can come inside," I replied, looking back at him. "I need all the support that I can get."

"Okay." Jayden and Mark exited the car and followed us.

"We're going to have to go in through the garage since we don't have our keys," Troy said, walking toward the garage. She then used the keypad to raise the garage door.

"You coming?" she asked me, because I was the only one left standing outside. I nodded my head as I made my way into the garage.

When I got inside, I peeped an all-purple Benz, sitting on rims. Since that was my favorite color, I had to stop and admire it.

"That joint is tight," I heard Mark comment.

"Yeah, it is," Jayden responded behind him.

"You like it?" Troy asked.

"Yeah, that mug is clean," I said.

"Good, because it's actually your car," she said, shocking me.

"Really?" I asked, not believing her.

"Yes. You bought it the minute you got down here. It took a minute for you to apply the paint and rims, but it was bought with your hard-earned money."

"Where are the keys?" I asked.

"They're in the house. You never drove it much. You drove your other car a lot." She sounded like a proud mother.

"Really? Where is it?" I wanted to know because I didn't see it.

"Umm, it's in the shop. You were driving it the day you were shot, so the police took it in as evidence." She lowered her eyes to the ground.

"It's okay, Troy. I'm okay. I'm alive, so you don't have to feel sad anymore," I said, using my finger to raise her face up.

"I know. I'm actually happy about that. It's just that I should have been there for you and I wasn't."

"Look at me, Troy," I said, stepping toward her. "What happened to me wasn't your fault. You didn't know that I was gonna get shot. It was Kaylin who shot me. It was his fault, baby girl, not yours."

I grabbed her and hugged her extra tight. She'd been more than a friend to me over the years. In fact, I didn't consider her my friend. I considered her my sister. She'd been there for me when I didn't have anyone, and I couldn't and wouldn't choose anyone else.

"I love you, sis," I said to her.

"I love you too. Now, come on. Let's go get your memory back," she said, walking toward the door in the garage that led to the house. She stood up on her tiptoes and searched above the door for what I assumed was a key. When she found it, she unlocked the door and allowed me to enter first.

The minute I entered the house, I got an unsettling feeling in the pit of my belly. It felt like it was trying to tell me something. I walked into the foyer, where I spotted more yellow tape and bloodstains on the floor by the front door.

"I'm sorry that I didn't get anyone to clean it up yet. I was trying to wait until everything was over with," she said, apologizing.

"It's okay," I replied softly, frozen in place. Seeing the blood on the floor made me feel incredibly sad.

She looked over to the guys and mumbled something, and then they left the room. I didn't hear what she said because I was still in a daze. I looked over to the left, where I noticed a bunch of toys paired up on the floor. When I walked over and picked them up, I was visibly shaken as a flashback of my four kids crying entered my mind.

"Are you okay?" Troy asked, walking up to me.

"Um, ye . . . yeah, I'm okay," I stuttered.

"Do you want me to get you a glass of water or something?"

"No, I'm okay," I said to her. "Where did you say my body was when you came in?"

"It was over there by the stairs." She pointed toward the back of the house.

I swallowed hard, as a lump had formed in my throat.

"Do you need me to go with you?"

"No, I'm okay," I reassured her.

"Well, I'll be right here if you need me."

I respected her because she gave me all the space that I needed. She wasn't trying to treat me like a baby, or cripple me like most people would've done. "Okay," I said, nodding my head.

I took a deep breath as I made my way toward the back of the house by the stairs. With each step that I took, the pain in my stomach became worse. It was in knots as I realized that was where I had died. I knew it was the exact spot because there was a chalk outline forming a perfect shape of the position that my body was lying in. I grabbed on to the wall as my knees started to buckle.

"Mimi," I heard Troy yell from behind me. I wanted to turn around, but I couldn't. It felt like a magnetic pull was holding me in that spot. The moment that my knees hit the floor, every minute that I wasn't able to remember came flashing back in my mind. It was as if the last few weeks of my life were playing on a projector screen. I saw everything Troy had told me: the moment I spotted Kaylin at the gas station, the minute I met Jayden, seeing Tyreek and Kayla, the hotel rooms with Jayden, the times I sat up with my kids waiting for Kaylin to come home. What hurt the most was when I returned to the house and saw Stacy posted up in it with a child Kaylin had fathered. It added insult to injury to find out that this child's name was Kaylin Jr.

My body started to shake as I recalled the flashback of Kaylin pulling a gun out and shooting Tyreek first, then turning the gun on me. In my mind, I felt the four shots enter my back again as if it were happening now.

"Why?" I screamed.

"Oh, my God. Mimi!" Troy screamed again. My head started to spin as I heard lots of footsteps running up behind me.

"Mimi! Mimi! Mimi!" Troy cried, pulling me into her arms. My body was there, but my mind was gone.

"Talk to us, ma," Jayden said, but I couldn't actually see them because a bright light blinded me.

Looking closer I saw an outstretched arm. Then I heard a voice say, *"I'm very glad that you're back, but I need to tell you something."*

I already knew who the owner of the voice was because I remembered hearing it before. I just didn't know what she wanted to say to me.

What's going on? I asked her in my mind. I still could hear Troy and Jayden in the background screaming for me to say something, but I couldn't respond to them.

"You have to get to Louisiana as soon as possible. Your kids are headed there with their father, and they're in danger. They need you, Amina."

What? I asked, not sure if I heard her right.

"Your kids are in danger, and you need to get to New Orleans now. I will be watching you along the way, but you have to get going, now!"

But—

"No buts. You have to get going and make sure you take your friends along with you because you're going to need their help!" Just like that, the voice was gone.

As I returned to my normal self, I jumped up out of Troy's arms.

"Thank God. You scared the hell out of me!" she said, standing up to her feet. I didn't answer her though. I hurriedly ran to the kitchen, with everyone in hot pursuit.

"Ma, what's going on?" Jayden asked.

"I have to go!" I yelled, searching through one of the kitchen drawers.

"Go? Where are you going and what's wrong?" he asked, walking over to me.

"I have to go. I need to find my car keys," I screamed, searching through another drawer. "Troy, where are my keys?"

"They're in your bedroom in your nightstand. What's wrong, Mimi? Where are we going?"

I didn't answer her. I bypassed all of them as I ran up the stairs to my bedroom. Spotting the nightstand, I quickly snatched the drawer to get my keys. Once I retrieved my keys, I ran out of the room, running into them headfirst.

"Ma, slow down. Tell us what's going on and where are you trying to go," Jayden gasped, trying to catch his breath.

"I have to go to New Orleans. My kids are in danger, and they need me. They need their mommy," I said, breaking down.

"What do you mean they're in danger?" he asked me.

"I don't know, and I can't explain it to you right now. All I know is that my kids are in danger and I'm going to get them," I replied, moving past them, headed for the stairs.

"Hold up, ma. If you're going, then I'm going with you."

"And you already know I'm coming," Troy replied.

"I don't even need to say it," Mark added.

"Well, come on, we don't have much time. They're already on their way there," I said, running down the stairs toward the garage. I got in my car and started it up.

"We can't go in your car, ma. They'll recognize it. Let's take the rental," Jayden stated, opening the passenger door.

"I don't care what we go in. Let's just go." I jumped out of the car, slamming the door so hard I almost broke the window. Troy was shutting the garage door as I hopped in the car.

"Are you going to tell us what's going on?" Troy asked as she hopped in too.

"I'll tell y'all on the way. Let me use your phone." I shook my head to clear it. I needed a minute to process everything.

"We need to stop back at your crib to pick something up," Mark said from the back seat.

"Well, hurry up then," I snapped. I couldn't help it. I was getting impatient. I was a mother, and I did what any mother would do if someone told them that their kids were in danger. I silently said a prayer as I begged God to watch over my kids because if something were to happen to them, I'd make someone pay—with their life.

We made it to the house exactly ten minutes later. I didn't even get out. I was nervous and anxious that we weren't getting on the road fast enough. I watched impatiently as Mark quickly dashed inside to get whatever it was he had to have. Two minutes after that, he was back in the car, and we were on our way to New Orleans.

I didn't know what was going on, but I knew one thing for sure: if anybody hurt one strand of hair on my kids' heads, I would personally add to the total that gave New Orleans the nickname the Murder Capital, and I wasn't playing.

Chapter 12

Jade

Something told me to double back and see what was going on at Kaylin's house. I didn't know why, but I actually listened to whatever that was. I parked down the street and noticed the car still parked in the driveway. I got out and snuck down to the front of the house so I could see what was going on.

When I made it to the front door, I noticed that the garage door was open, so I quietly made my way over to it. I got pissed off again thinking about how that bitch was living the lifestyle I wanted. I was standing there fuming when I heard screaming coming from the house. Just when I put my ear to the door, I heard someone screaming Mimi's name. I thought I was tripping at first, but then I heard it again.

I heard some more screaming. Then someone mentioned going to Louisiana. That's when I hauled ass to my car to wait and see what was going to happen next. When I got in the car, I rolled my window down a bit as I mentally replayed what I heard. I knew Mimi wasn't in there because she was dead. So why were they in there screaming her name? I didn't have time to answer my own question because I vaguely saw someone running to the car that was parked in the garage. They jumped in and started it up.

As I watched the scene play out, someone else went to the car, but then he shut the door and started walking out of the garage. When the person exited the garage, I noticed that he was the dark-skinned dude with dreads who was with that bitch Troy. He walked to the car that was parked in the driveway, got in, and started it up. Following him were the light-skinned dude and a chick. When I saw her, I gasped in shock. It was dark, and my eyes were obviously deceiving me because the chick looked just like Mimi. Taking a second look, I damn near bugged out. This chick didn't just favor Mimi. It was Mimi herself.

"Oh, hell no. I thought she was dead!" I exclaimed. I watched as she got into the car as well, with Troy following close behind.

The car then pulled out of the driveway in a hurry. I started my car and followed them. As I drove along at a safe distance, I tried to figure out how Mimi was actually alive and not dead.

"Fuck!" I screamed, banging on the steering wheel. "I thought this bitch was already dead and gone! Now I got to add her to my list of people to get back at!"

I followed them at a steady but careful pace. I didn't want them to get suspicious and figure out that I was following them. Ten minutes later, they pulled up to a house, and the passenger's back door opened.

"What the hell are y'all doing?" I asked softly, as if they could've heard me. I watched as dude got out of the car and ran inside, while everyone else stayed inside the car with it still running. I parked my car a few houses down with the engine still on, as I tried to figure out what they were up to. A few minutes later, dude came running out of the house with a bag in his hand. He then walked to the back of the car, placed the bag in the trunk, and got back in. Then they pulled off, and I followed at a safe distance.

The minute they got on the interstate, it confirmed their destination for me. In fact, we were headed to the same place: Louisiana. I guessed they also knew where Kaylin was and they were going after him. I wasn't about to let them get to him before me though. I quickly switched lanes and picked up speed because, just like them, I was on a mission. This time, I wasn't about to let Mimi defeat me. I guessed Louisiana was about to get turned up a bit, because I wasn't planning on leaving without what I came there for.

Chapter 13

Mimi

Five Hours Later

We made it to Louisiana in no time. I didn't sleep the entire trip. My whole ride was spent worrying about my kids, wondering where they were and if they were okay. I tried to think happy thoughts, but I couldn't. My mind was getting the best of me. We drove through the Ninth Ward, and I swear it felt like we never left. I could honestly say that nothing about this place had changed. There were still crackheads and drug dealers on the corners, kids playing in the streets, and many buildings still abandoned and run-down. *Typical New Orleans,* I thought, sadly shaking my head.

I realized we were on the same street as my old building, and I told everyone we were going to make a detour. There were old questions I needed answers to, and the only person I knew who could give me those answers was the bitch who gave birth to me twenty-seven years ago. Quickly, I mentally prepared myself for the visit. I hadn't seen this woman in years, and if it weren't for the fact that I had to come down here, then it would've stayed that way. I really didn't have much to say to her, because she was never the mother I needed. She was more like my master than my mother. I remembered there were days and nights I used to go without eating. There were times she would wake me up out of my sleep on school nights just to clean up after her. I reflected on the many hurtful names that she called me because she couldn't have the one person that she wanted the most: my father.

I never really understood her. I mean, how could you let a man bring you down like that? She never gave a fuck about me. She only had me because she thought that it would keep him, but I guess she was surprised when it actually pushed him away instead. That was the reason why she treated me poorly. She was the main reason why I'd always felt low. It was because of her that I was never too sure about myself, until I met Kaylin. Now that he'd done this to me, I didn't know what to think about myself anymore. I was starting to believe that I was a black widow or something, like it was meant for me to be alone.

Pulling up to the building, I just sat there and looked. The building itself looked like it was going to fall down any minute now. I didn't know how anyone could live there. I was nowhere near prissy, because I knew where I came from, but I knew that I wouldn't have continued to live there with the building in that condition.

Grabbing the jacket that was sitting on the back seat, I put it in and threw the hood over my head. I wasn't ready for everyone to know that I was still alive just yet. I knew that if people saw me, then it would get to Kaylin and Stacy, and I didn't want them to leave with my kids. I wanted them to be surprised when they saw me. I wanted to see the panic and shock on their faces as they saw the fury on mine.

"Do you want me to come inside with you?" Troy asked.

I swallowed hard, trying to remove the lump in my throat. I managed to croak out, "Yes."

We got out of the car and made our way into the building. It was too early outside for these crackheads to be out here looking for crack. I spotted the dude Lucky and quickly picked up the pace, because if he saw me, then Kaylin would know for sure.

I was walking so fast that poor Troy had to run to keep up with me. Like all ghetto hallways, the one in this building smelled just like strong piss. I had to cover my nose to keep from gagging. Walking up the stairs, I notice a big-ass rat sitting in a corner. All I could do was shake my head because the City of New Orleans was wrong as hell for this shit. They'd rather spend money on stupid shit than fix up the projects around this city.

With each step, I came closer to the apartment my mother stayed in. My heart began to beat faster and faster. Hell, I hadn't seen this woman in years. This would be one hell of a reunion, considering we never really liked each other. When I got to the door, I paused.

"It's okay. Take your time," Troy whispered behind me. I nodded my head as I took a minute to calm my nerves down. When I was ready, I softly knocked on the door.

"If you keep knocking like that, we'll be out here all day," Troy said. She was right. I knocked like a punk. Stepping aside, I let her knock. She began beating on the door so loud, I stepped farther to the side because I didn't want the occupant to fire a shot through the door.

"Bitch, chill out. You knockin' like you the police," I said, grabbing her hand.

"Hell, it was better than that punk-ass knock you did," she said, rolling her eyes. I was about to answer her when I heard a voice coming from the other side of the door.

"Who the hell is it? Shit, knockin' on the damn door hard like that and shit," a female voice yelled, but I couldn't tell whose voice it belonged to.

"It's Troy. Is Marie there?" Troy yelled back.

"Yeah," the person responded, opening the door. My mouth instantly flew open at the person before me. She was so small, like she was suffering from malnutrition or something. Her hair was broken off, and her clothes were just hanging off her. I kind of felt sorry for her.

"Um, is Marie here?" Troy asked again.

"Yeah, it's me, Troy. What do you want?" she replied, catching an attitude.

Troy didn't answer her. She just stood there staring with her mouth wide open. I stood off to the side where Marie couldn't see me, but I could catch glimpses of her.

"Um, you just gonna stand there, or you gonna tell me what you came here for?" Marie asked with her hands on her frail hips.

"Um, I came to talk to you. Can we come in?" Troy said, finally snapping out of her state of shock.

"Sure." She shrugged, walking away from the door.

Troy and I exchanged a quick glance. "Come on," she mouthed while motioning with her hand.

"Go ahead, I'm comin' right behind you," I said to her.

She walked inside, and I followed right behind her, making sure to close the door behind me. When I walked inside the apartment, I gasped. There was not one piece of furniture in there. The place had beer cans and bottles all over the place. I wanted to ask her how she could live like this, but it wasn't my business.

"What do you want? I already know about Amina's funeral, so if you've come all this way to tell me that, you wasted your time," she said, not turning around. I wanted to say I was hurt, but I wasn't, because I already knew how this woman was.

"Um, you don't have to worry about that, because there won't be a funeral," Troy said to her.

"How come?"

"Because I'm not dead. I'm alive," I said. I watched as her back stiffened. I could tell that she wasn't expecting me to be here.

"What are you doing here?' she asked with her back still turned.

"I came here for answers."

"Answers? Answers to what?"

"Answers to things I should've asked you," I said, stepping from behind Troy.

"I don't have anything to say to you, so you've wasted your time coming here."

"Why do you hate me? What could I possibly have done to you that made you so evil toward me? As I can recall, I don't remember doin' anything to you."

"Amina, please leave."

"No, turn around and face me. I need to know why you treated me bad for so long," I said to her. I wasn't about to go anywhere.

"Get your ass out of here." She didn't even bother to turn around.

I got fed up, walked over to her, and spun her around myself. "Look me in my eyes and tell me why you've mistreated me for so long. I need to know because from what I recall, you treated me like shit. Was it because that nigga didn't love you or was it because you couldn't love yourself? Were you mad because I was prettier than you? No, it must be because I had a head full of hair. Which one was it?" I asked, with tears pouring out of my eyes. I wanted to know, and she needed to give me an explanation, because I sure as hell wasn't leaving without it.

"Come on, tell me!" I screamed. "After all these years, now you wanna be quiet? You've always said what was on your mind. Why won't you say the shit now?"

She just stood there, still as a statue, looking at me. In all my years of living with her, I never knew her to be this quiet.

"You know what? Don't even worry about it. I already know the answer," I said to her. "Just so you know, all the things you said and did to me ain't did shit but make me a better woman and mother than you could ever be. Every day I prayed and asked God to give me the strength to forgive you, and you know what? He has, and I'm actually glad that I have. Otherwise, I would've been a bitter bitch just like you. Come on, Troy, let's get out of here!"

I stepped back from her and took her in from head to toe. I was about to say something else, but I changed my mind. She wasn't even worth it. She was always going to be the same bitter bitch she'd been since I was a teenager. I shook my head at her and turned to leave. I was almost out the door when she decided to speak.

"You want to know why I hate you, Amina?" she asked, making me stop in my tracks. "Is that what it is? You want me to tell you why I hate you?"

"Yeah, that's what I want to know," I said, turning around. I walked back over to her and stood in front of her. "Tell me why you hate me."

"Hate you. You think I hate you? What I felt toward you wasn't hate. I never did hate you. I think the proper word would be envied. I've always envied you. In fact, I've envied you since the day you was born," she said, looking at me. "From the minute I brought you into this world, you was a happy baby. No matter what went down, you always had a smile on your face. I always found myself wondering how you could be so happy when you was brought into a world like this. We were poor, your father wasn't here, and yet you was still happy. You didn't have enough food to eat or clothes on your back, but you was still happy. While I was falling into a deep depression over a man I knew would never be mine, you was here being happy. No matter what happened in your life, whether it was good or bad, you never let anything get to you. You had a 'fuck what people think' attitude that I wished I had. You had a shitload of courage and confidence, but I had nothing. That's why I treated you the way I did. It wasn't because I hated you. It was because you was the woman I wished I could've been," she cried as I watched the tears fall from her face.

"Happy? You thought I was happy? My whole life, you treated me like I was shit. I was never happy. In fact, I was far from it. I just knew how to actually hide my feelings, unlike you." I didn't know how she could figure I was happy, because I wasn't. I never was happy when I was with her. She made sure of it.

"I'm sorry. I'm so sorry. I've lived my life for years regretting what I've put you through. If I could turn back the hands of time, I promise I would've done things differently. Can you please forgive me?" She reached for me, but I took a step back.

"I've already forgiven you, Marie. I don't hate you anymore. I've given all of that to God already. I only came here because I had no choice. I needed to know."

"Thank you. That means a lot."

"Uh-huh," I said. I'd heard what I needed to hear. Now it was time for me to find my kids and bring them back home with me.

"Amina, wait, there's something else you need to know."

I turned around and found her walking up to me. She stopped right in front of me and just stared, making me feel uncomfortable. "Well?" I was starting to feel uneasy.

"For all these years I've struggled with this, but I think it's time you know what was going on around you." She was beginning to scare me. "The reason Kaylin and Tyreek went to jail when they were young was because I reported them. I saw when they killed Joe and removed his body. I was drunk, but the next morning I remembered everything. At first I thought that I was trippin', but when I couldn't find Joe for a couple of days, I reported it to the police."

I didn't say anything. I just turned around and reached for the doorknob.

"And the reason Stacy hates you so much is because she wants to be you. In fact, she's related to you."

When she said that, I removed my hand from the knob. "Related to me how?" I asked, not turning around. Suddenly, it became quiet as I waited for her to tell me what was going on.

"She . . . she's your sister. You both have the same father."

Thinking that I heard her wrong, I turned around. "Say what?"

"You heard me right, Amina. The reason Stacy hates you so much is because she's your sister. I didn't know it at the time, and by the time I found out, she had done slept with Kaylin. When I went to go and ask Julius about it, his wife happened to be there. She heard everything and threw him out."

I looked at Troy who had an "oh, shit" look on her face. I bet she was thinking the same thing I was thinking: *that backstabbing bitch.* I quickly turned around, opened the door, and ran out of there.

"Mimi!" I could hear Troy screaming behind me, but I didn't stop. I kept running until I made it all the way to the car. When I got there, I threw up the little food I had on my stomach. I puked for all of five minutes, until nothing came out.

"Are you okay?" Troy asked. "Do you want to talk about it?"

I shook my head, indicating that I didn't. I needed time to process this shit. I couldn't believe that the bitch who was my former friend was actually my sister. Now I knew why that ho was always hating. She really wanted to be me.

It turned out the warning I'd gotten was right. Troy got a call from Weedy, and he said that something had happened. He didn't see it himself what happened, but he knew there were gunshots at the house my babies were staying at, and one of them could be hurt. I sat in the back seat of the car feeling hopeless. I honestly didn't know why God picked me to go through all of this mess, but I was really hoping that He'd end it all soon. I laid my head back and closed my eyes. I needed to think about something, anything, positive that could stop me from going crazy, because all of these negative thoughts were eating me up. It seemed to be taking forever and a day for us to get to where my babies were. I wanted to scream so badly, but I didn't. Even though my nerves were on edge, I had to remember that Jayden wasn't from around here and he didn't know anything about New Orleans. It would take him longer than it would take Troy or me to get there. If it weren't for the GPS system, I was more than sure that he'd be lost.

I silently sat there and prayed. I prayed as I had never prayed before, asking God to please be with and protect my kids, because I didn't know what I'd do if I were to lose them. I'd probably be lost. I did know one thing: if anything did happen to any one of them, I'd be painting the whole city of New Orleans red, and that wasn't a threat. It was a promise.

"Are you okay?" Troy asked, giving my hand a gentle squeeze.

"To be honest, I don't know what I'm feeling right now," I said pulling my hand away from her. I really didn't know how I was feeling. I was just in a zone, numb. On one hand, I wanted to find my kids, rescue them, and move out of state, where no one knew who we were. On the other hand, I wanted to fuck everything up. It was like a push-and-pull battle going on inside of me, and I didn't know what to do.

"We're almost there," Troy said interrupting my thoughts. My heart pumped an extra few beats, as I realized that I was finally about to be reunited with my children.

"What are you going to do?" she asked a few minutes later. "You do know that there will be a lot of people out there when we get there. If you get out of the car, you risk the chance of someone seeing you, and that will probably get back to Kaylin."

Damn, I never really thought about that. To be truthful, I had completely forgotten about that fact that I was supposed to be dead. The only thing on my mind right now was my children and getting them back.

"I'm not worrying about all that shit. The only thing I'm concerned with is the safety of my children." I side-eyed her.

"I don't think that will be a good idea, sis," she replied, shaking her head.

"Well, what am I supposed to do? You expect me to just sit here while my kids are hurt?" I asked. I could already feel my eyes getting misty. I couldn't believe she wanted me to sit there while my kids could possibly be in there hurt.

"We don't know how bad it is. When we get there, just let me see what's going on first and, if it's bad, you can show your face."

"Okay, but if it's that serious, I don't care who's out there. I'm showing my face," I said, serious as a heart attack.

"Well, let's hope and pray for a better outcome. Right now it can only get better, because we're most definitely living through the worst. But if it's not as serious as we think, I'll just handle it while you sit back in the car."

"Okay, cool," I said just as the car came to a stop. She looked at me, and then out the window, and then she looked back at me.

"No matter what happens, know that I'll always have your back, regardless. I'll be on your side and in your corner until the death of me," she said, pulling me into a tight hug.

"Thank you," I said, hugging her back.

"Sit tight. I'll be right back," she said and got out of the car, with Jayden and Mark following right behind her.

It was hard for me to see out of the window, but I could see a little bit. There were cops everywhere. I watched as Troy walked over to Weedy and gave him a hug. They said a few things to each other, and then she backed up. She then proceeded to introduce him to both Jayden and Mark. I notice the look that Weedy had given to Mark, and I made a mental note to ask her about them.

Once everyone was acquainted, they all walked over to the cops who were standing around a tan-colored van. Troy said a few things to the cops, and then a young black guy pulled her to the side. They spoke a few words to each other, and he pointed to a few areas that were blocked off with yellow crime scene tape. They talked a bit more as he began to write on his notepad. When they were done, he handed her a business card, shook her hand, and walked off.

Throughout all of this, I didn't see an ambulance anywhere, but I did see a coroner's van parked by a curb. Seeing that made my heart fall straight to my ass. I just knew that there was one of my kids in there. I wanted to get out and check for myself, but as I realized that one of my kids could possibly be in that van dead, I stayed put. I didn't want to see it. I needed to be sure, and if it was one of them, I needed some time to get it together. I pulled my phone out of my pocket and was about to dial Troy's number when I noticed her pointing to the car that I was currently sitting in. Again I feared the worst, so I hung my head down and did the only thing that I could do right now.

"Lord, please. I know I haven't been all that good during these past twenty-seven years, but I'm asking that you please spare my kids and don't let them pay for whatever it is that you think I did wrong. Please let me pay my own consequences," I said. That was the only thing that I could do to help my kids. I felt so helpless. I felt that if I didn't get a grip on this situation soon, my world would continue to come crashing down. Soon I wouldn't be able to do anything at all to help them.

I was deep in my thoughts when someone started knocking on the window. At first, I didn't hear them because the knocks were super soft, so they knocked a little louder. Turning to see who it was, my eyes got buck as shit. Wendell, or Weedy as we called him, stood there looking as good as the last time I'd seen him. I realized how Troy once fell in love with him in the first place. He was sporting a fresh fade as if he just stepped out of the barbershop today, with a Rick Ross goatee, a light brown complexion, the prettiest set of green eyes that I'd seen on a man, and a banging body. I knew why all those bitches threw themselves at him. I couldn't lie. Dude was fine as fuck, but he was a dog and he knew it, which was why Troy left his ass in the first place.

I swung the door open, motioning with my hand for him to get in. I waited until he was seated all the way in the car before I spoke to him. "Hello, Weedy," I said to him.

He just sat there staring at me with his mouth open. He was yet another person who couldn't believe that I was actually alive and not dead.

"Boy, close your mouth before something flies in it."

"I'm just . . . What's up, ma?" he asked, stumbling all over his words. He reached over and gave me a hug. "I can't believe that you're alive, Mimi."

"Well, believe it, because this is me. Here in the flesh," I replied, quickly hugging him and sitting back in my seat.

"I see that, ma, I see that," he said, shaking his head.

I sat there and waited a few moments for him to collect his thoughts. I knew his mind was all over the place. After waiting, I got straight to the point. "So what's up? What happened? What did Kaylin tell you? Talk to me, Weedy," I said, getting serious.

I watched as he shifted uncontrollably in his seat before he lowered his gaze to the floor. He then took a deep breath and looked out the window. Finally, he brought he gaze back to me.

"Ma, I can't tell you too much. Like I said over the phone, I wasn't here when everything went down," he said, shaking his head as he rubbed his legs. "But what I can tell you is that ya boy done got himself into some serious shit and your kids are in deep trouble. Your girl Stacy and her pops are around here, playing for keeps. Since they couldn't get to you, they went after your mother, getting her strung out and everything. When they tried to get at you, Kaylin stood in the way of all that, so Julius sent Stacy after him as a distraction, but she ended up falling in love with him, and that's when Kaylin Jr. came about. Word around the street is that they've been trying to get at you for a while now. I'm still trying to find out why, but once I find that out, you'll be the first person I call."

I hung my head low as I sat there, taking in everything Weedy was saying. Life was definitely a bitch, and I'd seen that ho firsthand. I knew that Weedy wasn't on that bullshit, which was why what I was about to say next would probably throw him.

"You can stop looking for that reason, because I already know why they want my head," I said, raising my head.

"As it turns out, Stacy's my sister, my blood sister. We have the same father."

He gave me a look that said, "What the fuck?"

I continued, "Yeah, my mother fell in love with a nigga who already had a woman. As a matter of fact, the nigga was married, with kids already. Stacy and I were actually born in the same year, with me being the youngest. When my father found out about me, he gave my mother an ultimatum. It was either she got an abortion, or else she would never see him again. She called his bluff and decided that she would have me, thinking that he wouldn't leave her, that he'd be there for us."

I paused for a moment, taking a deep breath before speaking again. "On the day that she went in, she called to tell him. He answered and told her that he was at home with his family and for her never to call him again. From that moment on, my life has been a living hell, because of him. I never had a normal life. I don't know why he's bitching, because I've been going through hell my entire life. Yes, he may have lost his family, but why should I give a fuck? I lost my whole childhood. I was forced to grow up way before I had to. I didn't tell him to cheat on his wife. He did that shit himself. He could always get married again. My childhood was a once-in-a-lifetime thing. I can't get that shit back. I was beaten and raped. Do you think he cared about it? No, because he was too busy being part of a family. Should I be sad about his situation? Hell no, and I'm not. I don't give one fuck about him or his family, because I never had one until now."

I hadn't noticed that I was crying until he cradled me in his arms. I felt like shit. Lately, I hadn't been doing anything but crying. The shit made me sick. I was never this weak. I was always a strong woman. I was actually somewhat glad though. I'd been holding that cry in for a long damn time. A good cry was what I had needed.

"Damn, ma. It's going to be okay. You just have to tough that shit out. Bring back the child I once knew. You know, the one who ain't took no shit from nobody, the one who'd fuck something up without thinking twice about it. Bring her back. You gotta show them that they're not the only ones who can get grimy," he said, wiping the tears that had fallen from my eyes. "If you need me, you know where to find me."

"Thank you, Weedy," I said, sitting up and hugging him.

"Anytime. Make sure you take care of yourself, and I'm serious. If you need me for anything, don't hesitate to call me," he said before he got out of the car.

I sat there thinking about what he said. He was right. Troy and I used to fuck a lot of shit up together back in the day. I wondered where that girl went, because I most definitely needed to find her and bring her back. As I sat there reminiscing, it was in that moment I realized that I hadn't asked him about my kids.

I picked my head up, trying to see if he was anywhere in sight, but he was gone. Pulling my phone out of my pocket, I dialed Troy's number. I placed the phone to my ear as I waited for her to answer it.

"What's going on? Why y'all taking so long?" I asked once she had answered the phone.

"We're coming back to the car right now," she replied. "Jayden and Mark wanted to look at a few things before we left."

"Okay," I said and hung the phone up. I sat there pissed. My nerves were back, and they were playing around and shit. I wondered what the hell it was that they were trying to see. I reached in Troy's purse to grab a cigarette and lit it, just as they entered the car. Once they got inside the car, Jayden turned the key inside the ignition and pulled off.

"What's going on, Troy? Why y'all ain't saying anything, and where are we going?" I asked as Jayden entered an address into the GPS system. Getting a good look at it, I noticed that the thing said University Hospital. "Why are we going to University Hospital? Troy, where are my kids?"

I watched as she took a deep breath, and then she turned toward me. When she turned my way, I noticed that her eyes were glossy.

"Troy, you're scaring me. What's going on?" I asked. If she wasn't about to tell me, I swore before God that I was going to start mixing on her ass.

"The boys weren't there," she replied.

"Well, where are they?" I asked her.

"Right now, they really don't know. They've put out an APB on them, and there's now an AMBER Alert on the boys," she replied.

"Oh, my God. I can't believe this," I said. I could already feel a headache coming along as I sat there realizing that I wouldn't be reunited with my kids today.

"Mimi, it's Kailay. She . . ." she said, starting to get choked up.

"What about Kailay, Troy? What's wrong with my baby?" I asked, already fearing the worst.

"Kailay was the one who got hurt during the accident. They don't know how or why. They just said that she was at University Hospital and for us to get there as soon as possible," she said as the tears started to roll down her face.

I could feel my heart breaking into a million pieces as the different scenarios played out in my head. I tried to say something, but my mouth went dry, and the words got stuck in my throat, so I didn't say anything at all. I just did what I did before, and prayed. I prayed for God to give me the strength to handle whatever it was that I was about to face. I also prayed for guidance and forgiveness, because when I found Kaylin, Stacy, and Julius, I was going to make sure that they got exactly what they deserved.

Chapter 14

Jayden

Just when we thought nothing could get any worse than it already was, it could and it did. Here we were on our way to the hospital with Mimi, to go check up on Mimi's daughter, who was now in the ICU. We didn't know what happened to her exactly, nor did we know how everything went down. I just hoped that we heard something good when we arrived at the hospital. I couldn't believe that we were at this point again, but life sometimes has a way of knocking you down beyond your lowest point. I was ready for everything to turn around but, from the looks of it, that wouldn't be happening anytime soon.

When we pulled up to University Hospital in New Orleans, the place was crowded. It looked like damn near everybody who stayed in New Orleans was sick today. It was hard for me to even find a parking space, which frustrated the hell out of me. After about two minutes of riding through the parking garage, we were finally able to locate a parking spot. After getting out of the car, we rode the elevator to the emergency room, where we went straight to the nurse's station.

"Um, excuse me, but do you have a patient by the name of Kailay Williams in here?" Troy asked as Amina stood off to the side. She looked like she was stuck in place, as if her body was there but her mind wasn't. My heart went out to her. I couldn't imagine myself being in her situation right now. Hopefully, we could hear something great right now because, honestly, I didn't think she could handle it if it wasn't good news.

I stood off to the side as the girls did what they had to do. I wanted to give them the space that they needed, and yet still be there for them at the same time. I watched the way Mimi stood off, letting Troy handle things. I knew she didn't want anyone to know about her still being alive, and I was sure that the shit she was going through right now was eating her up. That look in her eyes was something that I'd never seen before. It wasn't the look of shock, surprise, or death; it was the look of fear. I went to try to talk to her, but my phone started to ring, bringing my movement to a halt.

Pulling my phone from my pocket, I noticed that it was Shelly calling. I wanted to ignore her, but I wanted to check on Cam and see how he was doing right now.

"Hello," I said, answering the phone.

"Nigga, I know you didn't think I was playing with your ass. Why haven't I seen your face yet?" she asked.

I silently cursed myself. This shit with her was beginning to get old, and I was just about tired of her shit. This was why I never wanted to answer the phone for her. She always came with some bullshit.

"Shell, for real though, ma. I'ma need you to chill with the attitude you giving me right now. I'm going through some shit, and I don't need you to add to it," I said. I signaled to Mark that I was about to walk outside and he nodded his head.

"Nigga, I really don't care much. I asked you to show your face and yet I still don't see you. I see you really trying to play with me right now, huh?" she asked, getting a little too loud for me.

"Look, bitch, I'ma need for you to shut your fucking mouth up before you make me do it for you. I've just about had enough of your fucking shit," I said, walking into the parking lot. "Don't you ever in your life come at me like that again!"

"Nigga, you actually think I give a fuck about your threats? You don't scare me at all. I think you and I both know that you ain't 'bout what you be talking about. Your bark is way worse than your bite," she said, which just pissed me off. I thought it was time that I put this ho in her place, once and for all.

"Bitch, you and I both know that the reason why I don't put my hands on you is because of Cam. Had it not been for him, your ass would be right where you belong. Now I told you not to fuck with me, but yo' ho ass stay letting your mouth write a check that your ass can't cash," I said, a little too loud. I looked up to see a few people staring at me, so I walked farther away from the hospital. "You already know what the fuck it is!"

She laughed a crazy laugh that made me even madder. "You and all these little tantrums that you're throwing are actually kind of cute. You think I, Lashell Monae Richards, give a fuck about what it is? Because I'm telling you right now that I don't. I told your flunky, fuck-boy ass to show your face, and yet it's been weeks and you're still not here. You really trying me right now, huh? You really thought that I was playing when I said that I'd come looking for you and whatever bitch you tripping on me for? I'm not. So if you know like me, you'd stop playing me like I'm some bird bitch!"

"Bitch, where Cam at?" I asked, ignoring her ass. This ho just wasn't getting the point. She really couldn't see that I was through with her dumb ass.

"Why the fuck do you care, huh? You ain't so worried about him that you came to see him yet," she said.

I swear, if this bitch were in front of me, I'd whoop her ass from Saturday to Sunday.

"Bitch, I care because I'm his motherfucking father, that's why. You know, the nigga who's paying for everything that y'all got? The nigga who makes sure that you have a roof over your head, a car to drive, and food to eat. Keep playing with me and I'll—" I started to say, but she cut me off.

"You'll what, nigga? Huh? You'll what? You talking all of that slick shit, but that's your fucking job. You're supposed to do that shit!"

I had to laugh to keep from exploding. "No, bitch, what I'm supposed to do is take care of Cameron. He's my seed, my responsibility, not your ass," I said, setting that ho straight. I didn't know why this ho thought I was just supposed to take care of her ass because, really, I wasn't. I only did the shit because I didn't want the bitch to run off with my son.

"Tsk tsk. We already had this conversation, Mr. Smith. You'll take care of me as long as I'm the mother of your child. Which will basically be for the rest of our lives," she said, laughing.

"Bitch, you got me all the way fucked up. As a matter of fact, I want you out of my house before I get back. If I get back and you're still there, we will have a lot of fucking problems," I said, about to hang up. "Oh, and don't take my car either. Since your ass got a lot to say, I want to see you take care of your muthafucking self, because I won't be anymore!" I hung up the phone, blowing out air in frustration. I was tired of playing with her. I was about to show her just how hard things were about to be without me.

I slipped my phone back in my pocket and started walking back toward the hospital when it started to ring again. I already knew it was her, so I didn't even both to look at the caller ID.

"You must not remember who I am. You think them little-ass threats are scaring me, but they ain't. Whatever bitch you fucking must be really good at her job to have you tripping on me like this, but just remember what Shelly said. We ain't over until I say we over and I haven't said that yet. Play pussy and get fucked, nigga." And with that said, she hung up the phone. I'd handle that shit the minute I found out what was going on with Mimi's daughter.

Before I could finish my thoughts, my phone started ringing again.

"What?" I yelled, answering the phone.

"I know you better watch the way you answer that phone, boy. Now, I don't know who done made you mad, but you better not ever talk to me like that," my mother stated calmly into the phone.

"Ma, I'm so sorry. I didn't know that it was you calling. I thought it was someone else," I replied, lowering my tone.

"Let me guess. You thought I was that baby mama of yours. She's the only one who gets you this upset. I told you that broad ain't no good," she said, sounding like she had a bad taste in her mouth. My mother was never a fan of Shelly. From the first moment that she'd met her, she'd always said that she was nothing but a gold-digger. She would always express her dislike for her, even when she was around. My mother never sugarcoated shit. She kept it realer than most of these niggas out here.

"Yeah, that bitch—" I started to say before she interrupted me.

"Hey, watch your mouth now, boy. I know you don't like her, but I'm still your mother. Show me some respect," she replied, chastising me.

"Sorry, Ma. I'm just so frustrated right now," I said, spotting a bench and taking a seat.

"I been told you to cut that little gal loose. I don't know why you continue to keep her around. She ain't no good, no how," she said, as always. I'd heard this same speech over and over again.

"Ma, you know why I keep her around."

"You say that, but you and I both know that Cam is and will always be good. She ain't trying to take him nowhere. She just had him so she could be tied down to you anyway. You know damn well that girl ain't in no position to take care of a child."

"Ma, what woman you know would just leave her child behind?" I asked her.

"The girl you chose to lay there, stick your thing in, and not pull out of, getting her pregnant in the first place," she replied.

"Come on, Ma, can we please change the subject?" I said, faking as if I were about to cough up a lung.

"No, we can't," she said, laughing. "You acting like you got something I ain't never seen before. You better remember that I was the one changing your diapers and shit."

"Ma, come on!"

"All right, baby, I'll leave you alone," she replied, still laughing. Then she got serious. "But how are you? How have you been? Why haven't you been calling me? Why haven't you come home yet? You better not be down there getting into no trouble."

"Ma, I'm good. I'm just down here handling a little business, that's all. I'll be back home in a couple of weeks, I promise," I said to ease her mind.

"Jayden Anthony Smith, you better not be getting your ass into no trouble. You know your ass ain't too old for me to go upside your damn head!"

"Ma, I already told you that I'm not. I'm fine. I need you to do something for me though," I said, trying to change the subject.

"Yeah, uh-huh, make me come out of retirement for your ass. Make me hook my foot up your ass. I'm not playing either," she said as if she could really beat me. "What you need?"

"Yeah, yeah, yeah. I need for you to make a trip to the house for me."

"Oh, hell no. You know that girl is there and you know damn well that I can't be alone with her ass, or else I'll end up in jail," she said. I waited for her to laugh, but it never came.

"Come on, Ma. I'm not there, and I need you to do this for me. If you want, I'll send Chucky with you."

"It better not be no illegal shit, I'm telling you now," she said, huffing into the phone.

"Ma, you know good and well that I'd never send you on no bullshit like that," I said. My feelings were hurt.

"Well, what is it then?" she asked.

"I need you to go and get Cam and kick Shelly out of the house," I replied.

"You sure about this? Because I'm not going over there only for you to take her back."

"Yeah, Ma. Besides, I got a new woman. Ain't no going back this time," I said, knowing she would want to know who she was.

"You do? Tell me about her. She better not be another one like the one you got now!"

"Trust me, Ma, she's nothing like Shelly. This girl is the total opposite, and she has class."

"Yeah, you say that, but I have to see it to believe it. When will I get to meet her?" she asked.

"Soon, Ma. I gotta go, but don't forget to do what I asked you to," I said, cutting her off because I knew how she could be.

"Uh-huh. Call Chucky. Tell him to meet me. As for you, I'll handle you later," she said.

"All right, I'll talk to you later. Love you, Ma," I said to her.

"Love you too. See you soon, baby," she replied. I hung up the phone as I stood up from the bench. Damn near ten minutes had gone by and I knew Mark and them were probably looking for me by now.

I hurriedly walked back toward the entrance. Once I entered the waiting room, I didn't see Mimi and Troy anywhere. I was about to walk over to the nurse's station when Mark called out to me.

"Over here, man," Mark said. He was ducked off in the corner, which was why I didn't see him in the first place.

"What's going on, man? Where are the girls?" I asked, sitting in the seat next to him.

"Man, you ever looked at your life or the life of some-one you cared about and wondered why they're going through the things that they're going through?" he asked, ignoring my question. The way he was looking made me scared to hear where this was going.

"Yeah, man, all the time," I said, answering him. Then everything got silent between us. I asked, "Well, what did they say? Which one of her kids was hurt in the accident? As a matter of fact, where are her kids?"

Hanging his head low, he shook his head from side to side before replying, which let me know that whatever he was about to say wasn't good news. "It was her daughter. She suffered an injury to her head, which left her with a great amount of head trauma. Right now, she's bleeding on the brain. They're waiting on someone to come for her, so that they could get papers signed, saying that she can undergo surgery," he said, as my heart broke into pieces. "I feel for Mimi. She's been through enough. It's like she can never get a break."

"Damn, man," I said as I wiped a hand over my face. I couldn't imagine my son going through anything like that. I hoped he'd never have to. On the outside looking in, one would think that Mimi was just a magnet attracting bad shit. I was sure that's what she was probably thinking right now. She needed to know that no matter what happened, I would always be there for her and I would have her back through all of this.

"I can only imagine what she's going through right now, man. For her sake, I hope that little mama pulls through, or else shit will only get worse, and her thirst for revenge will only increase," he said, just as Troy walked into the waiting room. I was thinking the same thing too.

A few minutes later, Mimi came walking out of the back room. I got up to meet her when she ran straight into my arms.

"It's going to be all right, ma. If she's anything like her mother, then she's a fighter. She'll pull through this in no time," I said as she broke down crying. She didn't say anything. She just laid her head on my shoulder and continued to cry her eyes out. My heart broke to see her in pain. I walked backward, trying to get to the seat that I was just sitting in. When I got there, I took a seat and pulled her into my arms.

"It's going to be fine. Just wait and see. She'll be just fine," I kept saying repeatedly as I rocked her.

She pulled back, looked me straight in my eyes, and said, "I really hope that you're right, because if I lose my baby, I promise you it's going to be hell on earth for them."

"I know, baby, I know," I said, as she laid her head back onto my shoulder. I silently prayed that God spared that little girl's life. I really hoped that little mama pulled through this, because I honestly didn't think that Mimi would be able to handle it if she didn't. If she lost her daughter, she was going to fall off, and if she fell off, we wouldn't be able to get her back.

Chapter 15

Shelly

Hey, everyone! How's it going? I know you probably don't know about me, but my name is Lashell Monae Richards. I was Jayden's baby mama, and I knew him and that bitch Ambria had probably told y'all some bad things about me. Which was why I didn't want Ambria to be the one to tell my side of the story, for one reason: she was team Mimi. She was in love with the fact that my man and her main bitch Mimi done got together and became an item, but what I wanted her to know was that I was about to fuck all the shit up. She had me bent and twisted if she thought I was about to let that shit slide. Ain't no bitch gonna just come up out the cut and take my man from me and I ain't do nothing about it. Oh, hell no, I wasn't that type of female.

Honestly, I didn't know why Jayden would try me. He already knew how I was. We already went through that shit with that bum bitch Janet Jones, and just like I was about to do with this shit, I shut that shit all the way down.

You see, Jayden called himself trying to play he was King Tut or somebody and have a bitch and a side bitch, thinking I wasn't going to find out. Oh, but I did, and I went berserk on his ass. I whooped Janet's ass every time I saw her, until the bitch left the state. I needed to show her and Jayden's asses that I wasn't to be played with

like that. I really believed that Jayden actually hated me
though. The dude never had anything nice to say about
me. Hell, he never said anything nice to me, so I knew
his ass was definitely feeling a little different about me
now than he was when he first met me. I really didn't
care though, because I played my part and I had my spot
locked down. I was wifey, the mother of his firstborn and
the bitch who was never going to go anywhere. I knew
damn well that I had it going good. Well, that was before
this new bitch came into the picture. Now I had to come
out of character and show her ass who I was and why she
shouldn't be fucking with another bitch's man.

At times, I would find myself asking if Jayden was
worth this shit. Should I really give a fuck about this
nigga? Or was it the shit he did for me that I didn't want
to lose? I was tired of making myself look like a fool for a
nigga who didn't want me, but when money was involved
and I knew damn well that I didn't have that, I pushed
that shit to the back of my mind.

My family always said that they couldn't believe that
Jayden and I were once in love because we never acted
like it. We were always bickering and beefing, and we
stayed fighting. He was always provoking me though. He
never did the things that I'd ask him to do. He stayed
doing the complete opposite, which always made me go
postal on his ass. He was barely home, and he was always
on the go with Mark's little bitch ass.

That's another thing: Mark was always around. It was
like he didn't have his own life or house to go to. He
was always there. Shit, I was starting to believe that
them niggas were gay or something. That's how much
they were always with each other. No matter what time it
was, when you saw Jayden, you were bound to see Mark
following him. The shit was gayish, and I was going to put
my foot down about that, among other things.

I was sidetracked when the house phone started to ring. I ran, trying to get it, because I didn't want it to wake Cam up. "Hello," I said, answering the phone with an attitude.

"Hey, bitch. What's up with you?" my cousin Brittney asked me.

"Girl, I'm chilling right now. What's up with you?" I asked her.

"Same here. I'm trying to find out what we're doing tonight," she replied. "I'm getting tired of staying in this house."

"Shit, I don't know. I got to do something with Cam's ass first," I said, once I reached his room. I poked my head in a bit to make sure that he was still asleep. Once I had made sure that he was, I walked down the hall to my bedroom.

"Bring him over here for Tae. You know he can always come and play with Nevaeh and Da'Myren," she said, referring to her kids.

"Girl, I don't know. You sure Tae gon' want to babysit all them kids?" I asked, making my way into my walk-in closet, trying to find an outfit to put on.

"Tae will do what I tell her to do. Besides, she's grounded. She can't go nowhere. I'ma just give her phone back, and she'll agree. You know she can't live without it."

"All right, but we still don't know where we're going, shit," I said, just as I spotted a black fitted dress. I removed it from the hanger and went to lay it across the bed.

We tossed around some ideas as I went into Cam's room and quietly laid out a bag to get him packed up for the evening, but we still couldn't decide where to go.

"Once you drop Cam off, we'll figure it out," she left it, just as the doorbell began to ring.

"Girl, all right. I got to go now. Somebody's at the door."

"Let me find out that you over there checking on Jayden again. He's going to fuck your ass up," she said, laughing.

"Girl, fuck Jayden's little bitch ass. He know better. He ain't going to do a damn thing but give me his money. He knows damn well not to play around. He already knows what it's hitting for. I got something that he's dangerously in love with," I said, letting it be known. I was the type of bitch to do a nigga wrong today and have him back tomorrow, just how I did with Jayden the first time. And you know why? It's because the power of pussy is a motherfucker. I had a lot of things that most bitches would die for.

At twenty-eight, I had a banging-ass, flawless body and a beautiful face, and my sex game was on point. I hadn't yet met a man who wouldn't give me anything that I wanted. I made sure that every nigga I fucked with was able to take care of me so that I wouldn't have to. I never had to get a job or anything. I believed that was why God blessed me with a powerful pussy, so that I wouldn't have to work. All I had to do was make sure that my body stayed right and my pussy stayed tight, and those niggas were putty in my hands.

"Shell! You still there?" Brittney asked me, pulling me from my thoughts.

"Yeah, but I got to go. I forgot that I had somebody at the door. I'ma have to talk to you later," I said, hanging up the phone, not waiting for a reply.

Before going to answer the door, I plugged my phone into the charger. As I made my way down the stairs, whoever it was started beating on the damn door.

"Damn, hold on. I'm coming," I screamed in a nasty tone, but the person ignored me and started to beat some more while ringing the doorbell at the same time. I put an extra pep in my step so that I could get to the door faster and chew out whoever it was. Once I made it to the door, I jerked it open, ready to give whoever it was a piece of my mind, until I realized just who it was.

"Well, it's about time you answer the door. I thought you was going to have me standing out here forever," Jayden's mother, Mrs. Carol Smith, said, making me eat the words I was about to say.

"Um, hello, Mrs. Smith, how may I help you? If you came here looking for Jayden, he's not here right now," I said with a fake smile, pretending to be nice. I always had to pretend as if I liked this trick when I knew damn well she didn't like me. She didn't say anything. She just stood there looking at me with a look of disdain written all over her face. I was starting to feel uncomfortable.

"Wha . . . what's wrong, ma'am?" I asked, stuttering. This little old bitch was beginning to hit a nerve.

"Where's Cameron?" she finally opened her mouth to say.

"Oh. Um, Cam's in his room sleeping," I said, confused. "Why?"

She looked at me, rolled her eyes, and then she headed for the stairs.

"Where are you going? I told you that Cameron was in his room sleeping," I said, chasing her, but she ignored me and kept right on walking. I wanted to grab her ass and knock her out. She was starting to piss me the fuck off.

When we entered Cam's room, he was up in his bed. She turned and gave me a snobby look before turning back to Cam, who was now reaching for her. She picked him up and then turned back to me. I didn't know why she always acted as if Cam were still a baby. He was now a four-year-old, and too big for her to carry him.

"You look as if you were about to go somewhere. Did I interrupt you?" she asked, noticing Cam's bag that was on his dresser.

"Oh, yes. I was about to bring Cam to my cousin's house."

"Well, why would Cameron be going by your cousin's house? Are you going somewhere?" she asked, looking at Cam.

"Well, yes. Me and my cousin were about to go shopping," I said, lying. Her old ass didn't need to know what I was doing. What she needed to be concerned with was her son and why he hadn't come back home yet.

"Yeah, I bet," she said under her breath as if I couldn't hear her. She then looked up at me with a smirk on her face. I knew some shit was about to go down.

"I'll keep Cameron until his father gets back. In the meantime, you can go and start packing your things. Your time here has come to an end. I want you out of this house in an hour," she said, just as the doorbell started to ring again. She pushed past me with Cameron in her arms and went to answer the door. I was right on her heels.

"What do you mean my time here has come to an end?" I asked, confused.

"Just what I said. It's time for you to pack your things and leave my son's house," she said as we walked down the stairs. She walked over to the door, opened it, and found a big, bald black guy standing there. "You're right on time."

"On time? On time for what?" I asked, still confused. I needed to know what the hell was going on.

"That shouldn't matter to you. All you need to be doing right now is going upstairs, getting your things, and then getting out of here."

"I don't know what you smoked, but I'm not going anywhere," I said, finally putting my foot down. I was tired of this old bat thinking she could do what she wanted in my house.

"Oh, darling, yes, you are," she replied, giving me an evil glare.

"No, I'm not. I'm here because my man, Jayden, your son, my baby's daddy, wants me here. I talked to him not too long ago, and he did not tell me that I had to leave. Therefore, I'm not going anywhere. This is my house. The only person who needs to be leaving is your ass," I said, taking a step toward her.

"You see, now that's where your little ass is wrong. Jayden is the reason why I'm here in the first place. He was going to do it himself, but since he's not here, he sent me to do it for him. And, to be honest, I'm really happy that he's finally seen you for the lying, two-timing hussy you really are," she said, taking a step closer to me. "Now, you can either go and get your shit and leave the easy way, or I can make you leave."

I stood there matching her stare. I couldn't believe Jayden sent his mother over here to do his dirty work. I stood there, standing face to face with the devil himself. I wanted to slap the fuck out of her old ass.

"You know what? Fuck you and your little punk-ass son," I said before I turned to walk up the stairs to my bedroom. Once I was inside of the bedroom, I went straight into my walk-in closet. I grabbed my suitcases out of the corner and began pulling clothes off the hangers and tossing them into them.

"This nigga must don't know who the fuck he playing with," I said, pulling more clothes off the hanger and throwing them into the suitcase. "I don't know what chick you take me for, but I can bet you my last dollar that you'll regret it. I done told him time and time again not to push me, but it looks like that's the only way I'm going to be able to get through to you," I said, talking as if he were right in front of me. Jayden just didn't know what he'd done. He done did the wrong thing. He was getting ready to see a side of me that he'd never seen before.

I exhaled furiously. "Fuck them and fuck this house. Jayden will definitely pay for this," I said as I zipped up my suitcase. I hadn't realized until now that I had packed all of my suitcases. When I was done, I rolled all three suitcases out of the room and into the hallway. I placed them by the door, then went to Cam's room and got his things. Once I had everything that he needed, I rolled Cam's suitcase out of his room, before stopping to pick up mine, and then I headed down the stairs. Once I had placed our stuff by the garage door, I went to the kitchen and grabbed my keys, before going in the living room to get my son.

"What are you doing with Cameron's things?" she asked, once I had entered the living room.

I had to look at her twice. "What do you mean?" I asked her.

"Like I said, what are you doing with Cameron's things?" she asked with a raised brow.

"What do you think? If I got to go, I damn sure ain't leaving my baby behind with you people," I said, attempting to walk over to where Cam was, but she stopped me.

"Little girl, it's in your best interest for you to leave out of here now. Cameron is staying with me until his father gets back," she said, stepping in front of me. She gave me a look that said "hell yeah," and I completely lost it.

"You must be out of your damn mind, lady. Cameron is my son. I gave birth to him, not you, and if I say that he's coming with me, then he is," I said, pointing my finger in her face. She looked at the finger that was in her face, then back at me, before she picked up her hand and slapped me in the face. "You bitch!" I yelled.

"No, you're the bitch and a stupid bitch at that. I've held my peace with your little ass for a long damn time, but that stops today. From the first moment that I laid eyes on you, I knew that you weren't shit, but my dumb-ass son was too busy thinking with his little head and not his big head. You had gold-digger written all over your face. You didn't want my son. You only wanted what he could've done for you and like a fool his dumb ass couldn't see it until it was too late," she said, and then she pointed at Cam, who was sitting on the couch. "You and I both know that the only reason you had that child was because you wanted to trap my son. You don't really want that child. You're only using him as a crutch against my son, which is the number one reason why he didn't put your ass out a long time ago."

"Look, you old hag, you don't scare me at all. Just like you, I've wanted to hook my foot up your ass among other things, but I didn't. You're right about one thing though. I don't want your son. I only want what his punk ass can do for me," I replied with a smirk on my face. She let the bitch out of me now, and she was about to see just how fucked up things were about to be. I got all the way in her face and raised my hand up to slap the shit out of her, but someone caught my hand midair.

"Bitch, I wish the fuck you would." Chucky had come in, and he pulled my arm so far back that I thought he was going to break it. He then picked me up and began walking to the door.

"Put me down, muthafucker" I yelled, kicking and screaming, but he ignored me and kept walking. "Chucky, I'm not playing with you. You better put me down, nigga, or I'ma fuck your fat ass up." I was about to try to bite him when I felt myself being lifted in the air.

'What the fuck are you do—" I started to ask, but before I could finish asking the question, I was being thrown onto the ground. I tried to get up, but he pushed me back down.

"Bitch, if you knew like I knew, you'd stay right down there where you are," he yelled.

"Chucky, this some fucked-up shit and you know it. Wait until Jayden hears about this. Your ass will be through," I said ranting.

"Bitch, if you ain't hear Ms. Carol when she said it, please let me be the one to tell you. Jayden was the one who sent us down here in the first place. He wants your ass out of his house, and I'm glad. He done finally seen you for the lying, two-timing, evil, vindictive, gold-digging bitch you are. He done finally found him a good chick and your time here is up, Bitch, be gone," he said, giving me a look of disgust, and then he walked away.

I sat there on the ground stuck. I couldn't believe that Jayden actually wanted to go there and take it this route with me. Did he not know the bitch I really could be? I was the type of chick to fuck a nigga today and not give a fuck about him tomorrow. I was that crazy bitch you knew, the one with a bunch of different personalities, the one who had to take beaucoup medicines to calm myself down. I knew damn well that the nigga didn't want to fuck around with something like this, but since he wanted to go down, I was about to bring it to him. I guessed I was about to go on a little world trip. I was making my way to Atlanta to find his ass. Either we were going to handle this thing properly like two adults, or I was going to cause hell on him and everything that he stood for.

Finally pulling myself off the ground, I pulled my phone out and made a call to my cousin Brittney asking her to pick me up. Ten minutes later, she pulled up. I grabbed my luggage, placed it in the trunk, and got in the car. The moment I got inside of the car, I wished like hell that I hadn't called her. She fussed a little bit about me letting Jayden and his mother do what they were doing to me, but I half-ass listened to her. She thought that since she was a few years older than I was, she could tell me what to do and how to do it.

"Look, Brit, you need to chill out. I'm really not trying to hear all of that right now," I snapped at her. She was beginning to get on my damn nerves.

"Don't catch no attitude with me. You need to check that nigga on his shit," she replied as if I didn't just ask her ass to shut the fuck up.

"Girl, I got this," I told her, and then a thought came to me. I pulled my phone out and made a phone call. The phone rang a few times, before going straight to voicemail.

"Who you calling?" she asked, pulling up into her driveway.

"I was calling that stupid bitch Jade, but she ain't answering," I said, dialing her number again, but like before, the phone rang a few times and went to voicemail.

"Your sister?" she asked, surprised.

"Yes."

"Girl, I haven't seen her ass in a minute. I thought you and her didn't fuck with each other like that," she said, looking at me sideways.

"We've talked a few times before, so it's not like that. Besides, she lives in Atlanta, and that's where I'm heading in a few days, so I thought I'd give her a call," I said, as we got out of the car.

"Okay," she replied. She looked as if she wanted to say something else, but instead, she left and went inside the house, leaving me there to get my own things out of the trunk.

I knew she was probably worried about Jade and me getting together, because every time that we linked up, we always ended up in trouble. This is why our mothers had chosen to split us up when we were little. Even as kids in school, we were getting into trouble. It worked for a little while, until somehow she found me and we'd kept in touch ever since. Now I needed her help, and I knew that it was going to take a minute, but she was my sister. She was going to help me either way. I just hoped that we didn't get ourselves into any trouble as we always did.

Chapter 16

Troy

We'd been sitting in the hospital waiting room for hours now, waiting on Kailay to get out of surgery. The doctor said that it wasn't going to take long, but it did. I hoped that nothing went wrong, because if it did, I'd lose it. Kailay, along with her twin sister Kayla, were both my godbabies. I treated them as if I had given birth to them myself. Once I found out she was the one who was hurt in the accident, I lost it. I was calling everybody and their mama trying to figure out if they'd seen or heard from Julius, Stacy, or Kaylin. I wanted so badly to make them bitches pay for what they'd done, once again.

I looked over at Mark, Jayden, and Mimi, who were all sleeping. I knew they were tired, but I couldn't sleep. When something was weighing on my mind heavily, I couldn't sleep. Kailay was that something, which was why I hadn't closed my eyes yet. I was too worried about her and wondering how she was doing. *Wherever Julius, Kaylin, and Stacy are, they better hope and pray like hell that she pulls through this, or else shit won't be too pretty for them.*

I looked over to where Mimi was sitting on Jayden's lap asleep, and I sighed. She'd been through so much these past few months that the shit didn't even feel real. My girl looked so worn out that it made me want to cry. Had anybody said that we'd be living our life like this, I'd have bet my last dollar that they were lying, but we were, and I would've been a broke bitch. We never imagined that our life would take a turn like this. Hell, we never imagined ourselves stepping foot back into Louisiana, because when we had left, we vowed not to, unless it had something to do with Kayla. Otherwise, we never fucked with it.

I was deep in my thoughts when my phone started to ring. I quickly grabbed for my purse to retrieve it. Once I had it, I got up and walked a few feet away from the waiting room area.

"Hello," I said, answering the phone.

"Oh, my God, I've been calling and looking all over for you. How have you been?" Candy frantically said into the phone. "I thought you was dead or something."

"Calm down, *mami*. I'm alive and I'm doing fine, as you can see," I said with a light chuckle. "I'm just out of town taking care of some business."

"Well, it's nice to know that you're alive. When are you coming back so that I can cuss your ass out face to face?" she asked, sounding a little mad. I laughed a bit. I barely knew her when she started working at the salon, but we became good friends.

"Girl, chill out with all that. You and I both know that I'm not going anywhere no time soon," I said, laughing a bit. "Anyway, how's everything going at the salon? Is anyone giving you trouble?"

"Everything is actually fine. I had to give Summer a few days off. She came over here on some bullshit, hollering about we were slaving for y'all while you're out there having a good time," she said, catching me by surprise.

"You talking about the light-skinned chick with the buck teeth in her mouth, making her look like Bugs Bunny's sister?" I asked, wanting to know if we were talking about the same person.

"Yes, that's her," she replied, confirming what I thought.

"But, I thought she was the quiet one. The one who kept to her business and not worrying about nobody else's," I said, wanting to know what happened that made her think she could play the game like that.

"Baby, she ain't quiet anymore, honey," she replied.

"Well, you know what? Since little mama want to have a big heart, fire her ass."

"But if I do that, then we're going to be short-staffed," she replied as if I gave a fuck. I didn't want anybody around if they thought that they could talk some slick shit about me.

"Well, put a want ad in the paper, pass out fliers, and place a NOW HIRING sign in the window or something. Just get the bitch out of there," I said, just as Mimi walked up on me.

"What's going on, Troy?" she asked. I raised a finger up, indicating for her to hold on.

"Okay, I got you. Now when will you be back?"

"I'll be back as soon as I can. In the meantime, make sure you take care of the salon. Make sure people are paying their dues, make sure that we stay fully stocked, and make sure that the books are right," I replied. "I have to go. I'll talk to you later."

"Okay, see you soon," she said before I hung up the phone.

"What's wrong, Troy?" Mimi asked again.

"Nothing," I replied.

"Well, who was that you was on the phone with?" she asked, putting her hands on her hip.

"That was Candy," I said.

"Well, what did she say? What's going on at the salon? Is she having problems out of anyone?" she asked, looking concerned.

"She only said that some chick was saying some slick shit out of her mouth and she gave her a few days off," I replied, hunching my shoulders.

"Well, who was it?"

"The little chick Summer."

"You talking about the little quiet chick, who never says anything to anybody?" she asked, looking surprised.

"Yeah, that's her, and it seems that she's not quiet anymore."

"Well, what did she say and what are you going to do about it?" she asked. I opened my mouth to answer her when my phone started to ring again. I looked at the caller ID, only to see that this time it Weedy calling. Not really wanting Mimi to know who it was, I let the call roll to voicemail.

"What's up? Why didn't you answer the phone? Who was it?" she began to ask, but the doctor interrupted her.

"I'm looking for the family of Ms. Kailay Williams," he asked, looking at his chart, then around the room.

"Umm, over here," Mimi replied, just as Mark and Jayden got up from where they were seated and came over to us. "What's going on? Is everything all right with Kailay?" Mimi asked, blurting out question after question.

"Well, Kailay's just now getting out of surgery, and I'm pleased to say that everything went well," he said, which made me release the breath that I had been holding.

"Will she survive this? Will she be able to have a normal life?"

"We were able to stop the bleeding, which means that Kailay's expected to make a full recovery. She's going to be hospitalized for a week or two maybe. All depending on how fast her wounds heal," he replied with a smile on his face.

'Oh, thank you so, so, so much," Mimi said, wiping the tears from her eyes. I guessed those were tears of joy. She then reached in and gave him a big hug.

"It's my pleasure. She'll be in her recovery room in a minute. You'll be able to see her. I'll send someone out here as soon as they're done," he said.

"Thanks, man," Jayden said, reaching his hand out for the doctor to shake it.

"You're welcome," the doctor replied, shaking his hand. "See you all later." And with that said, he left.

I turned to Mimi, giving her an extra tight hug. I was both relieved and happy that Kailay was going to be just fine.

"Are you fine? You feeling better?" I asked as we went to take a seat.

"Now that I know my daughter will be okay I'm doing better, but I will never be fine until I end the lives of the people who caused me all this pain," she said, raising her head up. The look in her eyes was one that I'd never seen before. I hope that Kaylin and Stacy were ready, because they were about to feel the revenge of a kept bitch.

Chapter 17

Kaylin

I never in all my life thought that I'd be in a predicament such as the one that I was in now. I once had my life planned out to a T. I was going to marry the love of my life, make an assload of money, and start my own family. Well, I had two out of the three things, but because of my poor lack of judgment, and thinking with my little head instead of my big head, I didn't have anything but money. I didn't care what anybody said, money couldn't buy you happiness. I wished I could say that this was somebody else's fault, but I knew that I had no one to blame but myself. Had I not been a typical male instead of the man that Mimi needed me to be, I wouldn't have been in this situation right now.

I woke up from a horrible dream that I was having. I was rolling through the streets of New Orleans with my kids and Stacy, when out of nowhere a car collided with the van that we were in. Next thing I knew, I was hearing a bunch of loud screaming and crying. Then a man opened the door and tried to pull me out. I tried reaching for my gun, but he somehow saw me and punched the hell out of me so hard that I was seeing stars. I turned to try to check on my kids when I noticed that there was blood on the window. That's when I saw Kailay on the floor, unresponsive.

"*Kailay,*" *I said, trying to reach for her, but dude reached in and stopped me.*

"*Where do you think you're going?*" *he asked, turning me back around to face him. I swore dude's face was so familiar, but I couldn't remember where I had seen him.*

"*Look, I don't know who the fuck you are and I damn sure don't know what you want, but I'm trying to get to my daughter. She's in the back seat, and she's unresponsive,*" *I said to him. What he said next had me wanting to take his fucking head off.*

"*I don't give a fuck if her little ass dies. She's not my problem, nigga,*" *he said. He then opened his mouth to spit some more shit, but before he could do that I had punched him dead in his muthafucking mouth. I didn't know where all that energy had come from, but I was on top of his ass like white on rice. I wasn't a fool, and I knew damn well that Stacy's no-loyalty-having ass had something to do with this.*

"*Bitch-ass nigga. How could you say some shit like that?*" *I asked, giving him a three-piece combo to his face that drew blood instantly. He tried to push me off him, but that left hook that I sent to his jaw had him in a daze. I knew the shit had to hurt, because I heard when it cracked. Standing up, I proceeded to stomp and kick all over his body. "I bet you're going to think twice when you come at me again.*"

I was about to get up and go see about Kailay when something hard connected with the back of my head. I moved my hand to grab the back of my head when I was struck again. The thing I remembered seeing before everything went black was Stacy standing over me with a gun in her hand.

That's when I woke up. I opened my eyes but closed them again immediately. The sun was so bright that when

I opened them, it was starting to give me a headache. It took a few minutes, but when I was finally able to open my eyes, I had no idea where I was. I moved my arms to try to sit up, but my hands were tied down. "What the fuck is going on?" I asked myself. I tried to recall how I got there, but somehow I couldn't remember anything.

"Well, well, well. Look who finally decided to join the party," I heard a male voice say, but I didn't see anyone.

"What the fuck is this shit and who the fuck are you?" I asked, getting angry. I was tied to a bed somewhere, and now someone was playing with me.

I heard him laugh, and then he said, "You're one tough cookie to crack, man." Again, I tried to turn to see if I could see him, but I didn't see anything. I had an idea of who it was, but I silently prayed to God that I was wrong.

"I must admit, you almost had me back there, but as always my little girl had come to my rescue," he said with a light chuckle. My heartbeat quickly sped up as I heard footsteps approaching me. "I owe you one, little nigga," he said, and then his fist connected with the side of my face. My head snapped back so hard, I thought I had whiplash. When I turned to get a good look at him, I almost bugged out. It was the same man from my dream.

"Man, what the fuck are you doing here and why the fuck am I all tied up and shit?" I spoke through gritted teeth.

"You and I both know the answer to that question," he said, walking around to the foot of the bed. "But what I need to know is where the money is."

"I don't know what you're talking about and there's no money. So you might as well just let me and my kids go," I spoke to him calmly. He erupted into a heap of laughter, as if I had just said something that was funny. He was starting to annoy the fuck out of me, because I for one didn't see shit that was supposed to be funny.

"You're a real funny guy, Kaylin," he said, taking a seat in the chair that was sitting by the bed. "But if I were you and I were in your position, I wouldn't try to be funny right now. Your kids' lives are at stake."

"Man, I don't know what the fuck you're talking about. Where are my kids? If you touch one hair on either one of my boys' heads, you'll regret the day your mother had you!" I said, my voice laced with venom.

"Tsk, tsk, tsk. We don't want your sons to end up like your daughter. Now do we?" he asked, with a smirk on his face.

I was about to answer him when the sound of a female's voice interrupted me.

"Did he wake up yet, Daddy?" Stacy asked, entering the room. Her mouth flew open when she noticed that I was sitting there awake and alert.

I didn't say anything. To be honest, I couldn't. All I could really do was laugh and shake my head. The bitch who I cheated on my girl with was now betraying me. Go fucking figure.

"So I'm getting fucked over by my side piece I see," I said, looking straight at her. The bitch couldn't even look me in my eyes. "So what? Is this supposed to make you feel better? What you trying to get back at me for? You was always my bitch, my bottom bitch at that. I never had any plans on making you my woman, because you wasn't worthy enough of becoming her and this is the number one reason why. You're a disloyal, untrustworthy person, a snake, and a bitch who would turn on her mama if you had to. You actually think that I want a bitch like you as my woman? A bitch, my bitch is always what you'll ever be. I hope that whatever it is you're getting out of this will make you happy."

She didn't say anything. She just kept her eyes down to the floor, so I continued, "Not only did you take away a mother, who left four kids behind, but you also took away that little girl's father. Now you want to take away a father and leave those same three, plus your own son, fatherless," I said, trying to build as much guilt on her conscience as I could.

"Don't put that shit on me. I wasn't the one who shot them; you were. It was your gun that killed Mimi and Tyreek, not mines. So save that bullshit. Speak for yourself, nigga," she said, taking a step toward me.

"Bitch, please. It was only because of your bitter ass that I even found the shit out in the first place. You couldn't just stay in your lane. You had to do what side bitches do: cause problems."

"Nigga, fuck you," she said and walked out of the room. I lay there wishing that I could rip both her and her fucking father apart. When I looked up, I caught the nigga standing there staring at me.

"What the fuck are you staring at?" I asked, mugging the nigga.

"You. I could never understand how y'all niggas let pussy be y'all downfall. Y'all claim to be that nigga, but the minute a bitch with a powerful pussy comes into y'all niggas' lives, y'all get as soft as a fucking teddy bear." He chuckled and then shook his head. "Your generation of men is weak-minded. Had you been born back in my time, you'd have known better. We didn't get pussy whipped; we did the whipping. Had bitches eating out of the palms of our hands, and then sucking our dicks after. We had bitch after bitch, and we never had a problems, because they knew about each other. Our bitches got along and never caused any problems, and you know why? Because we had it like that. Keep letting your little head get you fucked up and you'll find yourself in many more situations like this," he said, laughing. He looked at me, and then walked out of the room, leaving me with my thoughts.

I wasn't trying to hear none of that shit that wannabe pimp thug was spitting. I was only concerned with finding my kids and getting the fuck up out of here before it was too late. I was sitting there thinking when an idea popped in my head. I wasn't sure if it was going to work, but right now, I didn't have a choice. I was willing to do anything to get my kids and me up out of here, even if I had to die trying.

Chapter 18

Stacy

Something in my gut was telling me not to go through with this plan. I just had a bad feeling that something was going to go wrong and it did. As I was sitting there on the passenger side of the van, my mind kept on telling me to call my father and call the whole thing off, but I didn't, and now I was really regretting it. How the shit went down, it was never supposed to happen like that, and the way my father just blew Kailay off and left her there had really pissed me off.

I only agreed to help him with it because he guaranteed that no one was going to get hurt. He lied to me, and the bad thing about it was he acted as if he didn't give a fuck whether the child lived or died. I knew my father well, and gave him a serious side eye, because I knew for a fact he didn't care one way or the other. That child was actually his grandchild, and he didn't care, which led me to believe that if he and I ever got into it one day, he wouldn't give a fuck about my son either.

I was really starting to hate everything about this. I couldn't see it before, but I was a pawn in this game. My father really didn't care about me. He just wanted to get back at Mimi any way that he could, and it didn't matter what he had to do. I couldn't see it before, but I actually think this man used me this whole time. When my mother left him after finding out about Mimi and her mother, Marie, he didn't even try to fight for us. It was as if he was ready to leave. I really don't know why he's basically blaming Mimi for losing his family when he didn't want them in the first place. He knew from the beginning that he and my mother had a lot of problems, since before his infidelity. I got this funny feeling that he wasn't the only one wanting to see Mimi fall. I believed he was working with somebody else besides me and I was going to find out whom.

"Stacy," he said, calling my name.

"Yeah, Daddy," I replied.

"What's up with you? You haven't been yourself lately," he said, looking me straight in the eye.

"Ain't nothing wrong. I'm fine," I said. "What's up though?"

"I'ma need you to keep an eye on him. I have to go handle a few things. I'll see you all in the morning," he said, grabbing his keys and cell from the table.

"Where are you going?" I asked, popping up out of my seat.

"You don't need to know all of that. I told you that I'll be back in the morning. Just keep an eye on him," he replied, pushing past me. I wanted to say something else, but I knew better. I was about to let him know that I kind of knew what was going on, but I decided to leave him clueless, like he thought he was doing to me.

I waited until he was gone before I went to check on Kaylin. I knew what I said to him earlier, but the truth of the matter was I still loved this man. I just wasn't trying to take the blame for all of this, because he was as much to blame for this as I was, which was why I said what I had said to him. I knew he probably thought that I didn't have a conscience at all, but I did, and it was starting to get the best of me.

When I walked into the room, he was sitting there staring at the wall. I wanted to walk over to him and give him a hug and kiss, but I knew I couldn't. Instead, I stood there staring at him. I wanted to say something, anything, but the words were stuck in my throat. Reluctantly, I turned around and started walking out the door, but I stopped when I heard the sound of his voice.

"Where are my kids, Stacy?" he asked, which froze my steps. I just stood there, with my heart feeling as if it were going to hop out of my chest at any minute. The pain in his voice was unbearable, and it was evident that he was hurting inside as well.

"Is it really worth it?" he asked as his voice boomed through the room. I turned around to find him now staring at me. For a minute, I could've sworn that I saw tears well up in his eyes, but he didn't let them fall. "All of this that you're pulling me and my kids through. Is it worth it? I mean, you're basically leaving all of these kids without a parent, and you can't tell me the shit sitting right with you!" I opened my mouth to say something but immediately closed it when no words would come out.

"I hope you know that nothing good will come out of this. Yes, that man may be your father, but he has something else up his sleeve. I just hope and pray that you see it before it's too late," he said.

He looked over to me, waiting on a reply, but I couldn't say a word. How was I going to tell him, "Yeah, I fucked you over, and now I think my father has something else up his sleeve. He may even have someone else working with him, too." I just couldn't bring myself to say that. Not only would that make me look like a fool, but it would also make me mad that I fell for another nigga's lies.

"What happened to you? When I first met you, you wasn't this evil and vindictive. You was a little feisty, but to be lowdown and dirty wasn't you," he said, which pushed my buttons.

"You know what happened to me? My sister did. I got tired of seeing her with the things that I wanted, but I knew I couldn't have. She was always happy, while I wasn't. She could have anything that she wanted, when I couldn't even get the things that I needed. But, the straw that broke the camel's back was when she took my father from me. That sent me over the edge, and I never got over it," I yelled, looking over to him.

He looked confused as he tried to connect the dots, but he couldn't. "Next time, do some research before you go sticking your dick somewhere," I said and stormed out of the room.

I knew I sounded bitter, but I was young when my mother put my father out. We were forced to cut all ties with him and that had hurt me dearly, because I was a daddy's girl. I needed my father for any- and everything. No matter what reason it was, he came running. That all ended when my mother found out about my father's illegitimate child. She threw him out, and we didn't see him again until three years later. By then, I was hell-bent on finding that child, and I wanted to cause her the same kind of hurt and pain she had caused me.

At first, things were going smooth. I had succeeded. That was, until she met Kaylin. Dude was like her God. Whenever she was feeling down or hurt, he was there to take away all of her pain. He gave her any- and everything that she wanted and moved her up out of the hood. That's when I hatched a plan to go after him. I was more than sure that if I fucked him, she'd be heartbroken and she'd feel how I felt when I lost my father. So, I fucked him and, boy, was his dick good. When she found out she was indeed heartbroken and she left him, but a few months later, she ended up taking him back. I was fucked up because that wasn't supposed to happen, but it did, and I was now feeling some type of way, because I had fallen in love with him and the lifestyle that he had given me. So I said fuck the plan. I was going after the man, but here I was years later, and I still didn't have him.

As I sat there thinking about all of the things that I'd been through and what I'd put Mimi through, I couldn't help but to break down. She was dead, and yet I still couldn't have Kaylin. I did everything in my power to break them up, and he still didn't want me. I realized that it didn't matter what I did. If he didn't want me, I couldn't make it happen. It took me a while, but I finally got the hint. Now I was stuck here thinking about what I was supposed to do next.

Chapter 19

Jade

Before I came down here, my plans were simple. I was going to follow Mimi and her little crew to see if I could get any information about Kaylin and find him, but it looks like Miss Mimi had a few other things on her plate right now. I wanted to feel sorry for the bitch, but honestly, I didn't. The ho deserved everything that was coming to her. What she didn't get, I'd be sure to bring to her ass. I was going to make that bitch wish like hell that she had stayed dead.

I sat farther back in the corner of the hospital, peeping shit out. I made sure that no one could see me, but I could see everything. I wasn't trying to blow my cover just yet. I wanted to get what I wanted first, and then I'd shake shit up. I didn't want them to know that I was on to them. I wanted them to believe that I wasn't a problem, they didn't have to worry about me. I wanted me to be the last person on their minds so that when I decided to strike, they wouldn't see me coming.

"I hope they hurry the fuck up," I said to myself. I was hungry, thirsty, and I was beginning to get tired. I hadn't slept in days. I was so busy trying to find Kaylin's ass that I didn't take care of myself. I hadn't eaten in days, and I was losing a lot of weight. That stressing shit was not for me.

Thinking about Kaylin, I remembered that I had the papers and deeds to all of the properties that he had owned down here. I needed Mimi and them to finish over here so that I could go ahead and check on them. I was willing to bet my last dollar that the nigga was hiding in one of those spots and I was going to find him one way or another. I wasn't leaving New Orleans until I found his ass, and he was going to come back with me, either by choice or by force. Yeah, I knew that sounded a little crazy, but he made me that way. He should've known better than to fuck with me, because I wasn't the type of girl to let go easily. When I saw something that I wanted, I got it, no matter what I had to go through to get it.

"Bitch, you know damn well that man doesn't want you," I heard a voice say. I looked around, trying to find the person who had said it, but there was no one there.

"Yeah, I know you hear me talking to you. Kaylin never did want you. You was always just a piece of ass to him," the voice said again.

I looked around again, trying to see who said the shit, but there was no one sitting around me. The only people sitting in the waiting room were Troy, Mimi, their bodyguards, and me. I knew for sure that none of them had said it, because they didn't even know that I was there to begin with.

"You can keep looking around all you want. You'll never find me in here."

"I don't know who the fuck you are, but you better go ahead, if you know what's best for you," I replied.

"Child, you and I both know you ain't 'bout that life," she said, laughing an evil laugh that sent chills down my spine. It took me a minute to figure it out, but I realized that the voice was actually coming from inside of my head.

"Leave me alone!" I said, talking to myself.

"Nah, somebody needs to talk some sense into you. You need to leave that man alone."

"I'm not doing a damn thing, so you might as well just shut the fuck up!" I yelled a little too loud. I was starting to draw unwanted attention to myself.

"See? I told you before that you were a crazy bitch. Now other people will see too," the voice said, taunting me.

I got up so that I could walk outside and catch some fresh air when I bumped into somebody.

"Excuse me," he said.

I knew that voice. "That's okay," I replied, never lifting my head up. I moved to the side so he could pass. When he did, I hurried toward the exit. The moment I stepped foot outside, I released the breath that I didn't even know I was holding in.

"You got to get it together. You came too far to get caught now," I said to myself. I pulled my phone out and logged into the Where's My Phone app, trying to see if Kaylin had turned his phone back on, but again I came up with nothing.

"Fuck this shit," I said as I made my way toward my car.

"You know if you don't leave that man alone, you're going to get us killed," the voice said this time.

"Ain't nobody gon' kill us, so shut the fuck up," I said, just as I reached my car. When I got inside, I went straight for my purse. I had a bottle of pills that I usually took, but lately I hadn't been taking them. I opened the top, removed two pills, and threw them in the back of my mouth. I pulled out the bottle of water that I had and washed them down. Five minutes later, I started to feel mellow.

Since I parked a few cars down from the one that Mimi and them were riding in, I decided to wait for them out here. That way, it would be much safer, and I didn't have to worry about the possibility of them spotting me, because I had dark tint. I laid the seat back and prepared to wait. Lord knows that I hated to wait. I just hoped I wouldn't be waiting too long.

Chapter 20

Mimi

I sat there for hours, waiting to see what the doctor would say about Kailay. It had taken so long that I actually thought things were going wrong in that operating room. He said that it wasn't supposed to take long, but it did. Lord knows I wasn't good with waiting at all, so the minute Dr. Dallas came from the back and called out to us, I practically ran to him. I waited on pins and needles to hear what he had to say, wishing in my mind that it was all good news. When he came out and told me that Kailay's surgery was a success, I was ecstatic. Even though he said that no one could stay in the room with her, I wanted to jump for joy. I was even happier when he said that she was expected to make a full recovery. That moment was short-lived when reality hit me. I was sitting in the hospital for one of my daughters, my other daughter was currently with her grandmother, and my boys were still missing. Tears welled up in my eyes as I thought about them. Their birthday was coming up in a couple of months, and I wanted so badly to have them with me.

"Hey, girl, are you okay?" Troy asked, pulling me to the side.

"Yes. Well, no. I'm glad that Kailay's going to be around, but I will never feel comfortable until I have all of my kids back together. I miss my boys so, so much and my world will not be complete until I have them. To be honest with you, I don't care if I never get to seek revenge against Kaylin, Stacy, and my father. As long as I'm able to get my boys back, I'm fine with that. I just want my boys home, that's all," I said as the tears began to roll down my face.

"It's going to be okay. We'll get them back. I'll make sure of it. If that's the last thing I do, we'll get them back," she said as she wrapped her arms around me. "Come on, let's get out of here. You need some rest. We all do. We'll be back to check on Kailay tomorrow."

"Okay, but before we do that, I want to go ahead and check on my mother. I think it's about time that we put our past behind us," I said. She looked at me as if I were crazy. Hell, I couldn't believe the words coming out of my own mouth either.

"Okay," she replied as we went to get Jayden and Mark from the waiting room.

"Oh, and, Troy, I don't know what's going on between you and Weedy, but I can definitely tell you that y'all need to talk," I said, stopping her.

"What you mean?" she asked, all confused.

"I mean that I think Weedy still wants you."

"How do you know that?"

"Because when we went to see what was going on earlier, I noticed he give Mark this strange look. So I think you need to check on it before the shit turns into some drama, and you know damn well we don't need that," I said, walking off as I called out to Jayden so we could leave. When I looked back, she was still standing there. "Why you just standing there? Come on. Let's go."

It took her a couple of seconds to move, but she finally began to walk our way.

"Is something wrong?" Mark asked her.

"No, nothing is wrong," she said, wrapping her arms around him. Then we headed toward the exit.

Before I left, I made sure to give every nurse by the station my phone number. I wanted to make sure that they could reach me, in case they needed me for Kailay. After being reassured that they'd call, we left the hospital, making our way to my mother's house.

I wasn't too sure about what I was about to do. Hell, I even wanted to change my mind, but I knew that I couldn't leave her hanging. I mean, after all of the things that she had put me through, she's still my mother. Besides, I forgave her a long time ago. It was time that I started acting like it.

An Hour Later

We rolled through our old neighborhood feeling like outsiders. Everything was the same, and yet it was so different. We pulled up to my mother's building. It was now dark, and I wanted to be extra careful, so I invited Jayden and Mark to go up with us. It wasn't that I was scared of anything or anyone; I just didn't have the strength to protect myself if anybody did try something.

"Come on, let's go before I change my mind," I said, getting out of the car.

I walked over to the sidewalk and waited for them. Once everyone was ready, I started walking to where my mother lived. As soon as I made it to the building, I picked up my stroll. I had to cover my nose and mouth, because the smell was so damn rank and strong that I thought I was going to pass out. I was walking so fast that someone would've thought someone was behind me or that I was on drugs or something.

When I walked up to my mother's apartment, the door was cracked open, so I just walked right on in. As always, the living room was a damn mess. I was afraid to even walk up in there. I found a few needles and empty liquor bottles. I couldn't do anything but shake my head. "Some things will never change, I guess," I said to myself.

As I slowly made my way around the apartment, I thought that I was going to throw up. Besides needles and bottles, there were old newspapers, dirty clothes, and rat shit all over.

"Watch your step," Troy called out from behind me as I was about to step in a huge puddle of vomit.

"She needs to do better than this shit," I said, walking past it. I then made my way to my old room. I didn't know why I was even trying to go in there, being that I hadn't been there since the day that I was raped. When I opened the room, I was shocked to see that it was clean. My old bed was in there, and it was made. I walked farther into the room to see that the carpet was removed, and there were ceramic tiles in its place. The holes and dirt stains that were on the walls were no long there. Instead, a nice pink color adorned them. When I walked over to the closet, I gasped. All of my clothes from when I was a teenager were hanging neatly on hangers.

"Oh, my God," I said as tears welled up in my eyes. "She kept it. I can't believe that she kept it," I cried when I noticed the cover and sheets from when Gorilla Zoe had raped me. "Why would she keep this?" I asked.

"It's going to be all right. I'm sure there's a perfect excuse why she did that," Troy said, standing next to me. I turned to her, laying my head on her shoulder. She then wrapped her arms around me and tried her best to comfort me.

"I can't believe that she would keep it though," I cried in her arms. I wanted so badly to forget the memories as I stood in this room, but looking at those things, they came flooding back.

"Why did she let him do that to me?" I asked her.

"I really don't know, but come on. Let's get up out of here," she said, making her way to the door. I looked up to find Jayden and Mark standing there confused. I guessed they were wondering what the hell was going on. I wanted to tell them, but the thought of anyone else knowing what happened to me was too painful. Besides, I didn't need anyone judging me.

When we walked back into the living room, I took a minute to calm myself down. I didn't want to get my nerves all worked up and shit.

"Come on, let's go," she said, trying to get me to leave.

"No, I have to find my mother and get her some help. Did you even look at this place? I need to get her up out of here," I said stopping her. I was determined to put everything aside so that I could help her get her life together.

"I know that you want to help your mother, but do you think that will be a great idea? I mean look what just happened to you," she responded, which caused me to think about what I was about to get myself into. To be honest, I wanted to turn around and just forget about the shit, but something inside of me told me not to.

"I have to do this. I need to," I said, looking at her with pleading eyes.

"You know what? If that's what you want to do, then that's fine. I'm always here to back you up."

"Good," I said, flashing a small smile. I turned around and began walking toward my mother's room. I knew that she was in there, because there wasn't anywhere else she could possibly be.

With each step that I took toward the room, I could hear my heart beating in my ears. I wanted to turn around, but the voice kept on telling me not to. I kept saying that I didn't have to be like my mother, that I should help her and put the past behind me, so I kept going. When I made it to the door, I slowly raised my hand up, placed it on the knob, and I turned it. I opened the door to find my mother passed out on her bed, with some guy lying next to her. I couldn't believe that she still had this same routine going. I knew she had to be tired of doing this her-damn-self.

I walked over to the bed and kicked it, trying the wake them up. She didn't pop up; however, the dude she was with did, and it looked like he was surprised to see me standing there.

"Who are you and what are you doing in here?" he asked, struggling to get up.

"Who am I? Who the hell are you?" I asked him.

"Look, bitch, what the fuck are you doing in here?" he asked, with a groggy look. I took one good look at him and knew that he was on drugs.

"I'ma ask you to watch your mouth when you're talking to me," I said, pointing my finger in his face. "Now I'ma need you to get your fucking shit and get the fuck out!"

"I don't have to do a fucking thi—" he started to say but was stopped when he saw Mark and Jayden standing by the door. He got up from the bed, grabbed his clothes and shoes, and left, without even putting them on. I waited until I heard the front door opening and closing before I walked around the bed to the side where my mother lay.

I bent down and started pulling the covers back when I noticed that she barely had any clothes on. I turned to find Jayden, Mark, and Troy standing in the doorway.

"Umm, guys, I'm going to need a little privacy here," I said to them. They shook their heads and turned around to leave. "Not you, Troy. I think I'm going to need your help with this."

"Oh, okay," she said, turning around.

"Close the door," I called out to her. She did as I asked and then walked over to where I was.

"What's wrong?"

I pulled the cover back so that she could see. "I need you to help me put some clothes on her."

"Why hasn't she woken up yet?" she asked as she walked over to the dresser, and grabbed a pair of pants and a shirt out of it.

"She's probably drunk like always," I said, with a wave of my hand. She walked back over and handed me the clothes. I then bent down and started turning her over, when I noticed that she had a belt tied to her arm. Removing the belt, I then noticed a needle lying next to her. Pissed, I started to shake her so that she would wake up, but she didn't.

"Oh, my God, she's not moving!" Troy screamed, panicking. I stood there in a daze. I couldn't believe that something like this was happening right now. I mean I was already having a hell of a time with Kailay. I didn't need this shit on my plate right now.

"Mimi, we have to call 911," Troy screamed, but I stood there in a state of shock. It didn't register to me to call for help. *Why do these bad things keep happening to me?* I thought, wishing that I knew the answer.

"What's wrong? Why are you yelling?' Mark asked as he and Jayden entered the room.

"We have to call an ambulance, now!" I heard her yell.

"Why? What's wrong?" Jayden asked.

"Mimi's mother not moving. She won't wake up," she said to him. She then walked over to where I was and began to shake me. "Mimi, you have to pull it together, *mami.*"

I blinked a few times before I looked her way, remembered where I was, and ran to my mother's side. "Did anyone call an ambulance yet?" I asked them. They looked at each other, and then shook their heads, saying no. "Well, could y'all please do so?"

I watched as Troy pulled out her phone and walked out of the room. I then turned back to where my mother lay, and I tried to cover her up. "Can one of you guys please help me put a shirt on her before the ambulance gets here?" I asked, looking at them.

Jayden came over to where I was, picked up the T-shirt that Troy had gotten and helped me slip it over her head. "Thank you," I said to him, just as Troy walked back into the room.

"What happened?" I asked her.

"I called. They said they'll be here in about three minutes," she replied.

"Okay, thanks," I said to her. I sat there in a funk. I couldn't believe I was placed on this earth just to go through all of this. I hadn't been in this state for a full twenty-four hours, and here I was, into some shit again. I sat there trying to go over every inch of my life that I could possibly remember, trying to figure out what I did wrong, but I came up with nothing. I didn't know why it was happening, but I couldn't keep going through all of this. I knew there was a God up there somewhere and I wished He would help me before I went insane.

I was so into my thoughts that I didn't see when Troy had left the room. She came back a minute later with two paramedics following her.

"Excuse me, ma'am," the female said. I got up and stepped on the side so that they would be able to work.

"It looks like a drug overdose. We're going to have to transfer her before it's too late," the female said as the male left the room to get the stretcher.

"What's her name?" she asked, looking at me.

"Um, her name is Marie Washington," I replied, stuttering.

A few seconds later, the male paramedic returned to the room with the stretcher. I silently prayed as they placed her on the gurney and prepared to leave. Once we made it outside, I spotted a gang of people surrounding the building. I figured as much, because around here people never minded their business.

"Is everything all right with Marie?" some old lady asked me.

"Yes, everything is fine," I replied, never slowing my stride.

"Well, what's wrong with her?' she asked as she struggled to keep up with me.

I gave her a look that said, "Bitch, mind your own business," but it was a few seconds before she got the hint.

"Is anyone going to ride in the ambulance with her?" they asked once they had loaded her into the ambulance. I stood there looking at Troy, who was looking at me.

"I'll go," she replied.

"No, it's okay. I'll go," I told her. She had done more than enough for me with Kailay. I couldn't let her keep on doing this. It was time that I faced my own problems. I needed to handle them myself.

"And you are?" she asked me.

"Um, I'm her daughter, Amina Washington," I replied.

"Well, okay, come on. We have to go now," she said, walking off.

"I'll meet you guys at the hospital," I said, turning to Troy. I then followed the EMT to the front of the ambulance and got in. It was in that moment I made a promise to myself that I was going to get my life back in order. I was determined not to let any of this break me. I was going through all of this as tests. If these were tests from God, I was not going to fail. I was going to pass every one of them with flying colors.

Three Weeks Later

I was getting ready to have a mental meltdown. I hadn't had a full night of rest in three weeks. Hell, actually, you could say that I hadn't had a full night of rest since I got shot, and I was feeling it. I was so tired and burnt out that I really didn't have any energy left in me.

I'd been running back and forth between Kailay's and my mother's hospital rooms. To be honest, I was beat. All I wanted to do was take a hot bath and sleep for a couple of days. That's how tired I was. Besides sleeping, I really needed a strong drink or two, because my head was all over the place.

When we made it to the hospital that night with my mother, my nerves were on edge and my heart was in my ass. I really thought she was getting ready to check out of this world. Like before, I spent hours waiting for the doctor to update me on her condition. It wasn't until the morning that I was informed that she had a dangerous amount of heroin in her system and they weren't sure if she was going to pull out of it. I spent hours by her bedside, praying that she was going to make it. By the grace of God, she pulled through, and I was actually happy about it.

All in all, today was going to be a good day. Today was Kailay's release day from the hospital, and I was ecstatic. At first, I wasn't so sure, but the doctor said that she healed faster than he thought she would. She still wouldn't be able to do all of the things that normal little kids her age did for a while, but I was still grateful that my baby was alive and getting out of the hospital.

"Mommy, can I have some ice cream?" she asked as I helped her put on the clothes that Troy had brought for her. I turned and looked at the scar that was left on her head from where she was cut, and I almost cried, but that look in her bright eyes made me smile.

"Yes, baby. We'll get you some as soon as the nurse comes with your discharge papers," I said, helping her into her jacket.

"Okay," she replied as her little eyes lit up with joy.

"Okay. Now, why don't you lie down and watch cartoons until the nurse comes? I have to go check on someone," I told her.

"Can you put it on *Doc McStuffins?*" she asked.

"Yes, baby," I replied.

I got up from the chair, grabbed the remote, and searched the channels for Disney Junior. There were over a hundred channels on TV. I finally found it after searching a minute to find it.

"There you go, baby. I'll be right back," I said, placing the remote back on the bed.

"Thank you, Mommy," she replied before the TV had her full attention.

As I was about to leave the room, Troy came walking in. "What's up?"

"Nothing. I'm 'bout to go check on my mama. What's up with you?" I asked her.

"Nothing. I'm just ready to blow this joint. Hospitals are so damn depressing to me," she said, taking a seat on the bed next to Kailay.

"Who you telling?" I replied. "I'll be right back."

I didn't wait for a reply. I grabbed my purse and left the room. On my way out of the room, I bumped into the nurse.

"I'll be right back. I'm going to check on someone who's on another floor," I said to her.

"Oh, well, I have these papers here for you to sign," she said, referring to the papers in her hands.

"Okay, well, my sister is in there with her right now. You can just let her sign them."

"Um, okay," she said, then headed into the room.

As I started walking toward the elevator, my phone began to ring. I looked at the caller ID and noticed that it was Weedy calling. Since I already knew what he wanted, I answered.

"What you got for me?" I answered the phone, just as I was getting onto the elevator. I pressed the button for the third floor and waited for him to answer.

After a pregnant pause, he finally answered. "Ma, there's absolutely nothing in the street right now. We've searched high and low in and around New Orleans, and we still didn't find them."

"What about the house in Edgard?" I asked.

"We searched that one too and, just like the others, they haven't been there," he said, making my heart drop. Then everything fell silent. I sat there playing in my thoughts, wondering what I was going to do next. Then he said something that had me interested.

"Ma, I know you want to find your kids and get your revenge, which is why I'm willing to help you. I have this friend who knows some dude who's a private investigator, but the only thing about it is that he lives in West Virginia."

"Can you get his information for me?" I asked him. "Right now, I'm willing to do anything."

"Let me holla at my boy first and see. I'll holla back at you in a minute," he said, just as the elevator stopped on the floor that I was going to.

"Okay, and thanks for everything, Weedy," I said, stepping off the elevator.

"No problem," he replied. "I'll call you the minute I get that info for you."

"Okay," I said and hung up the phone. I had to stop to take a minute to gather my thoughts. Here I was yet again. No one could find Stacy and Kaylin. I could feel my anger getting the best of me, so I decided to put that to the back of my mind for now.

I was still standing by the elevator when I noticed the nurse and doctor walk into the room that my mother was in. I quickly got myself together and made my way there. When I walked into the room, she was sitting up as they were reading a few things from a clipboard.

"Um, what's going on, Doctor? Is something wrong?" I asked, getting their attention.

"Oh, no, ma'am. Nothing is wrong. Your mother is going to be released today. We were in here suggesting a few rehab facilities that she can enroll in," he said, turning his attention to me.

"Well, I wasn't aware that she's going home today. Are you sure that's right?" I asked, walking over to where they were.

He looked at his clipboard before he flipped a few pages and brought his attention back to me. "Well, yes. Your mother no longer has any signs of drugs in her system, and all of her vitals are strong, which is why we're releasing her."

"Okay, you said something about a rehab facility?" I asked.

"Um, yes. Although your mother's been clean a couple of weeks, the fact of the matter is that she has a drug problem. Without rehab, there's an excellent chance that she will relapse into using, which is why I suggest that she checks into a drug rehabilitation facility," he said, handing me a few pamphlets. I took one look at the info and decided that I was going to get my mother some good help, but I didn't think a facility in New Orleans would do that. I needed to get her out of this state and into a place that she knew nothing about, which was just how I was going to get to West Virginia without Jayden becoming suspicious. "Okay, thank you. When will she be discharged?"

"Um, actually we have the papers right here. We were just waiting for someone to come and sign them so that she could be released."

"Okay, well, I'm here. I'll sign them," I told him.

"Okay," he said and handed me the clipboard so I could sign the papers. Once I was done signing everything, he handed me a copy and said that a nurse would be right here to roll her out. They made sure that we had everything, they said good-bye, and left, leaving my mother and me there alone.

The room was so quiet that if you dropped a needle on the floor, we were going to hear it. I stood there in the same place that I was when the doctor left. She just sat there staring at me as if something was wrong with her. I wasn't scared or anything. I was more nervous. Here I was in a room with my mother, the same woman who managed to make my life a living hell, and I didn't know what to say. This was actually the first time we'd been alone in years, and it was awkward as fuck.

"Why are you helping me, Amina?" she asked, just above a whisper.

"What did you say?" I asked her. I was so nervous that I had to tap my hand against my leg to try to calm my nerves.

"I asked, why are you helping me? I mean after all of the things that I did to you in life, I figured you would be the last person to help me. So why are you doing it?" she asked again.

"To be honest with you, I don't know why. I mean, in my mind I keep hearing myself say that I want to put the past behind us and help you, but as I stand here right now, I don't know if I'm able to," I responded. She didn't say anything. She just sat there. I guessed she was trying to find the right words to say.

"Amina, I'm not looking for self-pity, nor am I looking for you to do anything for me. When I said that I was sorry a few weeks ago, I meant that. I know I wasn't a great mother to you at all and I wouldn't or couldn't be mad if you hated me, because I deserve it. You can leave right now if that's what your heart is telling you, and I wouldn't feel no type of way, but I want to thank you for being there for me when I didn't deserve it. Like always, you never cease to amaze me."

"Marie, if I wanted to leave, I would have. I told you what I came here to do. Yes, I know I just said that I wasn't sure if I wanted to, but I'm all you got. I wouldn't feel right if I left you hanging like this in your condition. If you let me, I want to help you, and after that, you can go back to your life, and if you choose to, whether we both like it or not, we're going to be in each other's lives. Point. Blank. Period," I said to her. She didn't say anything. She couldn't even look at me. She just sat there with her fingers entwined.

"Amina, I already told you that I don't need no pity party. I'm not looking for you to do anything for me out of guilt."

Here she goes again with this shit, making me start to rethink my decision. Fuck it. I walked over to the bed and took a seat by her foot. "I told you why I want to help you. I'm not worrying about the shit that you've done to me before. I just want to put the shit in the past and leave it there," I said, reaching for her hand. Her breath quickened as I slowly rubbed my thumb over the back of it. I couldn't believe that this moment was happening either. "In order for us to move forward, you have to let all of this go."

"Darling, I want you to know that I love you, and I know I haven't shown you that, but I do. Again, I want to say that I'm sorry for all of the things that I've put you through and there's no way that I could let all of that go. I've really done some things that I'm not proud of, and I can't believe that you are willing to forgive me for it, but I'm willing to try," she replied. I raised my head up and noticed that she was now crying.

"Aw, Ma, you don't have to cry," I said, hugging her. I used my thumb to wipe the tears that had rolled down her face, just as the nurse walked in with a wheelchair to take her out. "Now come and let's get up out of here before I go crazy."

"Okay," she said, with a light chuckle. She then reached up to my face, giving me a kiss on my cheek. I was confused at first, but it made my heart warm up. I didn't know what this feeling was, but I was happy to be feeling it. A few years ago, if someone had told me that my mother and I would be in this position today, trying to repair our broken relationship, I would've probably spit in their faces and cursed their asses out after all the shit she had put me through. But today was different. I was different. I was more forgiving, and I was happy about that.

I got up from the bed and waited to the side as the nurse helped her get dressed and then placed her in the wheelchair. Once everything was straight, and she was ready, the nurse handed the chair over to me, and then we left. Hopping onto the elevator, I hit the button for the fourth floor and waited for the doors to close.

"Where are we going?" my mother asked once she noticed that the elevator was going up instead of down.

"I have to pick someone up from here," I replied as the bell rang. Getting off the elevator, I bumped into the last person I'd expected to see.

"Amina, is that you?" she asked, looking confused as fuck.

"Yes, Darlene, it's me," I answered. I could believe that this bitch had the nerve to show up here, after all of the things that Kaylin had put me through.

"But how? I thought you was dead!"

"Nah, as you can see. I'm alive and fine now, no thanks to your son," I said, rolling my eyes at her.

"Well, does Kaylin know about this?" she had the nerve to ask.

"No, actually, no one knows that I'm still alive and I'd love for you to keep this to yourself."

"But you have to tell him. The last time I spoke to him, he sounded as if he was going to go crazy, thinking that you were dead."

"Darlene, what did Kaylin actually tell you?" I asked, because from the way she was talking, I knew damn well he didn't tell her what went down that day.

"He didn't say much. When he called me, all he said was that you was dead," she replied. "He's going to be so happy to know that you are alive."

"I wouldn't be too sure about that."

"Why? What are y'all not telling me?" she asked.

"Ms. Darlene, Kaylin was the one shot me and left me for dead. All because of Stacy," I said, bursting her bubble.

"No, that can't be true. My son would never do something like that to you. He loved you," she replied, shaking her head as if the shit weren't true.

"Loved me? Yeah, he loved me enough to fuck my friend—no, my sister—and get that ho pregnant. Then he let her come back years later and destroy our family. Now I don't know what Kaylin has told you, but whether you want to believe it or not, Kaylin was the one who did this to me, and I hope he rots in hell," I said, and then walked off, leaving her standing there with her mouth open. I didn't have time for this shit. I'd think about Kaylin's ass a little later. Right now, the only thing on my agenda was to get my mother and daughter up out of here, so that they could go home.

Chapter 21

Mimi

I'd been back home for only a few days, trying to keep myself busy. I was on my way to meet with my mother when the private investigator I hired phoned me. He told me that he had some information on Stacy and Julius I may be interested in. I immediately told him yes, and he agreed to meet me back at my house. As soon as I got off the phone with him, I phoned my mother and told her that I had to cancel our plans for today. Luckily, she hadn't yet left her apartment that I had just gotten for her. I expressed how sorry I was, and she said that it was okay. I then told her that I was going to call her later to reschedule. I then called the man back and told him where to meet me.

I swerved through traffic, breaking all kinds of traffic laws, trying to make it home. I was anxious, yet nervous. Here I was, finally about to get close to the people who had wronged me and I wanted so badly to get on with my life. As I sped through traffic, I thought of the many things that I'd do once I laid hands on them. I wanted to cause them the same amount of pain that they'd caused me. I wanted to make it quick and get the shit over with so that I could get my life back together.

I was so deep in my thoughts that I didn't even notice I'd made it to my home. Pulling up to the house, I noticed that dude hadn't arrived yet, so I killed the engine and sat there waiting. Lord knows I hated to wait, especially about something like this. Knowing that I'd soon be reunited with my boys had me on edge.

I sat there thinking about my babies. What did they look like? Would they remember me? Would they even want to be bothered with me? How were they? Did Stacy, Kaylin, and Julius hurt them? Where were they living? Were they living right? Those questions were rolling through my mind. Questions that I didn't have the answers to, but I soon would. As I sat there going back and forth, I hadn't noticed when David pulled up until he knocked on the window. I looked at him, grabbed my keys and purse, and got out.

"Hey, David," I said, greeting him.

"What's up, Amina?" he asked, giving me a hug.

"Ain't nothing," I replied. "What you got for me?"

"Yes, I have it right here," he said, pulling a yellow envelope from the inside of his jacket and handing to me. I reached inside my purse, pulled out the white envelope that contained the money, and tried passing it to him, but he stopped me.

"No, don't worry about it. You good. Weedy already took care of it," he said, shocking me.

"Um, okay," I replied, "and thank you, David. I'm sure that this wasn't easy to come by."

"Oh, but it was, and you're welcome." With that said, he walked back to his car, got in and left. A few minutes later, I made my way inside.

I placed my keys and purse on the coffee table and made my way into the dining room. Once I got in there, I threw the envelope on the table and went straight to the bar for a drink. I immediately took the drink to the head, poured another one, and did the same thing. Once I had calmed my nerves down a bit, I walked over to the table and sat down. Pulling the envelope in front of me, I sat there, just staring at it as if it were some type of disease or something. I treated it like something was going to jump out of it and bite me in the face.

After a few moments of just staring at it, I picked it up and opened it. There were a bunch of things in there, so I pulled everything out and placed it all onto the table. Before I started going through it, I said a silent prayer, asking God for strength. Once I felt that I was able to, I started going through everything. The more I looked at it, the madder I became. I couldn't believe they could ruin someone's life, kidnap their kids, and pretend as if everything was all right. When I got to a picture of Stacy, Kaylin, and the kids, I completely lost it.

"All this time. All this fucking time and these bitches have been right under my nose!" I yelled, throwing the drink that I had been nursing at the wall. "You'd think the police would be doing their jobs and handling the shit right now, but they ain't doing a damn thing. They have both the Atlanta and New Orleans police departments so-called after their asses, and yet they're still on the run. I don't know why I even tried to count on the police to find my kids anyway. All they want to do is sit on their asses and eat fucking donuts!"

I sat there talking to myself, trying to stop myself from going crazy. I was completely out of it. I knocked over any- and everything that was in my way. I didn't even know that I had that type of strength until I turned over the whole damn table. That's how mad and fucked up I was. I walked to the corner, fell to the floor, and cried. I was an emotional wreck right now. I was so mad, but I was also hurt. I couldn't believe that Kaylin and I, and the family we had built, had come to this. We were supposed to be that couple who withstood it all: that homie, lover, friend thing. I had once planned to marry this man. He was the father of my kids, and now he was nothing to me.

I had nothing now but hate toward him, and it was his fault.

I found myself thinking about the very first time that Kaylin and I first met. We were madly in love with each other. There'd been a time when we would've killed for each other, but not anymore and Stacy was the cause for all of that. Had I known about Stacy from the beginning, things would've probably gone much differently. I should've listened to Troy when she first said that Stacy was a hater, but no, I was always the bitch to try to give people the benefit of the doubt. Hell, I stayed doing it with Kaylin, but not anymore. Now I was wiser, and my heart was much colder.

"Ma, what's wrong?" Jayden asked, walking into the room. I'd forgotten anyone else was there. He looked around the room at the mess that I'd made, then at me slumped in the corner and he knew something was wrong. I silently sat in the corner, wishing that I could just snap my fingers and everything would go back to the way it was, with the only thing different being Jayden instead of Kaylin. I looked up into his eyes, just as the floodgates opened. Jayden walked over, sat down beside me, and took me into his arms. "It's going to be all right. Whatever it is, it will be okay," he said, rubbing my back.

I sat in his lap, crying my eyes out. I felt so hopeless, like a little girl who'd gotten her heart broken for the first time and was in desperate need of her father. Like that little girl, I needed to be loved.

"Oh, my God. Jayden, what's going on?" Troy was the next one to ask.

"Mommy!" Kailay and Kayla yelled, running toward me.

"What's wrong with my Mommy, Uncle Jay?" Kayla asked. I could tell by the sound of her voice that she was probably mugging him.

"Yeah, why is she crying, dude?" Kailay asked.

"I don't know, li'l bits. Mommy hasn't told me yet," he replied, looking up at them. I absolutely loved the relationship that Jayden and the girls had. He wasn't their father, but he treated them no differently than he would his own child.

"Troy, take the girls upstairs to their rooms," I said, finally speaking up.

"No, Mommy, we want to stay here with you," Kailay said, hugging me tight.

"Yeah, Mommy. We don't want to leave you again," Kayla replied, hugging me extra tight. Hearing them say those words had hurt me to my soul. The girls were still taking it hard. Kayla still had nightmares, and Kailay barely wanted to leave my side. They were both shocked when they found out that I was still alive, but even that didn't take away the fear of being separated from me again. It was so bad that I've been having to take baths with them, and in order for them to fall asleep, I had to be in the room. That shit really scared my girls, but by the grace of God and a whole lot of therapy and reassurance, they'd get over it.

"It's okay, girls. Mommy will be fine. I promise. Go to y'all rooms while Mommy has a talk with Auntie Troy and Uncle Jay. I'll be up to check on y'all in a minute," I said, reassuring them. They hesitated a bit but went anyway.

I wanted to wait until Troy got back before I decided to say anything. Knowing Jayden, I knew his mind was probably full of questions. I'd answer them, but for now, I just chose to lay my head on his chest. I wanted to address everyone at the same time. I knew what I was about to say was going to make them flip a little, but oh well. It was what it was.

"What's up? What's going on with y'all?" she asked when she walked back into the room.

"When's Mark coming back in town?" I asked them.

"In a couple of days. Why?" Jayden answered.

"I need you to call him and tell him to get here like yesterday."

"What you mean? What's going on, Amina?" he asked from behind me.

Getting up from where I was, I walked over to the table that I had turned over earlier. I picked it up, began to collect all of the information David had given me, walked back over to them, and handed Jayden the papers. I didn't say anything. I just walked over to the bar and poured myself yet another drink, because I knew I was going to need it.

"Hold up! Am I seeing this shit correctly? When did you have the time to do all of this?" he asked, heated. Jayden had gotten very protective over the last couple months, and I knew he was going to be mad, which was why I poured that drink.

"Yes, you are. I hired a private investigator a while back. I got tired of waiting."

"Ma, what were you thinking? I told you to fall back. I was going to handle the shit," he said, a little too loudly for my nerves.

"When, huh? When were you going to handle it? When these bitches take my kids and get ghost? When I'd never be able to see them again? Or when I die? Tell me, Jayden, when were you going to handle it?" I asked, mad as fuck. His ass was really starting to piss me off. "The longer I continue to wait, the longer my boys are away from me. I can't continue to live with two kids, knowing that I have two more out there looking for and asking about me. I can't do this, baby. I've tried, but I can't. I won't go another day, week, month, or year without my kids. It's time to do something about it."

By that time, I was in full-blown tears. He out of all people should have understood where I was coming from.

Over these past couple months, I'd had nightmares, and in every one of them, my kids were being taken away from me. He was there for each of them, comforting me, holding cold towels against my forehead when I'd wake up in cold sweats.

"Ma, I understand all of that, and I feel where you're coming from. I know what you've been through, which is why I said that I was going to handle it. I know you, and I've seen you break down many times. You're constantly doing things without thinking it through," he replied. "When I told you to chill and fall back, it was for a reason, but you never seem to listen to what anyone says. Not everyone is out to hurt you or do you wrong, Mimi, and I hope you learn that shit before it's too late," he remarked, pulling his phone out of his pocket. He then punched in a few numbers and placed the phone to his ear.

"What's up, man? What you got for me?" he asked whoever it was on the other end of the phone. "Hold up, man, I'm about to put you on speakerphone. Go 'head," he then said.

"Wait, are you alone?" Mark asked.

"Nah, I'm here with Amina and Troy."

"Hello, Mimi, Troy," Mark said to us.

"Hey, Mark," Troy and I said together.

"So you want me to say this in front of them?" he addressed Jayden.

"Well, we kind of have no choice. Amina hired a PI, and he gave her some information already," Jayden said, looking up at me. "Oh, and start from the beginning. I don't want to leave anything out."

"Okay," he replied. "Well, about three weeks ago, we got word about where Stacy and Kaylin were. At first, we thought it was a joke, because when the chick called us, she gave us the info, then hung up. Not knowing if it was true and knowing how bad you wanted your kids back, we sent a few pictures of the kids and them, along with the address and had one of my workers check it out. A week later, we got word back that it was them. So I went to check it out."

"Well okay. So what's new?" I asked, speaking up before Jayden could say anything.

"Um, well, I've been following them for a bit and I have yet to see Kaylin. I mean I see Stacy, her father, the kids, and some other woman, but I have yet to spot him."

"What about my kids? Are you able to get them?" I asked. "I'll worry about Kaylin later."

"Are you sure?"

"Yes. My number one priority is my kids," I told him.

"Okay. Well, how are we going to do this, Jayden?" he asked Jayden, who was just sitting there looking at me.

"I don't know. Maybe you should ask Mimi since she seems to be running the show," he said, giving me an evil stare.

"What the fuck is that supposed to mean?" I asked, snapping at his ass.

"Just what I said," he replied. "You always want to act like you're the one in charge. So why don't you tell him what we're going to do?"

"Jayden, I'm about to go there with you right now," I said, pointing my finger at him.

"Yeah, whatever," he said with a wave of his hand. Honestly, our relationship had been on the edge lately, and I knew it was because of me, but right now we couldn't do this. We were going to have to get into that at another time.

"Not right now, Jay, please," I said, begging him with pleading eyes. He looked at me, grabbed the phone off the table, and left the room.

"What was that?" Troy asked, walking over to me.

"It's nothing." I shrugged.

"Well what do you think he's going to do?" she asked me.

"Honestly I don't know, but I already have the information that I needed, and with or without his help I'm going to get my children, and that's that. There's nothing he can do to change my mind," I replied, just as he walked back into the room. He didn't say anything. He just stood there staring at me intently. The way that he was looking at me was making me feel very uncomfortable.

"Okay, we're going to head to West Virginia in a few days," he finally said. He then turned and said to me, "During that time, you need to find a spot that's safe for the girls to go to."

"Okay," I replied.

"Can you give us a minute please?" he asked, looking at Troy. She nodded her head and then left the room. Once she was gone, he turned back to me.

"Ma, I'm going to be honest with you. Shit like this ain't easy. You can't just go down there and think you can just up and get your kids back without a plan. That shit won't work. You have to listen and not let your emotions get the best of you. This time you're going to have to listen to what I say or else it's a done deal," he said.

He looked at me once and then left the room. I knew he was mad, because his face told me so. I wanted to run after him, but I knew he probably needed the space and time to think. I didn't. Instead, I just stayed there and thought about what he had said. I already knew the shit wasn't easy. It took us so long to find them, so I knew getting to them wouldn't be easy either. I just hoped and prayed that when the shit went down my kids wouldn't get caught up in this bullshit.

Chapter 22

Shelly

I'd been here for about three weeks, looking and searching for Jayden and still I came up with nothing. I couldn't believe that I traveled all the way down to Atlanta, only for Jayden's ass not to be here. It would be just like him to pull some shit like that. He really must have wanted me to go crazy on his ass or something.

I sat in the hotel room, pondering my next move. I couldn't stay here much longer. I was tired, and I was running out of money. Besides Jade, I didn't know anyone, and she wasn't answering the phone, which was beginning to aggravate the hell out of me. Any other time, I'd be able to get a hold of her, but not this time. I'd called her ass about a thousand times and still got no answer.

Fuck this shit, I thought as I grabbed my keys and my purse and headed out of the room. I didn't know where I was actually going, but I knew I couldn't stay in this hotel room one more night. Just looking at these walls had me about to go crazy.

I opened the door and headed straight for the elevator. After pushing the down button, I stood there and waited for a minute or two. Once I was in the elevator, I pushed the button for the first floor as the doors began to close, but someone's hand stopped them from closing completely.

"Sorry 'bout that," I heard a male voice say. I looked up from the floor, only for my eyes to be blessed by the most handsome man I'd ever seen. I mean dude was fine as fuck. Standing at about six foot two, with a light complexion and a tight-ass body, dude looked like he belonged on a cover of *GQ* and shit.

"That's okay," I said, flashing him a smile. I moved over to the corner, a few feet away from him, because I didn't trust myself. As fine as this dude was, I was liable to jump his bones and fuck the shit out of his ass right in this elevator.

I was very glad when the elevator had finally come to a stop on the first floor, because I honestly didn't believe that I would've been able to contain myself any longer. I almost busted my ass trying to get up out of there. That's how fast I was walking.

"Um, excuse me," the baritone voice said from behind me. When I turned around, I damn near went into shock. He was standing right there.

"Y . . . yes?" I stuttered. This dude had completely taken my breath away.

"I didn't get your name, beautiful," he said, staring at me with a pair of eyes that looked so dreamy, I thought I was going to drop my panties right then and there.

"My name is Lashell, but everyone calls me Shell or Shelly," I replied, reaching my hand out for him to shake.

"Kaylin, but everyone calls me Kay," he said, pulling me in for a hug. He shocked the hell out of me at first, but after a minute, I hugged him back.

"Um, okay," I replied. For a moment, we just stood there staring at one another. "Well, um, I should be going now. It was nice meeting you."

"Likewise," he said, and I walked off. "Wait, do you have a man?" he asked. My mind quickly went to Jayden, but then I remembered that he was fucking around with some bitch, so technically, I was indeed single.

"Um, no. Do you have a woman?" I asked.

He smiled, and that's when I noticed that he had two dimples. "Nah, I'm single right now."

"Oh, okay."

"Well, can I have your number, ma?"

"Um, yeah, sure," I replied. He pulled his phone out of his back pocket and handed it to me. I grabbed it, programmed my number in it, and gave it back to him.

"What you doing later?" he asked.

"Nothing really. I'm really not from around here. So, I don't know what there is to do," I said to him.

"Why don't you let me take you out then?" he asked. I thought about it for a minute. Hell, I'd known dude all of five minutes, and here he was, wanting to take me out. For all I knew, he could have been a killer or something, but then this little voice came into my head and said, *to hell with all that, this nigga is fine as all outdoors. What harm could he possibly do to you?*

"Uh, sure," I replied.

"Good then. Come on," he said as he began to walk off, motioning for me to follow behind him and I did.

"I finally took a good, long look at dude and I fugured out that actually, he was just average". He was like all of the rest of the dudes I was used to dating. He looked like a college boy. I needed a thug in my life. I followed him to the parking lot, where he got into a black Yukon Denali. *Humph, so dude got a little money I see,* I thought, before I hopped in the truck behind him.

"So where do you want to go?" he asked me, starting the car.

"Don't matter, surprise me," I said, letting my hair down. These past few weeks I been stressing about

Jayden. It was time for me to let my hair down a bit and enjoy myself.

"Okay," he replied, pulling out of the parking lot. He then hopped on the freeway and headed downtown.

"So, tell me a little bit about yourself," he said.

"What do you want to know?" I asked him.

"Whatever you feel free to tell me," he said, taking his eyes of the road to look at me.

"Well, you already know my name. I'm twenty-eight, from West Virginia and I have a son," I said giving him only a few details. "What about you?"

"Well, you already know my name. I'm twenty-eight also. I'm from Louisiana, born and raised, I'm a club owner, and I have three kids: twin boys and a daughter," he said, keeping it short also.

That figures, I thought once he said he had kids. There was no way a man this fine didn't have kids and a few baby mamas lying around somewhere.

"Where ya baby mamas at? I'm not going get you in trouble, am I?" I asked, looking over at him. I noticed his body stiffen, and then his whole demeanor changed. *Fuck me now!* I knew damn well this nigga didn't have any baby mama drama lying in the cut somewhere, because I for damn sure didn't have time for that shit.

"No baby mamas. I only had one, but, um, she . . . she passed away," he said, sounding as if he was about to cry or something.

"Oh, I'm so sorry. I didn't know, or else I would have never said anything," I said, feeling like a total ass.

"No, it's cool. I just rarely talk about her nowadays, you know," he said, clearing his throat. From the way he was acting right now, I knew he had probably taken the shit pretty hard. "Just trying to let her rest peacefully."

"Oh, okay," was all I could say. I was speechless. I couldn't imagine myself being in that type of situation.

The rest of the ride was mainly quiet. With the exception of the radio playing and his phone that was constantly vibrating, we didn't say anything else to each other. To be honest, I wasn't even up for it anymore, but my mind quickly changed when he pulled up to this little soul food restaurant. As I said, I wasn't from around here and I'd never been here either, but from the smell outside, I was sure these people could cook their asses off.

"Look, ma, I know what you thinking and I'm cool," he said, shutting off the truck's engine. "Let's just go inside and enjoy ourselves. It makes no sense to spoil each other's night."

He didn't wait for me to reply. He got out of the truck and walked over to my side to open the door. "Thanks," I said and got out.

"Hey, Kay," the hostess said once we were inside. The way her eyes were beaming and how happy she had gotten, I could tell that either he was a regular, she was fucking him, or she used to fuck with him.

"What's up, Mtisa? How are you?" he asked giving her a hug.

"I've been good. We haven't seen you in a long time," she said, hugging him back.

"Yeah, I've been busy. I don't get to much free time, ya know."

"I feel you. Oh, hey, boo," she said, finally acknowledging my presence. Her eyes were so focused on him that I didn't think she had even seen me standing there.

"Hey," I replied dryly. I didn't know this ho and for her to even act the way she was acting was nothing but thirst.

"Well, come on, we have an available table right this way," she said, grabbing two menus off the podium. She

then walked off, leading us over to a table to the left of
the restaurant. It also happened to be a few tables away
from the stage. "Okay, now. Here are the menus. Your
waiter will be right with you guys in a minute. Have a
great evening."

"You come here often?" I asked him, once she was gone.

"I mean I used to, but not anymore," he said, then his
eyes got all sad again, and I assumed that he was thinking
about his kids' mother again.

"Well, what's good here then?" I asked, trying to change
the mood.

"To be honest, everything," he said, flashing me a
bright smile.

"And how would you know that? Don't tell me you done
ate everything on this menu, Kay," I said, chuckling.

"Well, I won't tell you then," he replied.

"You mean to tell me that you've eaten everything on
here?" I asked, pointing to the menu that I had in my
hand.

"Yes! You don't think I came over here all those times
to eat the same thing, do you? Besides, I like trying new
things," he replied, with a serious face, and he then gave
me a sexy look that said, "I'd eat you too if you let me."

I was about to reply, but the waitress came to take our
orders. After getting both our drink and food orders, she
pranced her happy ass right to the back to place them.

"Now, where was I?" I asked him. "Oh, yeah, I bet you
like to eat, huh?" I asked, flirting back.

"Sure do. Maybe you'll find out," he said, licking those
thick, juicy, sexy lips of his.

"Oh, yeah?" I asked, challenging him.

"Most definitely," he replied.

Not too long after, the waitress returned with our food
and drinks. "Damn, that was fast," I said.

"Yeah, the service and food here are excellent," he replied, as she placed our orders on the table.

"Can I get you guys anything else?" she asked.

"Nah, we cool. Thanks though," Kay replied. She nodded her head, then left.

From across the table, I watched as he closed his eyes and began saying grace. I was stunned. He didn't look like the type who was all into the Lord and whatnot. I closed my eyes so that he'd think I was doing the same thing. When he said, "Amen," I repeated it right behind him. When I opened my eyes, he was staring at me.

"What? Why you looking at me like that? Is something wrong or something?" I asked shyly. I never liked it when someone just stared at me. It made me uncomfortable.

"Um, no, I'm sorry. I was just admiring your beauty," he replied, looking embarrassed.

"Oh, well, thank you."

"Welcome," he said, and then everything between us fell silent. "Well, let's eat then."

"That's a good idea. We wouldn't want our food getting cold now, would we?"

"Nah," he replied, and with that said, we began to eat. For the remainder of the night, nothing was said between us. We were both lost in our own thoughts. The only thing that could be heard was the sound of our forks scraping against the plates.

An Hour and a Half Later

Kay tried to get me to go to the club, but I wasn't feeling that. I was too full and too tired to go anywhere, so he offered to drive me back to the hotel room, and I agreed. When we pulled up to the hotel, he got out of the truck to walk me to my room. I would admit that dude was doing everything so well that I didn't want to let him go. I asked him if he wanted to come inside the room. At first he didn't answer, which kind of made me regret asking him.

"You don't have to come if you don't want to," I said, walking inside.

"Nah, I want to though," he said, walking inside behind me.

I didn't know if it was my hormones or the fact that I had four drinks at the restaurant and the liquor was starting to mess with my mind, but the minute he closed the door, I went at him. I covered his mouth with mine, making sure to slip my tongue in his mouth. I wanted to fuck him so bad. I wanted him in the worst way. I went to pull his shirt over his head, but he stopped me.

"Ma, are you sure about this?"

I had to take a minute to think. I didn't know dude from a can of paint, but here I was, ready to fuck him. Then that little voice crept into my head again. *"Bitch, get you some. This ain't nothing but a one-night stand,"* it said. That's when I made up my mind.

"Yes, I'm sure," I said to him.

"Okay," he said as he placed his lips on mine. He then picked me up and began walking over to the bed, never breaking the kiss.

I thought for sure that he was about to lay me on the bed, but to my surprise, he lay down, so that I was straddling him. I had on a dress, with nothing underneath, so it was easy for him to reach under it and begin playing with my clit.

"Sssh," I hissed as he rolled this thumb over my clitoris, which made me wet instantly. I bit down on my lip when he inserted two fingers in me. "Oh, fuck."

"You like that?" he asked as he slipped his fingers in and out of my pussy.

"Oh, yessss."

"Lift up for me right quick," he said. I lifted up a bit as he began taking his clothes off, leaving only his boxers. When he was done, he took my dress and pulled it over my head. "You ready?" he asked.

"I was born ready," I replied, slipping my hand into his boxers. I found his dick and began giving him a hand job.

"We'll see," he said as he pulled his dick out of his boxers. "Let me see what that mouth feel like." Normally, I wouldn't even give a nigga head, but there was something about the way he said it that made my mouth water. Slowly, I kissed my way down his chest to his dick. When I made it to his dick, I swallowed hard as my pussy started jumping. Staring me straight in the face was one of the biggest and prettiest dicks that I'd ever come in contact with, and I planned on tasting every inch of it. Reaching for it, I kissed the head, before inserting only a few inches in my mouth. I pulled back, sucking and flicking my tongue over the head.

"Ummmm," he moaned, which boosted my confidence a little. I made sure that my mouth was extra sloppy before I took him back into my mouth. Hungrily, I started to suck his dick as if it were a lollipop and my life depended on it. His dick grew harder and stiffer by the minute, which let me know that he was about to let loose. I went in for the kill, taking his dick all the way to the back of my throat. I looked up to see that his eyes were shut tight. He grabbed my head and pumped in and out fast, but I could still keep up with his pace. With each thrust he threw, my jaws became tighter. A few pumps later, he released his seed to the back of my throat, and I licked my lips and swallowed every bit of it.

"Damn, ma, that was some good shit," he replied, lying flat on the bed. Before he could say another word, I had his dick back in my mouth. Once it was hard again, I crawled up his body.

"I know you ain't trying to tap out on me," I whispered into his ear.

"Never," he said, kissing me. Like before, he guided his finger inside of me.

"Um, I'd rather something else be in me," I said in a sexy voice.

"You got that," he replied as he removed his finger. He grabbed me by my waist and then guided himself inside of me.

"Oh, my God," I said as his dick filled me up. I had to take a minute to adjust to his size.

"Aww, fuck," he said, once he was fully inside, grabbing hold of my hips.

"You ready for this ride?" I asked, looking into his eyes.

"Show me what ya working with," he said and smacked my ass cheek. I stood on my toes and began giving him the ride of a lifetime. Up, down, side to side, I rode him like a porn star. I knew all the right tricks to pull when I wanted to make a nigga nut and oh, boy, was it a tease. I knew he was trying his hardest not to, but when I started rotating my hips while clenching my walls together around his dick, I had him cumming within seconds.

"Shit," I said, collapsing on top of him. I was tired and out of breath.

"You good, huh, ma?" he asked, as he tried to catch his breath.

"Yeah, I'm great," I replied.

"Well, good, 'cause I'm just getting started," he said, rolling me over on my back. He placed his dick at my opening and with one thrust he was fully inside of me.

We went at each other like two dogs in heat, fucking each other's brains out like there was no tomorrow. Two hours later, we were both tired and exhausted, and we fell fast asleep. I knew for sure that in the morning my pussy was going to be sore as hell, but I wasn't worried about that. It'd been a long-ass time since I'd gotten a pounding like this and I was feeling great.

Chapter 23

Kaylin

I'd been free from Stacy and her father for about three weeks now. They only agreed to let me go if I'd give them the money. I thought about saying no, but then dude came in there saying he was going to hurt one of my kids and I couldn't let that happen. This was my kids' lives on the line. I agreed to pay them and let the shit be. Beside 350 Gs wasn't going to hurt my pockets at all. I had way more money than that. That little chump change wasn't even going to break my pockets, but I only had one problem. The money was back in Atlanta, and I was the only one who was going to be able to get it.

At first, dude wasn't going for it, but after a while he finally gave in, giving me exactly three weeks to hand over the money to him or else he would hurt my kids. I spent three weeks in Atlanta, because I had one of my homeboys place a tracking device on his car so that after I got my kids, I'd be able to go back and serve up some much-needed justice.

I'd been staying in a hotel in Atlanta, trying to stay off the police's radar. I needed a bit of fresh air, so I decided that I was going to go for a drive when I bumped into this fine-ass shawty getting on the elevator. I had a thing for dark-skinned chicks and shawty was a cute chocolate little thing, but still she, as well as every other female I'd come in contact with, couldn't hold a candle to

Mimi. Yeah, I knew that I shouldn't, but I found myself comparing chicks to Mimi all the time. I'd been doing that since we were young.

As I stood in the elevator, I couldn't help but to look at her. She had a cute face and a nice ass, which made my dick jump inside my pants. I hadn't had sex in I didn't know how long and all I knew was that I had to have her. When she walked out of the elevator, I went after her. At first, I thought she was going to shut me down, but she didn't. She agreed to go out with me. I took her this nice place that served soul food. The whole time we were there, my phone was blowing up with messages from Stacy and her dumb-ass father. I didn't want to be bothered with them and those idle threats they were dishing out, so I powered my phone off. I knew that they weren't going to lay a hand on my kids, because I had what they wanted. If they were stupid enough to fuck with my kids, not only would they not get the money, they'd also lose their lives in the process, so I wasn't worried about them.

I decided to turn my attention to Shelly. At first, I thought she was going to be gullible and whatnot, but she actually turned out to be a cool-ass chick. I hated when the night ended, but I loved that she invited me back to her room. Shawty surprised the shit out of me when she started kissing all over me. Shit, I thought we were just coming here to chill. Well, I surely thought wrong, because the minute the door closed, shawty was all on me. I wanted to make sure that she was sure about this, so I stopped her. When she said that she wanted to, I went all in.

I fucked her so good that I put shawty in a deep, deep slumber. She didn't even hear or move when I got out of the bed last night. I had to search for my clothes in the dark, trying my hardest not to wake her up. When I did find my clothes, I hurried up and threw them on, then headed to my room down the hall.

Once I got into my room, I plopped down on the bed, burying my face into my hands. I sat there, thinking about everything that was going on in my life at the moment. I wanted so badly for things to just go back to the way they were, when I didn't have any worries or anything. I just wanted the peace that I once had in my life, even though Mimi was no longer here. The way I saw it, the faster I got Stacy and her father out of my life, the better chance I had at getting my life back on track.

Not wasting any time, I grabbed my suitcase from underneath the bed and started packing my shit. I needed to get back to New Orleans like yesterday, get my kids, and get the fuck away from all this bullshit. Before I knew it, I was through packing my shit. I called down to the hotel room and told them to send someone upstairs to help me with my bags. While I waited for whoever it was to come, I made sure that I had the bag that contained the money. A few minutes later, there was a knock at the door.

"Sir, I'm here to help you with your bags," he said, once I had opened the door.

"Oh, yeah, right this way," I said, leading him inside the room, where the bags were sitting in the middle of the floor. He picked up as many bags as he could, then stood by the door and waited for me. Once I made sure that I had gotten everything, I picked up the rest of the bags, and we headed out the door, hopping straight onto the elevator.

Once we made it to the first floor, I told dude to wait for me in front of the hotel, while I ran to go and get my truck. My truck wasn't parked that far, so it didn't take long before I was pulling to the front of the hotel. I got out, opened the back of the truck, and began loading the bags into it. Once I was finished, I gave the dude a tip, hopped in the truck, and was on my way. I was heading back to New Orleans today, but before I did that,

I needed to drop by and check on an old friend.

I knew I was probably going to regret this, but I needed her right now, so I threw my feelings to the side. When I pulled up to Jade's building, her parking spot was empty. *Maybe her car's broken,* I thought as I got out of the car. Her apartment was in the front, and it didn't take me long at all to get there. When I got to the door, I knocked a few times and waited for her to answer. A few minutes went by, and she hadn't answered, so I knocked again.

"She not home. She hasn't been for a while now," a voice said from behind me. I turned to see her neighbor, Mr. Johnson, standing in his doorway.

"Do you know where she went?" I asked, walking over to him.

"No. I didn't know she was even gone until Selena came by a few weeks ago for the rent and she didn't answer," he said, pulling from a cigarette.

"Well, if she comes back, tell her that I came looking for her," I told him.

"Okay," he said and then went back inside of his house. I looked at Jade's door once more before I walked back over to my truck, got in, and pulled off. I couldn't worry about where she was. I had other things to worry about. My kids needed me, and it was time that I go and get them.

Chapter 24

Jade

Three weeks. Three whole fucking weeks that I'd been in New Orleans and still I'd come up with nothing. I was pissed off to the max. Hell, I was so fucking frustrated that I wanted to jump up out of the car and kill everyone in the truck that Mimi and her crew was driving. How could they be here three weeks and not know a damn thing? Shit, I'd gotten further than they had and yet here they were on their way to do only God knows what now.

Shit, I'd searched every address that I had gotten from the papers at Kaylin's place and still I couldn't find him. I went all around the city of New Orleans, damn near stalking people to try to find his ass, but still I couldn't fucking find him. I was beginning to think that Mimi and them couldn't find them either. Why else wouldn't they be staying in New Orleans to find him?

Pulling my phone out of my purse, I decided to call Shell, since she had been calling me these last few weeks. The phone rang a few times before it went to voicemail. *Stupid bitch,* I thought before I hung up. A few minutes later, my phone started to ring. When I looked at the screen, I noticed that it was Shelly calling me back.

"What's up?" I said, answering the phone.

"Where the hell have you been? Did you know I been calling you for weeks now?" she asked. I looked at the phone for a minute, before putting it back to my ear. She knew I hated when people questioned me and she was starting to aggravate me.

"I've been busy. What you want and what you talking about? You're in Atlanta now?" I asked, changing the subject.

"Yes. I came down here to find my no-good, cheating-ass baby daddy, but the nigga ain't even down here."

"Well, what are you going to do now?" I asked, not really caring about that. I already had problems of my own to deal with.

"Well, I was hoping that I could hang out with you since you live down here and all," she asked.

"Shell, I'm kind of busy right now. . . ." I said.

"Hello, Jade, are you still there?" Shelly asked.

"Look, I'ma need you to meet me. If you ain't here by the time that I get ready to go, I'm going to leave you," I said to her.

"Okay," she replied. I told her where to meet me and then hung up the phone. I didn't know why her ass even came down here. I hoped that she didn't throw a monkey wrench into my plans, or else I was going to have to do her ass in, too.

Chapter 25

Shelly

When I woke up, it was almost daylight. I rolled over to see that Kaylin was no longer in the bed with me. I'd be lying if I said I wasn't feeling some type of way about the nigga leaving in the middle of night, without so much as a good-bye, because I was. I'd given that nigga some ass, and he straight played the shit out of me. That shit don't normally happen to me.

Oh well, fuck him, I thought as I got out the bed and went to take a quick shower. When I was done, I started packing my clothes. I didn't want to, but I was about to head back to Virginia. I was almost finished when my phone chimed. When I picked it up, I noticed that I had a missed call from Jade. I looked at the time. It was only minutes ago, so I decided to call her right back.

At first, I thought she wasn't going to answer the phone, but at the last minute, she did. When she answered, she sounded as if she was busy, but I didn't care. I was going to fit myself into whatever it was that she was doing. So when she told me to meet her, I damn near grew wings, as I ran around the room, collecting the rest of my things. I didn't even bother to cut off the lights. I grabbed my bag and headed out.

Two minutes later, I was on the road to meet her. By that time, the sun had come out already. When I pulled up into the parking lot of the gas station, I didn't see her, so I called her phone. She answered on the first ring.

"Where are you?" I asked.

"I'm parked at the back of the gas station in the black Altima," she said. I went to say something else, but she had hung up on me.

"Stupid bitch," I said as I rode to the back of the gas station. I spotted her car and pulled up on the side of it. Popping her trunk, she then indicated for me to get out. I grabbed my bags from the back seat, then got out.

I walked to the back of the car, and placed my bags in the trunk, before walking around the passenger side and getting in.

"What's up?" I said, removing my glasses, but she didn't say anything. I then turned to her, but her vision was focused somewhere else. "Yo, what's up with you?"

"Shell, chill. Don't come over here with your bullshit now. Just sit your ass back in that seat and enjoy the ride," she yelled, not even looking my way. I wanted to chew her ass out, but I didn't have time for her bullshit right now.

"Chill out, damn!" I told her. She looked over at me, before starting the car and pulling off. She drove to the front of the gas station, where she sat to the side, so she could see the highway. I wanted to ask her why she was just sitting there, but I knew for sure that we'd have some problems. I just sat there and kept my mouth shut while she did whatever the hell it was that she was doing.

Chapter 26

Mimi

When I saw the sign that said WELCOME TO GEORGIA, I knew that things were indeed about to get real. There was no turning back now. I was going to get my kids back one way or another, but first we had to make a small detour. We were on our way to drop Kailay and Kayla off by Margie's house. Jayden thought that it would be a good idea for the girls to get out of Louisiana, in case anything were to happen. They'd be safe with her. No one would ever think to look for them there, because they didn't know her like that. Only I did.

"Call Margie and tell her that we're almost there," Troy said. I had been so lost in my thoughts that I didn't realize where we were.

"Okay," I replied softly. I reached for my phone that was plugged on the charger, and then dialed her number, placing the phone to my ear, as I nervously waited for her to reply.

"Hello," she said, answering the phone on the third ring.

"Hey, Margie. How are you?" I asked.

"I'm great, what about you? How are you doing?" she replied, sounding like her normal, happy self.

"I'm doing okay considering everything that's been going on," I answered, blowing out air in frustration.

"Chile, we've had this conversation already. So, don't you go getting all sad on me, because things are going to get better real soon. Now cheer up why don'tcha," she replied. "Now, where are the girls? I can't wait to meet them."

"Actually, that's why I was calling you. We're about to pull up in front of your house in a minute," I said, sitting up trying to see exactly where we were.

"Aww. Okay. I'm going to meet you guys outside," she said, and I had to laugh. Margie was a crazy little lady, but I was happy to know her, because she'd give you the shirt off her back if you needed it.

"Okay, well I'll see you in a minute," I said, hanging up the phone. A few minutes later, we were pulling up in the front of Margie's house. Like she said, she was waiting for us outside.

"Come, girls," I said to Kailay and Kayla. "Pop the trunk for me, Jayden."

"Hey, Mimi," Margie said to me.

"Hey, Marg," I said, hugging her. I then turned to the girls, who were looking on shyly as they stood behind me. "Come here, y'all. Kailay, Kayla, this is Margie, a friend of Mommy's. Margie, this is Kailay and Kayla," I said, introducing them. They hesitated, but then walked over.

"Hey, y'all. I'm Margie," she said, stooping down to them. "I'm a friend of your mother's."

"Come here, y'all," I said to them. "Mommy's going away for a few days to get your brothers. While I'm gone, you all will be staying here with Margie."

"No, Mommy, don't leave us," Kailay said, hugging me tightly, followed by Kayla. I knew that they would probably act this way, but I needed them to understand that they needed to stay here.

"Come here," I said, hugging them. I then pulled back and looked them straight in their eyes. "Mommy really needs y'all to stay here with Margie, so that I can get Kayson and Kaylon back safely. That way, we can be a family again. There are some bad people out there who are trying to hurt Mommy, and they would do anything to get back at me, which includes hurting the both of you. I'm trying to keep y'all safe, but I can't do that if I take y'all with me. Margie will keep y'all safe until I get back. So please do this for Mommy and stay here with her."

I knew they were only eight years old, and it was hard for them to hear it, but I had to tell them the truth. I needed them to be safe, and Margie was the only way that they'd be safe and out of harm's way.

"But what if you don't come back this time, Mommy?" Kayla asked me.

"Mommy will be fine, Kayla. I promise you that I'll be okay. Uncle Mark and Uncle Jay will protect Mommy. Margie will protect y'all while I'm gone. I'll be back to get y'all in a couple of days," I answered her. My heart broke when I saw a few tears escape their eyes.

"You promise that you'll be back?" she asked.

"I pinky promise," I said, reaching out my pinky to interlock with hers. It took her a few minutes, but she locked her pinky with mine. I then did the same thing with Kailay.

"I'll be back in a few days, be good for Margie now," I told them. "I love y'all."

"We love you too, Mommy," they said, hugging me again. They then let go and went to stand by Margie.

I went to the truck and removed their suitcases. "Thank you, Margie. I owe you big time for this."

"Chile, you don't owe me anything," she said, taking the suitcases out of my hand. I then reached into my purse and pulled out an envelope filled with cash and tried giving it to her. "Don't do this again. I'm not taking your money. Besides, I still have a lot left over from the last time."

"Are you sure?" I asked.

"Positive. Now go on and get those babies and be safe," she said, giving me a hug.

"I will," I said, hugging her back.

"I'll make sure to send up a special prayer, just for you tonight," she whispered in my ear when I pulled back.

"Thanks. I got a feeling that I'm going to need it," I replied. I took one last look at my girls before I headed back to the car.

"I love y'all," I said one last time before I got in the car and Jayden pulled off.

"Are you okay?" he asked after we pulled off.

"No, I'm not okay, but I will be the minute all of this is over and I get my boys back," I said wiping the tears from my eyes.

We were headed back to New Orleans to finish what was started. It was time for me to put all my of my emotions to the side and get ready to make a few bitches bleed. To me, it was wartime, and I was battling an ongoing war. I didn't start it, but I was damn sure about to finish it. There was no way that I was going to let Stacy, Kaylin, or Julius breathe another day, even if I had to die with them.

Chapter 27

Jayden

It took us some time, but we finally came up with a plan to help Mimi. When I first found out about what she did I was mad. I'd specifically said that I was going to handle the situation, but Mimi was always going to be Mimi, so she didn't listen. She actually found out where Stacy and Kaylin were, but it didn't matter, because we already knew. We just didn't tell her, which was actually a bad move. She flipped, and there was no stopping her. I knew there was only one thing for me to do: fulfill my promise and get her kids back for her as soon as possible.

Today was the day that everything would be going down and here I was, with my face in my hands. I wasn't nervous or anything, I only hoped that everything would go the way we planned so that Mimi could get her kids back. I was ready for this to be over with. I wanted my girl back, the girl I met in Atlanta that day at the gas station, not this one. The girl she was now, I don't recognize.

We had to come all the way back to Atlanta to drop the girls off, so that they would be safe and out of harm's way. Then we'd go back to New Orleans, where they were, and get the kids. Mark was already there scoping out the scene. If anything were to go wrong before we got there, we'd know, but hopefully everything would go smoothly.

When we pulled up to the house we were staying at, I was in a zone. I had spent the whole drive back to New Orleans in silence. I even went as far as turning my phone off, so that no one would interrupt me. I needed my mind to be clear of everything, and it was. Turning the car off, I waited until the girls got out, then I got out behind them.

"Jay, can I talk to you for a minute?" Troy asked, walking over to me.

"What's up, ma?" I asked her.

"I don't know what's going on between y'all right now, but you and Mimi need to get it together. She loves you, and what you're about to do tonight clearly states that you love her, but y'all got to get it together. The shit that we're about to do can cost us all our lives. So whatever the hell got y'all feeling some type of way, fix it," she said, and then walked into the house. I stood there thinking about what she just said. She was right. For the past few days, there'd been a distance between us. Right now was the perfect time to fix it and that was what I was about to do.

I popped the trunk, removing the bag with everything that we needed for tonight, and then headed inside. I placed the bag on a table and went to find Amina. I ended up finding her in the bedroom, sitting on the bed. I walked over to her and picked her up. Her eyes were red, which let me know that she was crying.

"What's wrong? Why you crying?" I asked as I sat down pulling her on top of me.

"I don't want to fight with you anymore, Jayden. All I want is for us to be a family and we can't do that if we hate each other," she said, looking into my eyes.

"Ma, I don't know where you got that shit from, but I could never hate you. Yes, we've been through a great amount of things these last few months, but I don't hate you. I actually love your little stubborn ass more than life itself," I said, putting her face between my hands and kissing her lips.

"I love you too," she replied, kissing me back. "I'm sorry

for being a brat and never listening. I promise to work on that."

"You're good, but when I tell you that I'll handle something, I'm giving you my word and trust me when I say that my word is bond. I keep my promises," I said to her, meaning it.

"I know, and again, I'm sorry," she said, then placed her lips on top of mine.

"Don't start nothing that you can't finish," I said, raising her off me.

"Oh, but I want to," she said as she starting kissing on my neck. I stopped her.

"We can't get into all of that like that. Mark will be here any minute, and we have to get ready," I told her.

"A'ight. I'm going to shower," she said, as she started to undress right in front of me. I knew what she was doing. I wasn't crazy. She thought that if she teased me, I was going to give in, but that wasn't going to work. I was only a few hours away from a mission, and I wasn't about to let pussy cloud my vision.

"All right, just meet me in the living room when you're done," I said. I gave her a quick peck on the lips and left the room before my little head started to take over.

Chapter 28

Stacy

I didn't know what Kaylin called himself doing, but I hoped like hell that he knew what he was getting himself into. I got my dad to agree to let him go to Atlanta to get the money so that everything could be over and done with, but he hadn't returned yet. I'd been calling and texting his ass like crazy, but he hadn't replied to any of my calls or messages yet. I was tired and stressing the hell out. Besides, my dad was over here about to go crazy, and I didn't know how long I'd be able to buy him some time. I knew one thing though: he needed to get his ass back to New Orleans before this crazy nigga ended up doing something that he, Kaylin, and I would regret.

I sat on the sofa thinking about everything that Kaylin had put me through. Most of it was good, but the majority of the shit was bad. I mean I played second fiddle to that chick for so long and now that she was dead, he still barely even looked at me. Then there was my father, the man who made me but left. I knew that my mother had put him out, but he should have been man enough to fight to be in my life.

"Stacy, have you talked to that no-good-ass nigga of yours yet?" my father asked for what seemed like the millionth time today. He was really beginning to aggravate the hell out of me.

"Yeah," I lied. "He said that he would be here tomorrow morning."

"He better be or else shit ain't looking too good for Thing One and Thing Two downstairs," he said, walking into the living room.

"Dad, please. It don't even have to be all that. All you have to do is wait and Kaylin will be here. He's not that type of father who would just leave his child out to dry like that," I said, throwing in that last part for him.

"You got something you want to say to me, Stacy? Because I'm right here. You don't have to try no slang. If you want to say something, then say it," he yelled, walking over to the sofa where I was sitting. I sat there staring at him. This was my father, the first man I'd ever actually loved, and he disgusted the hell out of me. I mean if he would want his daughter dead, then what would he do to me?

"Look, just be patient. Kaylin will be here, okay?" I said, ignoring his little rant.

"Well, he better be. I'm heading out. I'll be back in a minute," he said and then left, which made me happy as hell, because I didn't think I'd be able to stand his voice another minute.

Pulling my phone from my pocket, I called Kaylin's ass again, but like the thirty-four times before, he didn't answer. I sent him a text message. Again, he didn't answer, which pissed me off even more. I sat there hoping like hell that Kaylin got here in time to stop this bomb before it had a chance to explode.

Chapter 29

Shelly

I'd been with Jade for a while, and I still didn't know what the hell her stupid ass was doing, but I was not feeling this, and I didn't want no part in it. I wasn't sure what was going on until I noticed that she was following the same car that we had seen by the gas station on our way to Louisiana. I knew her ass was up to no good, when the car that she was following pulled into a driveway at a house and she parked her car a few houses down, sat there, and watched the house. I wanted to ask her crazy ass what was going on, but this was her problem, not mine. I pulled my phone out and began playing with it. I wasn't trying to see shit that didn't involve me. I just hoped like hell that nothing went wrong and she dragged me into her shit like most times, because I wasn't trying to have that. We were not little anymore. I had Cam to think about. There was no way in hell I was about to get into trouble. I was going to sit there and mind my own business. If she wanted to play Nancy Drew, that was on her. I was good. I wasn't getting out of that car for nothing and no one.

Chapter 30

Mimi

I wasn't trying to throw the plan off schedule, so I didn't take as long a shower as I would normally do. When I got out of the shower, Mark was already there, so I busted my ass to the room and got ready. Pulling the clothes out of the bag that Mark had gotten for us, I hurried up and threw them on, threw my hair into a ponytail, then went to meet them. When I walked in, they were already talking, but they stopped when I came in.

"What's up?" I asked, taking a seat next to Jayden on the sofa.

"Nothing much, we were just going over the plan again," Mark replied. "How are you feeling?"

"I'm okay," I said to him.

"Okay, well are you ready?" he asked.

"I'm as ready as I'll ever be," I told him.

"Well, let's get ready to do this," Jayden said, getting up from the sofa. He then walked over to the closet and pulled a huge duffle bag out of it. Walking back over to where he was sitting, he placed the bag on the coffee table and opened it.

"Damn," I said. My eyes bucked as I saw all of the guns that were in it. He reached in and pulled out two guns.

"Do you know how to handle this?" he asked as he passed them to me.

"Boy, please," I said, taking the guns out of his hand. I then watched as he passed two to Troy, about three more to Mark, and then took his pick.

"Are you guys ready?" Mark asked, getting up from the sofa.

"Hold up. Wait a minute," I said, stopping them. "Before we go, I just want to say thanks to all of you for everything that you've done and are about to do for me. I know I haven't been the best person to get along with, and that I've been hardheaded, but I appreciate everything, and I'm thankful that you guys didn't leave me when I needed y'all the most."

"Ma, chill out. You acting like we ain't coming back," Jayden replied.

"Ya never know, we may not, and I just want to thank you all for everything."

"You're welcome," he replied. "Now let's go and get your kids back so that we can finally move on with our lives."

"I love you, baby," I said, giving him a kiss.

"I love you too," he replied, and with that being said, we left out the door. We hopped into the car and were on our way to get my kids back. I was finally about to put this shit to rest, once and for all.

Chapter 31

Jade

I sat in the car watching Mimi's house like a hawk. I knew some shit was about to go down when dude grabbed that big-ass duffle bag out of the trunk. I wasn't a stranger. The only thing that could've been in there were guns, which confirmed what I had thought: something was about to go down, and I was not going to miss this. I parked my car a few houses down and waited.

Not too long after that, the little light dude I'd always see Mimi with pulled up and went into the house. By that time, it was getting dark. Almost an hour later, the four of them came out like they were about to go to war.

Oh shit, I thought as I watched them hop into the car, back out of the driveway, and pull off. Not wanting to be left behind, I started up the car and followed them. I didn't know where they were exactly, but I knew whom they were going for. They had no idea that I was about to fuck their whole plan up though.

Chapter 32

Kaylin

It didn't take any time to make it back to New Orleans. I didn't know if I was nervous or what, but I couldn't shake the funny feeling that I had in my stomach. I didn't have time to worry about it, though, because before I knew it, I was pulling up to the house where Stacy and her father held the boys.

When I got out of the truck, I noticed that the whole block was extremely quiet today. Not thinking anything of it, I grabbed the bag that the money was in and made my way inside the house. When I walked inside of the house, it was dark and unusually quiet, as if there was no one at home.

"Yo. Anybody here?" I asked as I tried to find the light switch.

"Damn, it's about time that you showed up. I thought I was going to have to come look for you and shit," Stacy said, flicking on the light.

"Well, I'm here now, ain't I?" I said, taking a seat on the sofa. "Your pops here?"

"Nah, he just stepped out. He'll be back in a minute," she replied like it was cool.

"I know he got a phone or something. Call him and tell that I'm here and I'm ready to get this shit over with."

"All right," she replied as she got up, grabbed her phone, and walked into the kitchen. She returned a few minutes later. "He said that he'll be here in a minute," she said, taking a seat on the sofa opposite me.

As I sat there looking at her, I couldn't help but to think of the many ways I could make her and her father disappear. I couldn't stand to see the sight of her right now.

"Kaylin, where do we stand after all of this?" she asked me.

"Honestly, Stacy, I don't know."

"Well, I thought you said that once this was over, we were going to be a family," she stated, sitting up. I didn't answer her. I didn't want to say too much that could jeopardize me getting my boys back and leaving here in one piece. "So you gon' just sit there and act like I ain't talking to you at all?"

"Stacy, chill. Let me just get the boys and give this nigga the money, and we'll go from there," I said, trying to satisfy her.

"Okay," she replied. I wasn't trying to have any more conversation, so I pulled my phone out of my pocket and turned it on. My phone immediately began to ring from all of the missed calls, text messages, and voicemails, which all happened to be from one person: Stacy. I looked at her, giving her the side eye before I found Shelly's number and sent her a text. I didn't have time to wait for her to reply before I heard the door opening. Stacy's father, along with the boys, came walking inside. I got up, but when I noticed a woman walking in behind them, I immediately sat back down.

"Marie?" I asked, not believing my eyes.

"Kaylin," she nonchalantly replied.

"What are you doing here?" I asked her.

"I came to collect what's due to me and mine," she said, confusing me.

"What the hell are you talking about?"

"The money, Kaylin. Where is it?" she answered.

I couldn't believe that she was working with these snakes. How could she even do that to her own grand-kids?

"I'm not giving anybody anything until I get my boys and know that we're getting out of here," I told her.

"All this time, it's been you?" Stacy asked, getting off the sofa.

"Of course, it's been me. How else was Julius going to know where Amina and the kids where?" she replied. She shoved the boys down the hall into a back room and pulled the door shut.

"So it was never about me and Kaylin Jr. You only had me in on the plan because you knew I had Kaylin's son," she said, turning to her father.

"Darling, you are weak. Just like that nigga was pussy-whipped, you was hung up on his dick. Even when you knew that nigga wasn't going to wife you," her father said to her. I couldn't do anything but chuckle. Here I was, thinking I was the only one who was being fucked, but it seemed that Stacy didn't know her father like she thought she knew him.

"So you had your own daughter killed, because of her mother?" she asked.

"What are you talking about?" I asked her.

"Yeah, you didn't know?" Marie asked. "Stacy and Amina are sisters."

"At least they were," Julius replied.

"No, they are," Marie replied, laughing. "You see Amina is actually . . ." she started to say, but stopped when the front door came crashing down.

"Am I too late for the party?" I heard a voice say.

I froze because I knew damn well this wasn't who I thought it was. When I turned and saw Amina standing there, I thought I had seen a ghost. "Hello, Kaylin. You miss me?"

Chapter 33

Stacy

I couldn't believe everything that was going on now. I knew my father was grimy, but I never thought that he'd fuck me over. To know that this whole while Mimi's mother was the one who was pulling the strings was crazy. They really didn't give a fuck that they had their own daughter killed and kidnapped her kids. I mean where the fuck they do that at? Those two muthafuckers were made for each other. They were snakes, and snakes belonged together.

As I stood there trying to figure out a way to get up out of there without getting myself killed, the fucking door came crashing down. *What the fuck?* I thought and, as if the situation weren't already fucked up, Amina came busting through the door. At first, I thought I was dreaming, but when she spoke up, I knew damn well that this wasn't a dream. This shit was actually a reality, and I knew from that moment on, things were going to get crazy.

Chapter 34

Mimi

The whole time I sat in the car all I could think about was my boys. I didn't want them to get hurt in this whole madness. I prayed that everything would go as smooth as Mark said it would be.

"Don't worry too much. Everything will be just fine," Troy said as if she could read my thoughts.

"I know. I'm just ready for all of this to be over and done with," I said to her.

"It's about time he decided to join the party," Mark said as we pulled up to the house.

"It's show time," Jayden said, checking his guns. Once he was sure that everything was okay, he got out of the car.

"Let's go," Mark said as he got out behind him, followed by Troy, and then me.

"Now remember what we said: if things start to go wrong, bail and we'll finish everything," Jayden said to me.

"I know," I replied as I held both guns in my hands. "See you in a minute." The plan was for us to go through the front so that we could distract them, while Jayden and Mark crept through the back. I didn't know if it was going to work, but I was not turning back now.

The street was unusually quiet as Troy and I made our way toward the front of the house. Like thieves in the night, we opened the gate and walked up to the front door. Once we made it to the door, we could hear a lot of fussing going on inside.

"I'm going to count to three, and we'll kick the door down," I whispered to Troy.

"Okay," she said, nodding her head.

"One," I said, as I began to count.

"Two," I said, just as I heard my name being called.

"Three," I said, as we brought our legs up and kicked the door off the hinges together.

"Am I too late for the party?" I asked, scaring the shit out of all of them.

I then turned to Kaylin who looked as if he had seen a ghost. "Hello, Kaylin. You miss me?"

"Mi . . . Mimi, is that you?" he asked.

"The one and only, baby," I said as I walked into the living room, with Troy behind me.

"But I thought you was dead," Stacy said.

"Nah, I can assure you both that I'm alive and well," I said to her. "What's going on? Did I interrupt something?"

"Yes, you actually did," the nigga who happened to be my father said.

"Well, well, well. Hello there, Daddy dearest," I said, walking over to him. "You don't look happy to see me."

"Because I'm not," he had the nerve to say.

"Oh, I can see that. It's too bad, though, because I don't give a fuck," I said. Out of the corner of my eye, I caught Stacy trying to get up. "Nah, bitch, sit right there. I wouldn't want you to miss the party," I said, pointing my gun at her.

"Look, Mimi, it don't have to be all of this," the bitch said, hitting a nerve. I walked over to her and hit her so hard in her face I thought for sure that I had knocked a few teeth out of her mouth.

"Bitch, was you thinking like that when you came up in my house and had my nigga shoot me?" I said, heated. I then turned to Kaylin who was standing there as if he ain't had shit to worry about. "And you. You let this bitch come between what we had, for what? To get played. I bet yo' dumb ass had no idea that this bitch was my sister. Hell, I didn't even know, until I went to visit Mommy dearest over there and she told me."

"So you knew this whole time that Mimi was alive and you didn't tell me?" Julius asked Marie.

"Actually I did," she said, pulling a gun from behind her back and pointed it at him, confusing the shit out of me, because I thought for sure that she was working with them. "You don't actually think that I would go against my daughter for you, now would you?"

"So you wasn't working with him?" I asked, now pointing the other gun that I had at her.

"I'm not going to lie to you. At first I was, when I thought that you were dead, but then I got hit with reality. This nigga was the reason why I was who I was. He was the reason why I did what I did to you. I didn't know that he was going to kill you. I really didn't, so when I found that out, I started to formulate a plan of my own. Then you came back into the picture," she said. "I was never going to let him harm one strand of hair on Kayson's and Kaylon's heads. I just needed him to think that I was."

I stood there thinking. On one hand, we'd bonded, or at least I thought we had, but here she was in bed with the enemy, and that shit didn't sit well with me. I wasn't buying her story. Why the fuck did she hook up with the nigga in the first place? Talking about a plan, for all I know this could be a part of her plan right now. I was not about to let her manipulate me again, so I pointed my gun and shot her in her head, killing her instantly. I didn't even blink, I just stood there. I was done letting people fuck over me.

"Stupid bitch," Julius yelled.

"Nah, she was the stupid one for thinking that she was going to cross me," I said, pointing my gun back at him. "I'm going to ask you one time. Where are my kids?"

"Eat a dick and die, bitch," he replied.

"Wrong answer," I said, shooting him in the leg.

"Ugh," he moaned in pain.

"Where are my kids?" I asked him again, but he didn't answer, so I shot him in his other leg. I walked over to him and pointed the gun at his face. "Where the fuck are my kids?"

"They're in the room down the hall on the left," Stacy yelled from behind me.

I turned to look at her when I spotted Jayden and Mark in the hallway. "Mark, take this bitch to the back and get my kids."

"Okay," he said, grabbing her. At first, she looked as if she didn't want to move.

"Bitch, if you know me, you'd run and get my kids from the back," I said to her.

"Mimi, please don't hurt him," she said, begging for her father's life. I looked at her, cracked a smile, and then shot the nigga in the head. At first, I was going to kill him while she was in the back, but I had another thought. I ain't give a fuck about the nigga, but since she did, I wanted her to watch him die. I killed him right in front of her eyes.

"Nooooo," she screamed, trying to get away from Mark.

"Bitch, I wouldn't do that if I was you," he said, placing a gun to the back of her head. "Come on, let's move," he said, pushing her to the back of the house. A few minutes later, they came back into the room with Kayson and Kaylon.

"Mommy," they both said, running over to me.

"Hey, boys," I said, hiding the guns behind my back.

"Where have you been? I missed you," Kayson said.

"I missed you all too," I said to them. "Troy, get them and take them outside. We'll meet you back at the car."

"Nooo," they started to scream.

"Not now, boys. I need y'all to go with Auntie Troy. I'll be out in a minute," I said to them.

"Will Daddy be coming with us?" Kaylon asked, shocking me.

"Um, yes, Daddy will be out in a minute. Now go," I said, pushing them in Troy's direction.

"Okay," they said as they hung their heads. I waited until Troy and the boys were out of the house before I turned back to Stacy. I was ready for all of this to be over.

I walked over to her and stared at her. "See, I didn't understand why you was always so jealous of me. You was my friend. Whenever I had, you had. We practically ate off of the same plate, and yet you stabbed me in the back."

"Mimi, I'm sorry. My father used my feelings toward Kaylin to get me to turn on you, and I really wish that I could take it all back," she sobbed as the tears started to roll down her face.

"See, the first mistake that you and Kaylin made was underestimating me. The second mistake y'all made was when y'all didn't check to see that I was dead back in that house," I said and shot her four times in the chest.

Turning around to Kaylin, I stood there staring at him. Here was the man I'd loved for over ten years of my life, the same man who fucked my sister and had a baby by her. He was also the same man who shot and left me for dead and right now the only thing I felt for him was hate.

"I want to thank you for what you've done to me. Because of you, I finally found and know what a real man is—" I began to say, but he interrupted me.

"Just cut all of the bullshit out, ma, and do what you came here to do," he replied.

"Okay," I said as I raised the gun and aimed it at him.

"Bitch, I wouldn't do that if I was you," I heard a voice say. When I turned, I was face to face with Jade, Kaylin's sidepiece.

"Damn, Kay, your bitches just don't know when to cut it, huh?"

"Bitch, please, you should've stayed dead where you was," she replied as she took two steps in my direction.

"And if I would've stayed dead, you still wouldn't be able to have Kaylin," I told her. "That is why you're here right?"

"It surely ain't for you," she replied. Like before, the bitch was never on point.

"Kill her," I said to Troy, who had snuck up behind her. She never even saw Troy coming. I heard several shots ring out, but I wasn't focusing on that. What I was more worried about was Kaylin trying to run. Raising the gun up, I let off several shots that hit him straight in the back, and then he went down. I bet he was probably wishing that he never took me to the gun range. I didn't even go over to check on him. I was more than sure I'd done what I intended to do.

"Let's get out of here," I said to Jayden and Mark.

"Hold up right quick," Mark said as he walked over to the duffle bag that was sitting by the sofa. When he opened the bag, there was an assload of money in it. Picking up the bag, he then began to spread money around the living room, and I knew just what he was trying to do. "Now we can go."

I took one last look at the bodies that were lying around the room before I followed Mark and Jayden out the door. I was very happy that everything was over and I now had my kids back. The hardest part was over. Now all I had left to do was to get my life back together.

Chapter 35

Shelly

I should've followed my first mind and left when I said I was. Now Jade's ass had me stuck in the middle of some shit. When she first got out of the car, I was cool. I stayed my ass right there and minded my own fucking business. It was about a few minutes later when I started to hear plenty gunshots that I got worried. I sat in the car scared out of my mind. I didn't know if I wanted to get out of the car and check on her or call the police. Going against my better judgment, I got out of the car anyway.

Tiptoeing and looking behind me every second, I made my way toward the house that I had seen Jayden walk to. The door was off the hinges, so I was able to see straight inside. When I walked inside, there was blood and dead bodies all over the place. I spotted Jade over by the sofa, and I ran to her side.

"Jade, get up," I said, taking her into my arms. "Get up, Jade," I kept repeating, but she didn't answer. I check her arm to try to find a pulse, but I couldn't find any. I attempted to pick her up when I heard coughing coming toward the kitchen, so I got up and went to check.

I almost lost it when I spotted Kaylin by the back door with blood all over him. "Oh, my God, Kaylin," I said, rushing over to him.

"Help me," he said

"Okay, don't talk. I'm going to get you some help," I said as I located a phone and dialed 911. "Um, hello, I need some help. Someone's been shot," I said once the operator came on the phone.

"What's the address, ma'am?" she asked. I located a piece of mail and rattled the address off to her.

"What's your name, ma'am?" she asked. That's when everything hit me. Here I was, sitting in a house with beaucoup dead bodies and I had no idea what happened. Instead of answering her, I hung the phone up.

"I have to go, but help is on the way, Kaylin. You just have to hold on," I said as I got up from the floor. I walked over to Jade and removed the keys from her pocket. I then gave her a kiss on her forehead and got my ass the hell out of there. I wasn't trying to get caught up in this bullshit. There was no way I was going to go down over something I didn't do.

I ran all the way down the street, hopped in the car, and pulled off. I silently said a prayer for Kaylin, wishing that the ambulance would get to him in time.

Chapter 36

Mimi

I couldn't believe that everything was over and done with. I could actually breathe. I now had my kids back, we were headed back to Atlanta in a few days, and I had Jayden. I was not going to say that the road was easy, because it wasn't. I'd had some trying times, and there were a few times when I wanted to give up, but by the grace of God, I was able to hold it all together. I had a great support system in Jayden, Troy, Mark, Weedy, and Margie by my side throughout this whole ordeal. I really had to thank God for Jayden. Without that man, Lord, I didn't know where I'd have been. I'd have probably been in a mental institution somewhere.

It was now summertime, and I was enjoying the weather, so I decided to have a barbeque and pool party. I invited my friends and the people I considered my family. I never got a chance to relax after all of the things that I'd been through these past twelve months, so I was actually enjoying this little peaceful time.

From a distance, I sat there and watched as my kids, Jayden's son Cam, and a couple of other kids from the neighborhood enjoyed themselves in the pool. As I watched Kayson, Kaylon, Kailay, and Kayla, my heart warmed up as I noticed the smiles that were plastered on their faces. I was so happy to be back in their lives. It felt good knowing that no one could come and mess this up again.

I was finally done with the bullshit. Stacy and Julius were probably somewhere in hell together. I made sure of that. Shit, I wouldn't have been surprised if they bullied the devil for his spot. As for Kaylin, he wasn't as lucky as they were. He was alive, but he was probably wishing that he weren't. I didn't blame him, though. If I were a paraplegic, I'd probably be thinking the same thing. I couldn't live my life knowing that I had to spend the rest of it in prison while being confined to a wheelchair. See, I thought about killing his ass, but death would've been too easy for his ass. I wanted that nigga to be able to live and think about all the shit that he'd done, for him to see the grass wasn't greener on the other side and how he should've never fucked with that duck-ass ho Stacy, because she'd been a snake. I wanted him to live his life knowing that he had kids he wouldn't be able to see. I wanted him to see how the shit felt when they were doing the shit to me. They asked me if I felt bad for him, but I said no. Honestly, I didn't. He never felt sorry for me, so I didn't feel sorry for his ass. He deserved everything that he got, and if I had to do it all over again, I would've done it all over again.

I sat deep in my thoughts, just thinking about all the shit that I'd been through in the past few years. Some things were great, as others were not so great, but still and all, I'd somehow survived every storm that was in my way. There were a lot of people who would've gone through the things that I'd gone through and given up, but not me.

"Hey, lady! I see you over here daydreaming and shit. You all right?" Troy asked, sitting in the chair beside me.

I took a minute to look around at all of the people sitting in our backyard. There was a crew of people dancing, some were in the pool, others were playing Spades, and the rest were eating. When I was left to die, I never imagined that I'd be enjoying life again, and yet here I was. "Actually, I'm fine. I'm still overwhelmed. Everything still doesn't feel real. I swear I thought I would spend damn near the rest of my life trying to get my life back in order, from what Kaylin and Stacy had put me through. I still can't believe that everything is over. I mean, I finally get a chance to sit there and breathe, to enjoy my family, my kids, my friends, and my man, in peace. I don't have to worry about looking over my shoulder or worrying about if someone is going to come and try to hurt me again. All of my enemies are gone, and I can't do nothing but thank God and you all, of course," I said to her.

"Girl, who you telling? That's me. I thought that this thing wasn't going to ever end. I mean, when I thought that you was dead, I was lost. Then Kaylin had taken the kids and Stacy's old dumb ass was lurking around here. Not to mention all of the things I went through with not being able to find your body for the funeral and Kaylin's little side pieces Jade and Star. Humph, shit was just all the way fucked up," she said, taking a sip from her drink.

"Girl, who you telling? I thought for sure that I'd end up in a casket somewhere before I'd ever get to see all of my kids together again."

"Who you telling? We must be some cats that got nine lives, because we done used about four of them already," she said with a light chuckle, which in turn made me laugh also.

"For real," I replied. We both sat there in silence, lost in our own thoughts.

"You think that the cops will find Julius's and Stacy's bodies?" she asked, looking at me.

"I don't know and to be honest, I really don't care. They're right where they need to be," I said, hunching my shoulders. "Besides, if they do, they don't have any proof that we were the ones who did it, so I'm good," I said, sitting back in my seat. I grabbed my drink from the table and took a few sips. The last thing on my mind was the police finding Julius's and Stacy's bodies. Hell, there probably weren't any more bodies, because where we threw them, I was more than sure, the bugs and animals ate them all up. We didn't need to worry about the police finding anything.

"Yeah, you're right."

"On another note, what's going on with you and Weedy?" I asked her.

Her eyes damn near bulged out of their sockets as she swallowed hard. "What you mean?" she asked, with this dumb look on her face.

"Don't play dumb with me. I know Weedy's the one ringing your phone when you claim that it's your cousin," I said, busting her bubble. "You don't have to lie. It's me you're talking to."

She sat there for a minute, without saying anything. I know she was confused. Hell, if I were her, I'd be confused too. On one hand, she had a man who she had history with. Now everything wasn't peaches and cream, but at the end of the day, they had a love that only they could understand. Then, on the other hand, she had the total opposite. Mark and she didn't have a lot of history, but I could tell you that he genuinely loved her. I mean what man do you know would kick it with a bitch he only met, have her back when the going gets tough, and wait patiently when it took her awhile to give up the cookies? He could've been like most niggas and bounced, but he didn't, which should've let her know that it wasn't all about sex. Hell, the odds were clearly stacked in Mark's favor. Weedy'd had a history of fucking a lot of bitches, bringing home diseases, and not being there when she needed him. Mark was the total opposite and the man she should clearly choose, but that was none of my business. I wasn't trying to tell her how to live her life, because I'd made a lot of mistakes on my own. She should have known better and learned from my situation. If a man cheated once, he'd cheat again, no matter how much he said that he changed.

"Um, hello," I said, snapping my fingers at her.

"Honestly, there's nothing going on between Weedy and me. We're just friends. I'm with and in love with Mark. He's the one I want to be with. I'm not trying to mess that up," she replied. I heard what she was saying, but her actions were telling a whole different story.

"Okay," was all I said. I wasn't about to go there with her. As I said, that wasn't my business. It was hers. I just hoped that she knew what she was doing.

"Hey, my darlings," Margie said, walking over to where we were. She gave each of us a hug before she pulled up a chair and sat down with us.

"Hey, Marg!" Troy and I said at the same time.

"How are my girls doing today?" she asked.

"We're fine and you?" I said to her. Ever since that day Margie had helped me when I was in the hospital, we'd grown extra close. She'd been like a mother to me and a grandmother to my children. She even had Cam calling her Nana. She'd been there a few times to comfort me and to check my ass when I needed it.

"I'm doing great. Where are my babies?" she asked, referring to my kids.

"They're in the pool over there," I said, nodding toward the area where the pool was. She looked their way and smiled.

"Look at my babies. They look so happy and full of life," she said, beaming with pride. I really didn't know what my kids did to Margie, but they'd really grown on her. She was always coming over to take them to the park or bring them things. We were lucky to have her in our lives. "Oh, that reminds me. There's a circus coming to town this weekend. Maybe we should take them."

"That would've been lovely, but Jayden and I are surprising the kids with a trip to Disney World this weekend," I said to her

"Aww, that will be so nice. The kids are going to definitely enjoy that," Margie replied. "Just make sure that y'all take care of my babies and make sure that they have lots of fun."

"We will, and I'm pretty sure that they will. Besides, we really do need this vacation."

"I'm saying," Troy said. "I think that's what Mark and I need our-damn-selves."

"Well, make it happen. I'm so used to thinking that I might not get a chance to live tomorrow, that I'm living for today and if tomorrow comes, then I'll be living for that day," I said to her.

"Girl, I feel ya. I just need a minute to enjoy my man," she said, laughing.

"I second that motion," I replied, grabbing my drink and downing the rest. It'd been a minute since Jayden and I did our own little thing, and the shit were long overdue.

Speaking of Jayden, I spotted him over by the barbeque grill with a drink in his hand, laughing at whatever it was that Mark was saying. Even though he had on an apron that was full of barbeque, I peeped out how sexy he was looking, in a wife beater, some True Religion, and some all-white Air Max 90s. The way the sides of his lips curled up and the deep print of his dimples when he laughed drove me crazy. He must have felt me watching him, because a minute later, our eyes met. I wanted so desperately to kiss him, to feel him, just to be near him, so I got up and walked over to him.

We held eye contact the whole time I was walking. I felt like there was no one else there, but him and me. When I made it to him, I threw myself in his arms, hugging him extra tight. No words were spoken as I placed my lips on top of his, parted his lips with my tongue, and gave him one of those deep, passionate kisses, the one that says, "I love you," without having to speak the words.

"Well damn, y'all don't worry about the house that's behind y'all. Why don't y'all just go at it right there in the back seat?" Mark said sarcastically.

"Shut up and mind ya business," I said, punching him on his arm.

"Ouch, damn. You know you can't be hitting on a nigga like that. You don't hit soft no how," he said, playfully holding his arm as if it was really hurting him.

"Boy, stop playing, you know damn well that shit don't hurt," I told him.

"Yeah, yeah, yeah. What's up with you though, ma? How you doing? You feeling good or what?" he asked, grabbing me and giving me a friendly hug.

"I'm doing fine. I now have my kids and life back, so I can't complain," I said to him.

"That's good then, but let me holla at you for a second right quick," he said, walking away from where the guys were standing by the grill.

"What's up?" I asked once we were out of earshot.

"Look, ma. I'm only telling you this because that's your girl and all, but something is going on with Troy and ya boy," he said. I wasn't surprised, though. Mark was the type of dude to observe shit. He knew shit that you thought he didn't know.

"Mark, right now I don't know what's going on with Troy, but I don't think that her and Weedy are messing around," I said, lying through my teeth. I also knew that something was going on between the two of them, but I wasn't going to tell him that. What kind of friend would I be if I were to rat my girl out?

"Ma, come on. You can't tell me that you haven't noticed the shit that she's been doing. I'm trying to give her the benefit of the doubt, because I love her, but if I find out that she's fucking with him, I'm done with her ass," he said, looking me in my eyes. I wanted to say something, anything, to make things right for them somehow, but I couldn't. There was nothing to say. He looked at me for a little while longer with those intense eyes that he had. For a minute, he seemed to be stuck, lost in his thoughts maybe. Then he walked off, leaving me there with my own thoughts.

I turned and spotted Troy over there looking at me. She raised an eyebrow as if to ask me what was up. In return, I hunched my shoulder while shaking my head, indicating that I didn't know.

"What's wrong?" Jayden asked as he wrapped his arms around me.

"Nothing. Why you asked that?" I asked him.

"Well, because for one, Mark came back with in a sour mood and for two, you're standing over here with a confused look on your face. So I'm guessing that something has gone down between you two," he said staring at me. There was something about the way that he looked at me, and I knew I had to tell him the truth.

"He came to talk to me about something with Troy and Weedy. It didn't have anything to do with me," I told him.

"Well, what's going on?" he asked me. "You know my boy is not about all them games and shit."

"Honestly, I asked her myself, but I really don't know. She say that it was nothing, but I'm thinking something different."

"Well for her sake, I really hope that it's nothing, because Mark's a real good guy. He's not about playing, and he really likes her. That shit is very rare. He don't really be 'bout that shit. Normally he's all work and no play, but with her, it's different," he replied. I heard what he was saying, and like him, I hoped that the shit with Weedy and Troy was nothing, because I knew if it wasn't, shit could get real sloppy and we didn't need no more of that in our lives.

"Well, I hope not then," I said turning to kiss him.

"You know if you keep on doing that, we're going to have to end this little get-together early," he said, palming my ass. He then leaned in and gave me a kiss that took my breath away.

"All right, you two. Cut it out. We have guests here," Ms. Carol, Jayden's mother, said, interrupting us.

"Ms. Smith, how are you?" I asked, leaning in to give her a hug.

"I'm doing fine and yourself?" she said. "And I told you to stop calling me Ms. Smith. You can call me Mom."

"I'm doing fine and okay," I replied.

"Amina, after all of the girls that Jayden has been with, I have to say that I like you. This time I can actually say that my son has finally found the right girl. I just hope he does right by you," she said, cutting her eyes at him.

"Ma, you don't even have to worry about all of that, because I plan on making her my wife one day," Jayden said, looking in my eyes.

"Boy, stop playing, you know you damn well that you don't want me to be your wife," I told him.

"I was waiting for the right time to do this, but apparently there's no time like the present," he said, reaching in his pocket. He pulled out a small red velvet box, and then looked back at me. I was no stranger to this move, being that Kaylin had proposed to me already. He then looked over to his mother, who in turn nodded her head in approval, and he got down on one knee, making my eyes get watery.

"Mimi, baby, I know that you've been through a lot of things this past year, but throughout all of this, you've survived. You're one of a kind, you're like a rare gem, and I cannot let you get away. When I thought you were dead, my whole world was turned upside down. I thought for sure that I had lost you forever, but by the grace of God, you're still here with us right now. You're a great mother and a wonderful woman, who I'd like to have my own kids with someday, not to mention that Cam loves you also. Yeah, I know that we've met under difficult circumstances, and we haven't known each other that long, but no matter what anyone says about it, I love you, and I want to spend the rest of my life with you. So what I'm saying is, will you do me the honor of becoming my wife?"

By the time he was through with saying all of that, I was in full-blown tears. He was right, I'd been through a lot, and he was right there by my side. He was everything that Kaylin wasn't, and I didn't have to worry about him cheating on me, because he made it clear that he wasn't that type of guy. Still, I was skeptical about marrying him. Hell, who was I kidding? This was the perfect man, my man, and here he was, down on one knee, asking me to marry him. I'd never find another man like that and, to be honest, I was not planning on looking. I had my knight in shining armor, and I was sticking with him.

"Yes," I said jumping into his arms, and then I gave him one sweet, long kiss on his lips. "I love you too, baby." He picked me up and swung me around like I was a big old kid.

"Yay! Mommy and Uncle Jay," my kids said, running up to us.

"Yay, Daddy and Mama Mimi," Cam said, running up behind them.

"Thanks, babies," I said, bending down, giving each one of them a kiss and hug.

"Congratulations, baby," Ms. Carol said, hugging us.

"Thanks, Ma," Jayden replied.

"Thanks, Ms. Carol," I replied.

"You are very much welcome. Now that you're about to be my daughter-in-law, you can definitely call me Mom."

"Well, thank you, Ma," I said, just to satisfy her.

"Jayden, baby, I have to go, but I promise to see you later," she said to him. "Don't be a stranger now, and, Mimi, remind that boy that he still has a mother, because sometimes he seem to forget that," she said, laughing.

"Ma, chill out, you know that ain't true. You gon' play on me like that, huh?" he replied, smiling.

"Yeah, I bet. You be good and take care of that girl now," she said, pointing a finger at him.

"I will, Ma."

"I'll see you later. We should do lunch sometime," she said, hugging me.

"I'd love to. Just let me know when and where," I said, hugging her back.

"Okay. Jayden come walk Mama to her car," she told him.

"I'll be right back, baby," he said, giving me a quick peck on my lips.

"Okay," I said, kissing him back.

"Congrats, bighead," Mark said, hugging me.

"You know about this shit, didn't you?" I asked him, poking him in his chest.

"I'm not saying that I did and I'm saying that I didn't," he said, laughing.

"Yeah, whatever," I said to him as Troy walked up. He looked at her, she then looked at him, and he walked off.

"Girl, what's up with that shit?" I asked her.

"I don't know. Shit, he be fucking tripping. Let me see it, girl. Quit playing," Troy said, reaching for my left hand.

I held it up so she could get a good look at it. "Girl, it's beautiful. Congratulations." She reached in and hugged me. When she tried to pull back, I pulled her closer to me, so that I could whisper in her ear.

"Whatever the fuck is going on between you and Weedy needs to end. You have to clean that shit up and dead it today. Mark's getting suspicious, in case you ain't know or you don't give a damn. Either way, the shit needs to end. Otherwise, you're going to end up losing your man, for the same man who left you high and dry," I said to her. I didn't wait for her to reply. I moved past her and made my way toward the house, leaving her there to think about what I had just said. I didn't want any part in that shit. I'd already been through too much drama already. I wasn't trying to get into this.

A few people who wanted to say congratulations as I made my way inside of the house stopped me. Most of them wanted to see my ring so that they could go talk about it among themselves, but I didn't care at all. Today was one of the greatest days of my life.

Bitter Bitch

I was on my way to Jayden's house. I was tired of playing games with his ass. It was time that I put my fucking foot down and dealt with him and his ma. I wanted my child from over there. I wasn't about to let no bitch think that she could come in and play mommy to my child. Fuck that. I spent thirteen hours in labor when I had my son, and I wasn't about to let the next bitch think that she was gon' come in and take my muthafucking spot. I'd be damned if I let that shit happen.

As I was driving, I received a collect call. I already knew that it was nobody but my little boo, so I answered the phone on the first ring.

"You have a collect call from . . ." the recorder started to say, but I pressed number five so that the call could connect faster. I didn't have time to be listening to that long-ass recording.

"What's up, ma?" he asked, once the call was connected.

"Hey, boo, how you doing?" I asked him. Lately, he hadn't been acting right. Hell, I still didn't know how he was in jail in the first place.

"I'm doing fine, ma, considering the situation that I'm in. How are you?" he asked in that sexy voice that I loved to hear.

"I'm good. I'm about to go pick up my son."

"I thought he was staying with his daddy," he said.

"Yeah, he was, but I'm about to go get him. I've missed my baby, and I'm ready for him to come back home. It's been too damn long since he's been with them. Besides, Jayden done moved his new bitch and her kids up here, and I'm not trying to have that ho thinking she's Cameron's mother," I said, getting pissed off. I hated Jayden's new bitch with a passion.

"Come on, he doing it like that?" he asked me.

"Yeah, last time I talk to Cam over the phone all he wanted to talk about was Mimi. At first I thought he was talking about his grandmother, until I asked him. He said he was talking about his daddy's new girlfriend," I said to him.

"You said her name was Mimi?" he asked.

"Yeah, why?" I asked him.

"What's her real name?" he asked, ignoring my question.

"Um, I think its Amina something. Oh, Amina Washington," I said, snapping my fingers. "Why?" I asked, wondering why he wanted to know what her name was.

"Nothing, I just thought she was somebody I knew, but I don't know her," he said. "Say, I have to go. We're about to go to chow. I'ma call you later."

"Okay, I love you," I said to him.

"Yeah, me too," he replied, and then hung up. I pulled the phone away from my ear and just stared at it. This nigga was just acting all depressed and shit, but now he was all jolly again and shit.

Not thinking twice about it, I threw the phone on the seat, just as I turned down the street where Jayden stayed. I noticed that there were a lot of cars parked up and down the street, so I was guessing that they were having some sort of party or something. *Oh, well, I'ma break this shit up if this nigga don't give me my child in peace.*

I spotted Jayden walking up to the front door, just as I was parking. I hurriedly exited the car and made my way over there, before he went inside.

"Say, Jayden, let me holla at you right quick," I said as I walked, trying to catch up with him.

I was guessing that he knew it was me, because before he turned around, he blew up air in frustration. "What do you want, Shelly?" he asked.

"I came here to get my son, Jayden. I want my child to come home."

"Well, if that's what you came here for, you might as well get back in your car and leave, because you ain't taking my son from over here," he replied, turning around to walk inside the house.

"Don't turn your back on me," I said, grabbing him. "I've played things by your rules for the past couple of months. I'm tired of the shit. It's time for you to give me my child back."

"You must be tripping. You know the drama that you've caused between me and you. Then you bring the shit to my home. As if my girl's life wasn't already fucked up, you had to come around here and show your ass. Adding extra shit to the punch," he said, snapping at me.

"Nigga, if you think for one minute that I give a fuck about your bitch, then you're wrong. I couldn't fucking care less about what that bitch was already going through. That wasn't my problem nor was it my concern. My only concern around here is Cameron Jahavon Smith."

"Bitch, I don't give a fuck what you think. All I know is that you ain't taking my child from here and that's a bet," he said, getting in my face.

"I'm really trying to be civil with you right now. Don't make this shit worse than it already is, because I can guarantee you that neither you nor your bitch will like it," I said, through gritted teeth.

"I know damn well this ain't who I think this is," I heard a voice say from behind Jayden. When he moved to the side, I came face to face with his bitch.

"Look, bitch, if you know like me, you'd go back inside and mind your business. This shit right here don't have nothing to do with you," I said, pointing my finger back and forth between Jayden and myself. "This shit is between me and my baby daddy. So butt the fuck out of this, or else you'll regret it."

"Look, bitch, I never whooped on your ass for the sake of my fiancé, because I knew no matter what, he'd have to deal with you, but I can guarantee that if you keep playing with me, I'll light your ho ass up," she said, stepping a little closer to us.

"Fiancé?" I asked, baffled.

"Yes, bitch, my fiancé," she replied, holding out her left hand so that I could see the huge rock that was sitting on her ring finger. The minute I laid eyes on it, I lost it. Here I gave this nigga a seed, was with his sorry ass for six years, and he gave this ho here a ring.

"Nigga, you ain't shit," I said, walking up to him. I proceeded to slap the dog shit out of him, knowing that he wasn't going to hit me back. He wasn't the type of dude to hit on females, which was why I stayed slapping and punching on his ass, because I knew he'd never hit me back.

I turned around and was about to walk away when someone tapped me on my shoulders. When I turned back around, that Mimi bitch's fist connected with my mouth, drawing blood instantly.

"Guess what, bitch? You picked the wrong fucking day to come over here with the bullshit. You want to hit on somebody, well I'm about to show you how the shit feels. See, you already know that Jayden will not put his hands on you, but that ain't going to stop me from giving you a ass whooping," she replied. I wanted to say something, but I was still in a daze. I really couldn't believe that that bitch had just hit me.

Chapter 37

Mimi

After the 1,001 congratulations that I had gotten from the people in the backyard, I went inside in search for Jayden. When I walked into the kitchen, I didn't see him, so I went to look for him in the garage, thinking he was in there, when I heard a female voice coming from the front of the house. At first, I thought that the person was in the living room, until I got there and saw that there wasn't anyone in there. When I peeped outside of the door, I had a front-row seat to the show Jayden and his baby mama Shelly were putting on.

I couldn't believe that out of all the days in this year, she had picked this day to come over here with her bullshit. Today wasn't a good day, though. I wasn't in the mood to fuck a bitch up. My man had just proposed to me, and I was happy, but when I stepped outside, the vibe that they were giving off was a muthafucker. I was actually going to try to calm them down, but the bitch said something that pissed me off, which ended up changing my whole mood and made me go ham on her ass. The moment she slapped Jayden in his face, the bitch had made a huge mistake. She already knew that Jayden wasn't a woman beater, which was why she slapped him in the first place. Jayden told me about the many times that they'd gotten into it, and she'd hit him only because she knew he wasn't going to hit her ass back. I was here to show that bitch something different. She wasn't about to hit my man while I was standing there and get away with it. I was about to show that ho just how it felt to be hit on.

When I punched that ho in her mouth, she just stood there in a daze. I wasn't trying to fight that bitch like that. I wanted her to be aware of that ass whooping I was about to give her.

"Bitch, don't just stand there. Pick your jaw up and hit me back," I said to her. I wanted this bitch to pick up her hands and fight me fair so that I could give this ho an ass whooping that she would never forget.

"Bitch, I know damn well you ain't just hit me," she finally said.

"From the looks of that busted lip you got, you can see that I did."

"Ho, you done fucked up now," she said, trying to run up on me, but Jayden had stopped her. "Nigga, let me go, so I can whoop this bitch's ass."

"Shelly, go 'head about your business. I don't have time for your shit," he said, walking her to the road. I followed him.

"Yeah, Jayden, please let this bitch go, so she can whoop my ass," I said, taunting her.

"Mimi, please go back inside the house," he said to me.

"Nah, I ain't going nowhere, until I whoop this ho ass," I told him.

"Bitch, please, the only ass that's going to be getting whooped is yours," she said, trying to break away from him.

"Nah, ho, you got me fucked up. I don't get my ass whooped. I do the whooping," I replied, letting this ho know.

"Bitch, please. Tell your nigga to let me go and I'll show you just whose ass is gon' be whooped, and I can bet my last dollar that it won't be me."

"Bitch, please. You'll be broke, because I can guarantee you that this right here ain't what you want. Jayden, pleeease, let this ho go. Please," I said, begging him.

"Mimi, baby, please just go back in the house while I handle this right quick, please," he said, pleading with me.

"You know what? This ho ain't even worth it. You got five minutes to get rid of this garbage before I come back out here and do it for you," I said, and then walked off.

"Yeah, bitch, you know better. Do what your massa say and go back inside the house," she yelled from behind him.

"Bitch, please, unlike you, ain't no nigga got shit on me. Yes, he's my fiancé, and yes, I'm about to listen to him, because I don't want to have to kick your ass, but don't get that shit twisted. I'm not anyone's slave. If I wanted to leave today or tomorrow, I could, because I'm a bitch who has her own shit. Unlike your needy ho ass," I said, leaving them there. I hurried up to get inside the house, because I know one thing: if this bitch said one more thing that I didn't like, I was going to bless that ho and Jayden wouldn't be able to stop me.

When I walked out into the backyard, I frantically looked around for Mark. I spotted him over by the barbeque grill, talking to the rest of the guys. I could still hear Jayden and his baby mama fussing in the front yard. The shit pissed me off even more. I stalked over to Mark as if my ass was on fire.

"What's going on, Mimi? Why you look so upset?" he asked, once I had reached him.

"Your boy is out front with his baby mama, and he got all of one minute to get that bitch away from here before I go back out there and fuck them up," I said, walking away and not giving him a chance to respond.

"What's wrong, Mimi?" Troy asked, walking up to me.

"I'm about to fuck Jayden's baby mama up. That's what's up," I said, walking inside the house.

"Mimi, slow down," Troy said, following me. I ignored her as I power-walked to the front of the house. When I opened the door to walk outside, they were on the other side of the street still arguing. I walked over to where they were and let their asses have it.

"I told you that you had five minutes to handle this situation right here, but it seems like you can't do it, so I'm here to help you," I said, nudging him in his back.

"Bitch, please. He ain't going to handle shit. What you need to do is get your black ugly ass back over to the house and mind your fucking business," I heard her say.

"Time's up," I said to him. I turned to where she was and charged at her ass. I popped her dead in her mouth, because the bitch was talking too much shit.

"I ain't know your ass for nothing but a minute and here you wanna come talk shit," I said, punching her in her face. Grabbing her by her hair, I pulled that bitch in the middle of the street.

"See, bitch, I done been through too much shit already and here you go with more shit. I tried to let that shit slide, but you're one of those bitches who need to be taught a lesson," I said, giving her a kick to her face. I then proceeded to fuck that ho up. I threw nothing but powerful punches at her face. With my left hand, I took and gave her two quick licks to her eye. I was trying to leave my ring imprint in her face.

"Ho, let me go," she said, trying to get at me, but she couldn't.

"You know what, bitch? Get up and fight me fair. Let me see if your bite as big as your bark," I said, letting her go. I watched as she picked herself up, and then looked at me.

"Bitch, you done fucked with the wrong one," she said, rushing me. She gave me a good lick to my face. She then grabbed my hair and tried to pull me on the ground. "I'm about to paint this concrete with your blood, ho," she said, kneeing me in my face. I had to admit that the shit did hurt, but still, the bitch couldn't fight at all.

"Nah, bitch, first learn how to fight before you come fucking with me," I said, giving that ho a lick to her guts, causing her to let me go. She was bent over, trying to catch her breath, when I grabbed her and kicked her again.

"I told you that you can't fuck with a bitch like me," I said, upper-cutting her ass. She grabbed a hold of me. Next thing I knew, we were on the ground. I managed to get on top of her, and that's when I blacked out. I sat on top of her chest and began to merk that face. I was trying to fuck her all the way up. When she went to look in the mirror, she was going to remember me. She was going to think twice before she ever came at me again.

"That's enough," Jayden said, grabbing me. "Mark, get Shelly, man."

"Let me go," I said, trying to get away from him.

"Nah, ma, that's enough. You made your point already," he said, still holding on to me.

"Nah, that bitch asked for that shit. Let me give her some more," I yelled, trying to go at her again.

"Nah, ma, you need to chill out. Troy, come get you girl and take her into the house," he yelled to her.

"I'm not a fucking child. You don't have to call nobody for me," I said to him.

"Well, you're surely acting like one now," he said, letting me go. I was about to say something to him when I spotted Cam running toward us.

"Daddy, what's going on? What happened to Mommy?" he asked, looking at Mark, who was helping her.

"Go in the house, Cam. Daddy will be there in a minute," Jayden told him.

He stood there stuck. He looked at me, then to his mother, then back to his father.

"Now, Cam."

"You don't have to talk to him like that," I said, rolling my eyes at him. "Come on, Cam, let's go inside, baby," I said, walking over to him. I grabbed his hand as he led the way inside the house.

We headed straight for the kitchen once we were inside.

"Are you hungry?" I asked him.

"No, ma'am," he replied.

"Well, you've been in the pool all day. I didn't see you eat a thing. Are you sure that you're not hungry?" I asked, turning around to face him

"I'm sure," he said, getting quiet. I knew he had a lot of questions flowing through his little mind. I just hoped that he waited to ask them until his father came.

"Ms. Mimi?" he said, taking a seat on one of the bar-stools.

"Yes, Cam?"

"Can I ask you a question?" he asked with a straight face.

"Sure, you can," I said, walking over to where he was sitting. I then took a seat on the stool that was next to him as I waited for him to ask whatever it was that he wanted to ask.

"Did my mama do something wrong? Is that why you and her were fighting?" he asked, catching me off guard.

"Um, well, your mother and I had gotten into an argument, and that lead to us putting our hands on each other," I simply said to him. I wasn't trying to say too much to him. This was a conversation that he should have been having with his father.

"Okay," was all he said as my kids came walking through the door.

"What's wrong with you? Why do you look like you just got into a fight? Were you and Jay fighting? Because he's making everyone leave and he told us to come inside," Kailay asked as she and her siblings took a seat at the table.

"No. Don't worry about that. Are you guys hungry?" I asked, ignoring her questions.

"Yes, I'm starving," Kayla said, rubbing her belly.

"Me too," Kayson replied.

"Me three," followed Kaylon.

"Y'all want some barbeque or y'all want to go and get something else?" I asked them.

"They can eat what we have here," Jayden said, entering the kitchen. He walked over to Cam and kneeled down in front of him. "Are you okay?"

"Yeah, Dad, I'm fine," Cam replied.

"Are you sure?" he asked.

"Yes," he said, nodding his head.

"Okay good," he said, hugging him. "Let me talk to you right quick," he said, walking up to me. I placed the towel that I was holding down on the stove as I followed him.

"What's up?" I asked once we were out of the kids' earshot.

"Are you okay?" he asked, examining the bruise that was on my face.

"Yes, I'm fine," I said, removing his hand. I still was feeling salty about the way he tried to handle me earlier.

"What's wrong, ma?" he asked, looking concerned.

"Nothing," I said dryly.

"Come on, ma. Don't do this right now. Talk to me please," he said, looking at me with pleading eyes.

"We'll talk about it, okay? Let me fix the kids something to eat. I'll meet you in the bedroom," I said to him.

"Yeah, a'ight," he responded. He then looked as if he wanted to say something, but instead, he just left.

I walked back into the kitchen and started to fix the kids a plate of food. When I finished fixing and warming their food, I started to put the rest of the food in containers.

"You need help with that?" Troy asked, scaring the hell out of me. I turned to face her and then rolled my eyes.

"Girl, you scared the shit out of me, but nah, I'm fine, I got it," I said, turning back to finish what I had started.

"Are you sure?" she asked, walking over to me.

"I just told you that I got it. What's up with you? Why you acting all strange?"

She folded her arm across her chest before she blew air from out of her mouth. "Mimi, what happened earlier?"

"Troy, you already know that bitch had it coming to her ass—" I started to say, but she cut me off.

"I'm not talking about the stuff that went down between you and Shelly. I'm talking about what you and Mark was talking about earlier in the backyard before that," she asked, looking scared and confused.

"Oh, it was nothing," I said as I started loading dishes into the dishwasher. When I turned back around, she was looking at me funny. "Why you looking at me like that?" I asked her, trying to downplay it.

"You know why. I know you're lying to me," she said, walking over to me. "What happened?"

"Fine. Mark knows about the shit between you and Weedy. The nigga ain't dumb. I don't know why you trying to play on him like that. Your shit is getting real sloppy, and you need to clean it up," I said, walking off from her. I didn't have time to play and watch over grown-ass people. She, out of everyone else, should have known better than that.

"Mimi, please," she said, walking behind me.

"Please nothing, Troy," I said, turning around, which made me bump straight into her. "Either you clean that shit up and cast Weedy out, or you're going to lose your man."

"Is everything okay?" Mark asked, walking in on us. I was pretty sure that he'd heard what we were just talking about.

"Yes, everything's fine," I said to him, but I was looking at Troy.

"You ready to go?" he asked her.

"Um, yeah. Let me go get my jacket and we can leave right after," she said. I knew he wanted to say something, but instead, he turned around and left the room.

"Mimi, you gotta help me. I don't know what to do," she said, looking at me with pleading eyes.

"Troy, honestly, there's nothing I can do. You gotta figure this out on your own. The only thing I am going to tell you, though, is to be careful," I said, walking to where the kids were sitting at the table eating.

"Are you guys done?" I asked them.

"Almost," Kailay and Kayla replied. I should've known that they weren't finished. My girls were very prissy. They'd take all day eating if they could.

"We're done," Kayson said, referring to him, Kaylon, and Cam.

"All right, why don't y'all go ahead and wash up. I'll be back to clean up later."

"Okay," they said as they ran up the stairs.

"Hey, hey, hey, stop that running now," I yelled to them. "I'll be right back, girls."

"Okay, Mommy," they both said at the same time, making me smile. I'd waited a long time to finally be able to be happy with my kids, and it felt damn good. Walking out of the kitchen, I walked over to the front door to make sure that it was locked. Once I had confirmed that it was indeed locked, I made my way up the stairs to my bedroom. On my way to my bedroom, I stopped to check on the boys.

"Hey, guys, what are y'all doing?" I asked them.

"We're about to take a bath, then we're going to play video games for a little while before we go to bed," Kaylon said, going through his drawer.

"Yup, Mama Mimi, I'm going to whoop Kayson's and Kaylon's butts in the game," Cam said, smiling. He too had a deep set of dimples just like his father.

"No, you're not. I'll be the one doing the whooping," Kayson threw in. I stood there smiling at the three of them. We were now staying in a three-bedroom house until we found something bigger, which meant that they had to share rooms. At first I thought that it was going to be a problem, but they quickly proved me wrong. I absolutely loved the way that they were getting along. Since day one, they'd had a great relationship, as if they were blood brothers.

"Okay, well, I don't want you guys to stay up all night, because we have somewhere to go in the morning."

"Yes, ma'am," they said in unison.

"All right, I'll be back in here later to check on y'all," I said and left.

When I walked into the room, Jayden was sitting on the bed watching TV.

"What's up?" I asked as I sat on the bed beside him. He sat up, turned the television off, and turned to me.

"Ma, I just want to say that I'm sorry about earlier. I didn't mean to go off like that. I was just in a zone, and I was trying to get control of everything, but I couldn't," he said sincerely.

"It's okay, Jayden. I'm not worrying about none of that. I just want your baby mama to know that she can't continue to come over here and do as she pleases. Her time is over, it's my time, and I want her to respect me, or else shit will not be all right for her, and that's a promise."

"You won't have to worry about that, ma. After that ass whooping that you gave her, I am more than sure that she won't try to no shit," he said, placing his lips over mine.

"Well she better not, because I'm not gon' take shit easy on her anymore," I replied.

"Okay. I got you," he said. "I'm 'bout to go check on the kids, because I know you tired."

"Yes, I am," I said as I lay back on the bed. Lately, I'd been feeling sluggish, and right now, all I wanted to do was sleep.

"I already told you why. I don't know why you ain't trying to hear me," he said, laughing.

"Boy, bye, I'm not pregnant. So I ain't even trying to hear that shit."

"Uh-huh. You can deny it all you want, but watch when you go to the doctor next week."

"Yeah, yeah, yeah," I told him. "Now get out. I'm about to get some rest."

"All right, I'll be back to check on you later," he said and left.

I sat there, thinking about my life before and how it was now. I was very happy and if I was pregnant by Jayden, then so be it. He'd been a wonderful father to my kids, and I'd have no regrets if I was having his baby.

"Yo, Mimi," Jayden said, walking back into the room.

"Didn't I tell you that I was tired? Why are you bothering me?" I asked him, but he didn't answer me. When I looked at him, he was standing there with a duck look on his face, holding something in his hand. "What's that?"

Again, he didn't say anything, so I got up and walked over to him. "What you got in your hand?" I asked, stopping in front of him. He still didn't say anything. He just stood there staring at me, so I took the shit out of his hand.

"What the fuck is this shit?" I asked. "Where the fuck did this shit come from?"

"Ma, I have no idea. When I went downstairs, someone knocked on the door. When I opened it, there was no one there. Instead, this was sitting on the welcome mat."

"Well, what are we going to do about this then?" I asked him.

"To be honest, I don't know," he said, then walked out of the room, leaving me standing there.

As I stood there with pictures of Stacy's, Julius's, Kaylin's, and Marie's bodies in my hand, I couldn't help but to think that I was born just to go through some shit. After all I'd been through, I still found myself in some shit. I guessed I would never have my happy ending.

I was still standing there when my phone chimed, telling me that I had a new text message. Throwing the papers on the nightstand, I grabbed the phone.

When I opened the message, I was confused at first, but after a minute or two, I got what she was saying. I replied to her message, then took the paper and walked out of the room. I found Jayden in his office sitting behind the desk. I walked over to him and gave him the papers.

"You can trash that," I said as I walked back over to the door.

"Why? We still don't know who is behind all of this," he said, getting up.

"Actually we do, but she won't be able to come for us anymore," I replied.

"What are you talking about?" he asked, walking over to me.

"Your baby mama," I said and walked out of the room. This time I had a smile on my face, because I knew for sure that right this minute, no one could hurt me anymore.

Chapter 38

Troy

We were on our way back over to Amina and Jayden's house. I had forgotten my purse with the keys to the new house that Mark and I were staying in, so we had to drive all the way back to come in get it. The minute we pulled up on the block, I noticed someone creeping over to Mimi's house. At first, I was going to jump out and get them, but I made Mark park down the street, and I got out.

When I crept around, I noticed Jayden's baby mama walking toward her car. Silently, I made my way over there. Instead of the crazy bitch pulling off, she just sat there, watching the house. I spotted Jayden as he opened the door. He looked at it, stooped down, picked something up, and then he walked back inside.

"Yeah, nigga, I know what the fuck y'all did, and I'm going to make your life a living hell," she said as she went to start the car.

"No, you're not, bitch," I said, pulling the blade out of my bra.

"What the fuck?" she began to say, but she stopped once I placed the blade to her throat and dragged it, cutting her from one ear to the other.

"You should've minded ya business," I said before I left.

"Come on, ma, I got the purse. We got to go," Mark said, scaring the shit out of me.

"All right," I said as I followed him back to the car. Once we got in, he pulled off. I pulled my phone out and sent Mimi a text. She texted me back within a minute. I smiled, placed my phone back into my purse, and sat back.

"Are you okay over there?" Mark asked me.

"Yeah, I'm fine, baby. I'm just fine," I said, placing my hand over his. I reached over and kissed him. It was in that moment I vowed to myself that I was not about to let Weedy or nobody else come in and fuck our life up. We'd come too far, and this peace and happiness was what we all needed. I wasn't going to let anyone fuck that shit up!

Epilogue

Mimi

Hey, everyone. How's it going? Well, I hope. Well, I know y'all are probably wondering how life turned out with Jayden and I'm here to tell y'all that everything was great. He was a wonderful man and father to the kids. I'm not going to lie. At first shit wasn't all that gravy. We used to fuss and fight like no other, but don't get it twisted. He never once put his hands on me. He was a real man, one that Kaylin wished he could've been. I'm not going to front on y'all though. There was a few times when I wanted to pack my shit up and leave, but I didn't, because every time I'd try to, I remembered everything we'd went through and it was a lot—too much to just try to throw everything away. Besides, that nigga was in love with my ass. He wasn't trying to let me go, no matter how many times I packed my bags and threatened to leave. He'd be like, "Mimi, we in this shit together. I don't care how mad any of us gets. We ain't going to leave one another. If I get mad or you get mad at me, we gon' talk this shit out. We ain't come this far to leave and go be with somebody else." So, yup, that nigga was everything I needed and then some.

"Babe, you ready to go?" he asked, walking in on me.

"Yeah, let me send an e-mail to Ambria right fast. I'll meet you downstairs in a minute," I said, looking up from the computer.

"Well, hurry up. You know the movers will be here soon, and we gotta get going before we be stuck in traffic," he said, standing behind me.

"All right, boo, I'm almost done," I said, reaching up and giving him a passionate kiss.

"Don't start no shit, ma," he said, pulling back.

"I'm not. I'll save that shit for when we get to our new house," I said, laughing.

"Uh-huh, keep playing and watch me put one in you."

"It's too late for that, nigga," I said, rubbing my growing belly.

"Yeah," he said, bending over and kissing my baby bump. "I can't wait to meet my princess."

"I can't wait to get her active ass up out of me," I said, faking as if I was mad. "She been giving my ass the blues lately."

"You better leave my baby alone," he said, beaming with pride. "She gon' be feisty, just like her mama."

"Daddy, the movers are here," Cam said from the door.

"Okay. I'll be right down," he said to him.

"Okay," he replied and left.

"Hurry up, before you make us late," he said, heading for the door. "And tell Ambria I said what's up with her fine ass."

"Boy, bye, I can tell you that girl is not checking for you," I said, laughing. "She already got a man."

"Who, that nigga Donovan?" he asked, turning around.

"Yesssssss, and he's so fucking cute. Me and her might have to trade niggas," I joked.

"Yeah, don't get yourself fucked up," he said seriously. "Tell li'l sis the minute that nigga act up, she knows how to reach me."

"I'm pretty sure that she can handle her own, but I'll tell her," I said, laughing. I didn't know how they became so close, but their relationship was so strong, you'd think that they were actually brother and sister.

"Yeah, yeah, yeah, I'm still going to have her back, just in case. Now hurry the hell up, before I have that nigga Donovan coming to pick your ass up."

"Well, in that case, I'll take my time then."

"You already know what it's hitting for, Mimi," was all he said before he left.

Well, y'all, it's about time that I get myself up on out of here. I'm hungry, and this little girl is in here kicking the hell out of my stomach. Oh, her name is Jakayla. She's due this fall, and I can't wait to meet her little ass. I hope that she won't be as bad as her brothers and sisters. Her father is more excited than I am. He's finally getting his first and last princess, because I'm tying my tubes after this baby. I'm not trying to be like that lady on *19 Kids and Counting*. All them damn kids ain't what I'm trying to do.

"Mimi," Jayden yelled.

"I'm coming, I'm coming," I said, getting up from the chair.

Well, I hope y'all enjoyed my story, and I thank you, Ambria, for helping me share the shit. Love you, sissy! Until next time, I'll see y'all later. At least I hope there won't be a next time.

"Amina," Jayden yelled again. This nigga was really starting to work my nerves again. He knew that shit wasn't good for the baby.

Anyways, see y'all baddies and hood niggas later. I'm Amina. Don't forget the name either. Peace!

ORDER FORM
URBAN BOOKS, LLC
300 Farmingdale Road, NY-Route 109
Farmingdale, NY 11735

Name (please print):_____

Address:_____

City/State:_____

Zip:_____

QTY	TITLES	PRICE

Shipping and handling: add $3.50 for 1st book, then $1.75 for each additional book.
Please send a check payable to:
        Urban Books, LLC
Please allow 4-6 weeks for delivery